CELIA

Celia stared at him wordlessly, temporarily struck dumb. He seemed nice: amiable, even-tempered. Not the kind of man to throw his pregnant daughter out on to the streets, if you can tell that kind of thing from meeting someone on their doorstep for two seconds.

"Who is it, Stan?"

A woman's voice: broad Lancashire accent. She came into view behind her husband and smiled at Celia.

"Can we help you, love?" Her voice was warm. She had a large, motherly bosom and startlingly red hair.

It was the hair that did it. Conscious of her own, escaping from her beanie hat and hanging about her face in stringy ginger strands, Celia took a tentative step forward.

"Hello," she said. It came out as a meaningless squeak. She cleared her throat, and tried again. "Hello. My name's Celia. I'm your grand-daughter."

Look out for Catherine Robinson's other title:

Tin Grin

Point

CELIA

catherine robinson

SCHOLASTIC

Scholastic Children's Books,
Commonwealth House, 1-19 New Oxford Street,
London, WC1A 1NU, UK
A division of Scholastic Ltd
London ~ New York ~ Toronto ~ Sydney ~ Auckland
Mexico City ~ New Delhi ~ Hong Kong

First published in the UK by Scholastic Ltd, 2002

ISBN 0 439 99236 2

Printed and bound in Great Britain
by Cox & Wyman Ltd, Reading, Berks.

1 2 3 4 5 6 7 8 9 10

CHAPTER 1

The rain started again at the precise moment
the invigilator – Miss Sykes-Jones, Senior
Mistress, aka complete cow – glanced at the
clock and said: "You have two hours. Turn over
your papers and begin. . . *NOW!*, with a theatri-
cal pause before the final word. The hall was
filled with the sound of rustling papers, squeak-
ing chairs and throats being nervously cleared,
before it settled down to the kind of expectantly
charged silence peculiar to examination halls
and dentists' waiting rooms.

Celia gave a resigned sigh, and turned over
her own paper. She opened her pencil case and
took everything out: pen, spare pen, pencil,
spare pencil, spare ink cartridge, ruler, eraser.
She laid everything carefully out across the top
of the desk, then picked up her pen and
unscrewed the lid. She wrote her name on the
front of the examination paper, carefully, and
slowly read through all the questions. Then she
sighed again.

*Can't answer any of those. It's even worse than
the first paper. Anyway, what's the point? I never*

wanted to do History in the first place. That was Dad's idea. I wanted to do Drama. Edward thought that was hilarious, of course, the little ratbag: calling me a drama queen, and saying I should get an A. But Dad had to know best. As ever. "Drama's a waste of a GCSE. You'll learn much more doing History. Besides, you'll need some good academic GCSEs to get to university." *Like me going to university is a foregone conclusion. What if I don't want to go? Not that what I want to do is ever considered.*

She sighed once more, heavily, and turned to the window next to her. It was steamed up with the combined breath of a hundred eager History 2 candidates. Celia rubbed a clear patch with the sleeve of her blazer, and peered out. Outside, the rain was running down the pane in rivulets.

Still chucking it down. I thought June was supposed to be hot and sunny?

She stuck out her index finger and drew a rudimentary face in the condensation – a circle, two dots for eyes, downturned mouth – and issuing forth from the mouth, a speech balloon containing the single word: HELP!

"Are you all right?"

Startled, Celia turned; Miss Sykes-Jones was standing beside her in the aisle between the desks, her voice lowered, an expression of enquiry on her face.

"Yes, thank you, Miss. I'm fine."

"Then what. . ." The teacher inclined her head towards Celia's artwork on the window. "Why did you do that?"

"I don't know, Miss."

Miss Sykes-Jones looked down at the exam paper, lying untouched on the desk.

"But you haven't even begun yet! Half an hour has gone by, and you haven't—" Her voice rose, and she checked herself. "Why haven't you started? Are you feeling unwell?" she asked in a loud whisper.

"No, Miss."

"Do you want anything? Would you like to go outside for a few moments? It's quite permitted – I can fetch you an escort."

Celia had a brief vision of a hunk in a dinner jacket, with a cheesy smile and a red rose in his lapel. A hysterical bubble of laughter welled inside her, and she bit her lip to stop it escaping.

"I'm fine," she repeated.

Miss Sykes-Jones was clearly not convinced. She peered at the front of Celia's paper.

"Celia, isn't it? Celia Duckenfield?"

"Yes, Miss. That's what it says on the exam paper," Celia agreed.

Sensing insolence, Miss Sykes-Jones glanced sharply at her. Celia smiled a sweet smile. The teacher was baffled; was the child simple? None of her twenty years' experience at Lady Margaret's had prepared her for this. She was used to bright, obedient girls who knew how to behave and what was expected of them. Girls who knew what to do in examinations, not like this one who clearly wasn't even making the slightest effort.

"Just try to begin," she urged Celia, giving her the benefit of the doubt. She was probably just overcome with nerves. "Read the questions through again, and try to write something. I'm sure it will all come flooding back once you make a start."

She smiled again, kindly, and hurried back along the rows of diligently bent heads to her desk, set authoritatively high upon the stage. Her shoes squeaked as she went.

Silly cow. How can it all come flooding back when it was never there in the first place?

Celia sat and stared out of the window again. The patch she had cleared and the mournful little face with its message had misted up already, its outlines barely discernible. She was aware of the Senior Mistress's eyes upon her, watching her. She opened the paper again, obediently, and, turning to the first question, began to write. She wrote in the space provided, but what she wrote bore no relation to the question; it was random words, thoughts jotted

down as they entered her head. *Help. HELP!!!!*
No use. Useless. Useless at History. History. His
story. Her story. My story. Whose story? What
story? History. Family History. Families. Mother
father brother sister. Mother. Mothers.

Celia looked at the words she had written,
and to her horror she felt tears prickling behind
her eyelids.

Stuff this. I'm not going to cry, not here in front
of everybody; I'm just not. STUFF it!

She unzipped her pencil case, savagely, and
crammed in everything she had laid out so carefully at the start of the exam. Then she pushed
her chair back; two of its rubber feet were missing, and the metal legs scraped across the
polished parquet floor with a squeal that resembled that of a pig being murdered. Every eye
turned in Celia's direction.

"What?" she demanded loudly, and stood up.
"What's your problem? Not the same as mine, I
bet!"

She ran from the room, clutching her pencil
case to her, aware of a sea of scandalized
upturned faces and the Senior Mistress's boom-
ing voice following her as she fled: "Celia!
Come back! Come back!"

She burst through the double doors at the
back of the hall and along the corridor, pausing
only to pull off her blazer. She shoved it with

grim satisfaction into a tall metal rubbish bin in the corner of the entrance hall, pushing it down hard amongst the dirty tissues and empty crisp packets and apple cores; then she was out, through the main entrance – strictly forbidden to pupils, apart from those sanctified beings in the sixth form – through the staff car park and on to the road. The rain beat down upon her, soaking her thin, striped cotton dress in seconds and turning her hair to sodden ginger rats' tails, but she scarcely noticed. *I'm free*, she thought, with a wild elation, *I'm free. I've actually done it! Now I just need the courage to do everything else.*

Celia couldn't remember a time when she hadn't known she was adopted: the knowledge had always been there, buried deep inside her psyche, as much a part of her and her perception of herself as her name and the colour of her hair and eyes. When she was small her parents had made much of the fact that she was chosen, and therefore implicitly special. "*We picked you out to be our very own little girl.*" She remembered the swell of pride she always felt when they spoke of it, could recall how she would prompt them to talk about the time they first saw her and what happened when the adoption was finalized and she was brought to them, carried into their house in the arms of the woman from the adoption agency ("*Wrapped in a soft white blanket like a little princess in a fairy story*," Dad would always say at this point). She remembered feeling faintly sorry for Edward during these conversations, glancing covertly at him playing unwittingly with his toys and pitying him for having entered the family in the normal, boring way, and not being special like her.

Of course, that was when she was small. What she couldn't remember was when it all stopped. When Mum and Dad stopped talking fondly about her triumphal entry through the Duckenfield portals. When she stopped feeling special, and began having the sneaking suspicion that Edward was, after all, their favourite, on account of their having created rather than chosen him.

"You are joking," Phoebe said once, when Celia was complaining about it.

"No, I'm not. They favour him. They definitely do."

"Oh yeah. Sure they do," Phoebe replied, sarcastically. "That's why they bought you that computer for Christmas. That's why they got you that mobile, so you can ring home for a lift whenever you need one. That's why—"

"OK, OK," Celia interrupted, irritably. "No need to go on. I know they buy me stuff, but that's just money."

"Right. Just money. Course it is; silly me."

"It is. I'm not talking about money."

"What are you talking about, then?"

"I dunno. The way they treat us, I suppose."

"And you're saying they treat Eddie better than they treat you?"

"Yes. No. Oh, I don't know." How come Phoebe always had this ability to make her feel confused, unsure of what she really did mean?

Phoebe looked at Celia for a long, steady moment. "My parents treat my sisters and me differently, you know. It annoys the hell out of me, I don't know why they do it, but I do know one thing. It's got nothing to do with being adopted."

"That's because none of you are."

Phoebe waved a dismissive hand. "You know what I mean. If they treat Eddie differently to you it's because he's a boy, or the youngest, or whatever. Not because you're adopted and he's not."

It had annoyed Celia. What did Phoebe know? Nothing, that's what. She just had to have an opinion on everything, even things she knew nothing about. She'd had something to say when Celia told her she intended trying to trace her birth mother, too – "Isn't that a bit of a cliché?" – and that had annoyed her, too, and upset her, although to give Phoebe her due she had apologized.

"I shouldn't have said that. Sorry."

"No, you shouldn't."

"I didn't mean to upset you. It's just that I know you haven't been getting on too well with your mum recently."

"Tell me about it." It was an understatement – they didn't seem able to be in the same room without snarling at each other. Things weren't exactly wonderful between her and Dad, either, and as for Edward: forget it. He was starting his GCSEs in September, and the way everyone was carrying on about it you'd have thought it was the most important decision since Neville Chamberlain waved that bit of paper about in 1939 (that much of History she did remember). Everybody seemed to have forgotten that she, Celia, was actually *doing* the damned things. But she was just left to get on with it.

"I just meant," Phoebe went on, "is it a good idea to start this just because you and your mum are going through the generation-gap thing?"

Celia stared at her. "You sound like one of those agony aunts in the teen mags. *Auntie Phoebe. Write to me about anything,*" she intoned, in a voice dripping with false sincerity, "*and I'll try to help.*"

"I didn't mean it like that. I just wonder whether you really want to do this – you know, setting wheels in motion, opening cans of worms, that kind of thing."

Celia told her it was something she'd been thinking about for ages, which was true, but up until then it had only been the vaguest of notions, an idea held at the back of her mind just on the outer edges of her conscious thoughts.

After that, though, it became larger and stronger. Celia found herself thinking about it, having thoughts about her birth mother, after every run-in with Mum, no matter how minor. *I bet my real mother wouldn't talk to me like that. I bet we would get on better than this.* It was as if she had a sort of insurance policy – something to fall back on in case of emergencies. She found herself most days taking her birth certificate out of the velvet-lined jewellery box she kept it in at the back of her undies' drawer, and poring over it, over and over the details she had first seen at the age of thirteen. Then, she'd barely given it a second glance – official forms had held no interest for her, and besides, the person it referred to, the tiny newborn baby, scarcely seemed to have any connection with Celia, as she could recognize none of the details apart from her date of birth. Everything was different now: mother's name, address, father's details (the box for "Father" was blank, empty) – even her name was different. How could this be her?

She had shoved the document into its box with hardly a second glance, and there it had stayed, all but forgotten. But now, three years on, Celia found herself scanning it with increasing avidity, as if by reading it over and over again she would somehow glean some morsels of knowledge in addition to the bare facts written there.

The letter, too, she took out and read. But not as often. The birth certificate was an official document: formal, impersonal, even though it belonged to her. But the letter was different. Short though it was, it was loaded with personal meaning: every word, every sentence, resonated with an intimacy Celia found hard to cope with. She could practically hear her mother's voice resounding through it, even though she couldn't remember what her mother's voice sounded like. How could she possibly? She was only six weeks old when she was handed over to her adoptive parents.

The birth certificate was the first thing she sought now, that wet June afternoon, after plunging through the front door and crashing up the stairs and into her bedroom. She stood on the carpet, shivering in her sodden school uniform, and clutched her birth certificate to her as if was her salvation. *This is it. I've got to do it now. After running out on old Sykes-Jones and History 2, I've got no choice.* She put the certificate back into its box, shoving it into a rucksack which she pulled out from the floor of her wardrobe. She dumped it on her bed, and began to open drawers and cupboards, yanking things out at random, discarding some, shoving others into the bag until she could fit no more in. She hurried into the bathroom next to her bedroom, picked up a sponge bag and filled it with various essentials: toothbrush, toothpaste, shampoo, soap; pulled open the airing cupboard door and tugged out a large bath towel.

Going back into her room, she added the new things to the top of the rucksack. Then she threw off her wet school clothes, pulled on jeans and a T-shirt, rubbed hastily at her hair with a towel and secured it back off her face in a messy ponytail. *No time for a shower. Eddie'll be home soon and if he catches me there'll be no chance of me seeing this through. Wonder when I'll next get the chance for a shower or a bath?* She pushed the thought from her mind – no use thinking like that. She knew she wouldn't even step out of the front door if she allowed herself even the tiniest negative thought.

She grabbed the rucksack from the bed and put one or two last-minute items – a map, her wallet – into the side pocket. Bending down, she thrust her arms through the padded straps and stood up, sagging a little under its weight. *Bloody hell! At this rate I'm not even going to make it to the station, let alone anywhere else!*

She let the rucksack drop down on to the bed again and pulled out several items of clothing and a pair of shoes. Then, as an afterthought, she shoved her mobile phone and building-society book on top of the remaining contents, pulled the drawstrings tight and eased it on to her back again.

Right. That's definitely it. No more wasting time – it's do or die time, as Feebs would say.

Clattering down the stairs on her DMs, she let the rucksack slide from her back on to the tiled floor of the hallway. She tugged her grey fleece and beanie hat from the coat stand in the hall and pulled them on. Then she tore off a sheet of paper from the pad that lay neatly beside the telephone on top of the polished walnut console table and, grabbing a pen from the onyx pot that accompanied the telephone pad, she scribbled a note. *Gone away for a few days. Don't worry about me. I'll be fine. Love C XX*

She slid the note under the pen-pot, where it would be easily seen by whoever was first in. She bent down, and eased the rucksack on to her back again. Then she opened the front door, slammed it behind her with a satisfactory crash that rocked the stained glass, and was gone.

CHAPTER 2

She didn't relax until the train reached Waterloo and disgorged all its passengers. She spent the entire journey huddled into the corner of her seat with her face turned to the window, pretending to be asleep, but covertly watching through her eyelashes as the pleasant pines and birches of the Berkshire countryside gave way to the suburban sprawls of Staines and Richmond, and finally the grimy grey rain-lashed buildings of London itself.

The train was quite empty – her carriage had only half a dozen or so other passengers, including a businessman in a crumpled grey linen suit who passed the hour's journey shouting down his mobile – but she couldn't shake off the odd feeling she'd had since leaving the house of being watched; observed, followed even. All the way to the station, puffing along the kilometre or so with her unaccustomed burden on her back, and even once she'd got there, queuing up at the ridiculously low little window to buy her ticket, she'd had a paranoid sense of being spied on.

All I need now is for someone I know to be on the train, going to London: one of Dad's partners from the golf club, or – oh God! – one of Mum's cronies from the church Lunch Club. Just imagine if Carole Baines got off at Waterloo and saw me! That would set the cat among the pigeons all right – she'd be on the phone to Mum in five seconds flat: "I've just seen your Celia at Waterloo with a great big rucksack on her back, off camping is she, I only ask because she looked really odd, terribly furtive, as if she was up to no good. . ."

Celia shuddered, and settled further into the prickly plush corner of her seat, pulling her legs up and wrapping her arms around them in a foetal position. She laid her cheek against the cool glass of the window, her rucksack leaning companionably against her on the seat.

"Tickets from Ascot, please."

Celia gave a guilty start. *This is ridiculous! Come on, girl, get a grip!* She dug her ticket out from her pocket and held it out to the inspector.

"Carnforth, eh? That's a long way. Going home, are you, love?"

"Er – no."

"Visiting relatives?"

"Something like that." *Trust me to get the world's nosiest ticket inspector. Why can't he just do what he needs to do to the ticket and then go away?*

He gave her a friendly smile. "You all right going across London?"

"What?" Celia frowned, not understanding.

"Your connection leaves from Euston. This train gets in to Waterloo. You'll have to go on the Underground, you'll need the—"

"Northern Line," Celia interrupted. "Yes, I know." She'd looked it all up beforehand on the Internet, checking and re-checking every detail of her journey. There was no way she was going to risk mucking it up through not reading some timetable properly. Not now she'd got so far. Figuratively speaking. In actual terms, she'd not got far at all, only a few kilometres.

The ticket inspector was still looming anxiously over her, as if he had personal responsibility for ensuring Celia reached her destination unscathed. With an effort of will, she smiled at him – no good drawing attention to herself by being sullen and grumpy, after all.

"Actually," she said, putting on her best Lady Margaret's drawl, "I was going to get a cab."

"Oh, right." He punched her ticket (*at last. . .*) and gave it back to her with another smile. "Change at Lancaster: but I expect you know that, too. Have a good journey."

I suppose he was only trying to be helpful. He was quite nice really, a bit like an older version of

Josh – Josh in an official railway uniform, twenty years down the line. Ha ha.

She didn't want to think about Josh. Thoughts of him definitely weren't going to help, she told herself firmly, and neither were thoughts of Miss Sykes-Jones, Dad's golf club mates, Carole Baines, or anybody else for that matter. The only person she could afford to think about now was herself, and with that thought in her mind she settled back determinedly in her seat, folded her arms, and dozed fitfully until the train finally pulled into Waterloo with a great screeching of brakes and slamming of doors.

She took her time getting her things together. *Just to give everybody else on the train time to get off first. No point in running the risk of being spotted by somebody who knows me.* She stepped cautiously down on to the platform, the rucksack on her back threatening to overbalance her and send her sprawling. She supposed she would get used to it eventually, even though at the moment she felt rather as she imagined a tortoise might feel if his shell were to be removed and replaced with a large and unwieldy chunk of paving stone.

By the time she got through the ticket barrier and on to the bustling station concourse she was exhausted. She looked at her watch – only four o'clock, plenty of time to get down to the

Tube and to Euston to catch her train which departed, so her ticket told her, in thirty-five minutes. However, she had reckoned without the twin handicaps of her weighty rucksack and the busyness of Waterloo station at four o'clock on a Friday afternoon. Despite her display of apparent knowledge to the ticket inspector she wasn't nearly as *au fait* with travelling around London by herself as she had pretended. Come to think of it, there weren't many forms of public transport she'd had to cope with; in fact, none. She'd always been able to rely on Dad or Mum or a friend's parents for lifts.

I'm a travel virgin, she thought, with gritted teeth, as someone bumped into her rucksack for the umpteenth time and almost sent her spinning like an out-of-control top. *It's about time I got used to it, then, isn't it?*

But by the time she reached Euston – hot and sweaty and with only moments to spare before the guard blew his whistle with a self-important blast – she was beginning to wonder if what she was doing was such a good idea after all. Especially the coping with the transport side of things; having been pushed and jostled and trampled on since getting off the train at Waterloo, she now couldn't seem to find an empty seat that didn't have an irritating little paper label sticking up from its back, indicating that it had been booked and was now awaiting its rightful occupant. She tramped up and down what seemed the entire length of the train, annoying people with her backpack as the train glided noiselessly out of the station at the start of its journey north.

Eventually, in desperation at the prospect of having to stand for the duration, she stopped and peered at one of the labels. CREWE – CARLISLE, it read. It would have to do. If its owner wasn't getting on until Crewe, she could sit here until then. She removed her rucksack, thrust it into the space between the backs of the seats, and sat down with a grateful sigh of relief.

"That's a big sigh." The woman opposite her – dumpy, grandmotherly, with spreading thighs and a damp beige raincoat – gave her a friendly smile.

"I thought I was never going to find a seat." The words were out before Celia could stop them. *Damn! I wasn't going to speak to anybody. I don't want anyone to remember me; what I looked like, how I spoke: nothing about me.*

It was too late. The woman stood up and removed her coat.

"Would you be ever so kind and stick this up there for me?" She indicated the luggage rack above their heads. "Only I don't think I can reach – I'm only a little titch, me!" Obligingly,

19

Celia took the coat, stood up, and thrust it into the rack. "Ta, love. You are kind. Eh, the rain's been that bad today, I thought it were never going to stop."

Celia smiled, a non-committal smile.

"In't it terrible for June? I don't reckon we're going to get any summer this year, do you, I mean here it is, what, the third week, and we've seen no sun as yet, have we?"

Celia smiled again, politely, and the woman caught her eye and leant forward in her seat.

"You going far, love?"

Short of actually being rude, Celia couldn't see how she could carry on being silent.

"Not that far, no. How about you?"

"Just back home to Lancaster. I've been to stay with my daughter and the grandchildren. I've had a grand time." She beamed with pride. "Here, I've got some pictures somewhere." She dug around in a handbag the size of a small suitcase, and brought out a large folder of photographs. "This is Lee, look; he's the eldest, he's going on ten and a right little monkey, I can tell you. And this is Annie Rose, she's just seven and a real little girl, all pink frocks and Barbies, a proper cutie. Then these are the twins, Ashley and Stacey, they're five, just started school last Easter, and. . ."

On she went, on and on, passing the photographs over and chattering incessantly. Celia nodded and made appropriate noises, but it made her head spin. *Please tell me I'm not going to have a crash course in this woman's family all the way to Lancaster – I can't bear it!*

At last the photos came to an end. Celia stood up hastily before any more could be produced.

"I'm just going to get a drink," she said. There must be a buffet somewhere – she kept seeing people swaying down the carriage, carrying folded paper bags and lidded Styrofoam cups. "Er – can I get you anything?" *May as well offer; she's hardly going to forget she's ever clapped eyes on me, is she? Not now she's shared her entire family history with me.*

"Bless you, love; but no thanks." The woman delved into her bag again, and produced an enormous Thermos. "I always bring my own. They can't make a decent cup of tea on these trains, can they?"

When Celia returned, lurching drunkenly along and bearing a can of Coke and a sausage roll, the woman had a newspaper open on the table in front of her and was engrossed in the crossword. Celia put her purchases carefully down on the table and bent to retrieve her rucksack. She took out the velvet box containing her birth certificate and a paperback copy of *Tess of the d'Urbervilles*. The woman glanced up as Celia sat down again and opened the book.

"Revision," Celia said, indicating the book with a rueful smile. It was a lie – English Lit. had been ages ago, and besides, *Tess* wasn't even one of the set books – but it did the trick. The woman went back to her crossword, leaving Celia alone with her thoughts and her book.

It wasn't the best choice of reading matter, under the circumstances, but Josh had loaned it to her and she'd promised him she would read it.

"I adore Hardy," he'd said. "And Tess reminds me so much of you."

At the time she'd been thrilled to be compared with one of English literature's most romantic heroines, but as she got into the story she became less sure. She privately thought Tess a bit of a wuss, mooning around after Angel Clare in that terribly drippy nineteenth-century way. And didn't she come to a horribly sticky end? Celia was sure she remembered that from the film. Thomas Hardy wasn't exactly renowned for his happy endings, after all.

Celia drank her Coke and ate her sausage roll, and managed to read about a page and a half before she felt her eyes beginning to droop, and after a bit she gave up fighting it. She closed her book, tucked the velvet box into the crook of her arm, laid her head back against the headrest, and fell into a shallow and wholly unrefreshing sleep.

She had met Josh at the golf club, of all places. She'd been dragooned by Dad, much against her better judgement, to accompany him and Mum and Edward to the club's Christmas do: "I'm sure you'll have a good time, darling, once you get there. Our club puts on a good bash." *Yeah, right*, she'd thought, *a festive dinner dance at the golf club, God, how sad is that*. And as she'd walked in there was this vision of loveliness standing at the bar, looking as sheepish and reluctant to be there as she felt. Josh. Joshua Peters, the Club Captain's son, all Liszt-like flowing locks and dashing dark good-looks. *Bloody hell*, she'd thought, *it's Heathcliff* (unlike *Tess*, *Wuthering Heights* had been one of her set books), and at that precise moment he turned and looked at her and that was it, *Boom*! – she was smitten.

Phoebe, of course, had thought that pretty much of a cliché, too.

"You mean it was love at first sight, kind of thing?" she'd remarked drily on the phone the next day, when Celia rang full of excitement to tell her all about it. All about *him*. "Eyes across a crowded room, and all that crap?"

What did Phoebe know? It was love, true

love – well, true lust at any rate. God, he was gorgeous.

It turned out he went to Lady Margaret's male counterpart, St Phillip's; was two years older than her, was doing English and Drama A-levels.

"I'm going to RADA," he told her seriously. It was one of their first conversations. "I'm going to be an actor."

She didn't doubt it. She knew little about acting but Josh had talent. Celia dragged Phoebe along to see Josh as the eponymous hero in St Phil's production of *King Lear*, and he alone stood out from the cast, the rest of whom were so wooden you could have lit a fire with them.

Even Phoebe was impressed. "He's good," she said afterwards, approvingly, as they walked home. "He's got presence, hasn't he? That 'never, never, never!' bit was amazing. I really believed he had his dead daughter in his arms, not some ratty little third-year lad got up in a frock. He's got – what do they call it? – charisma."

Thereafter she was a convert, and went around telling anyone who'd listen what a babe Celia was seeing, even though her own taste in men tended towards chunky blond rugby-playing types rather than those she normally dismissed as "arty-farty intellectuals". Given her friend's enthusiasm for him, Celia didn't really understand what instinct made her keep it a secret when she and Josh started sleeping together. Some things were just too private to share, she mused, even though she and Phoebe had discussed and giggled over absolutely everything in the past, every detail of every snog with every boy, even allotting them marks out of ten for technique and artistic content. *Maybe I just want to keep it to myself*, she thought, *keep it special, not pull it to pieces and snigger over it with Phoebe*. The fact was, what she had with Josh was a proper adult relationship, and she knew that discussing it with Phoebe would somehow diminish it.

She thought of Josh now, as the train pulled in to Lancaster – she realized, with a start, that her reserved seat's rightful owner had never turned up at Crewe or, if he had, hadn't the heart to wake her – and she struggled to retrieve her rucksack and stow away her belongings and stagger on to the platform with her head still woolly and stupid and spinning from sleep.

"You getting off here, too, duck?" It was the grandmother extraordinaire, carrying a neat tartan suitcase.

"Kind of. I have to change here." *Why couldn't I get all my stuff in one dinky little suitcase, instead of this ridiculous thing?* She struggled to pull the straps over her shoulders.

"Well, my Tom's come to collect me, better go and report back. Have a good journey."

"Thanks."

She watched the woman make her way along the platform to the exit, eager to share her tales of the grandchildren with her husband, and Celia wished with a sudden homesick pang that Josh was there to share this with her.

Don't be such a nit, she told herself savagely. *He's not here, OK? You wanted to do this thing by yourself, so just get a grip, girl!*

She bought herself a Fruit & Nut bar from a vending machine to cheer herself up, and presently her connection came along, a small chugging diesel with carriages that looked as if they dated from the nineteen-sixties. The journey to Carnforth took only a matter of minutes: she then had to repeat the rigmarole of hefting her pack off the train and along the platform, reflecting as she did so that at least it had stopped raining.

Right. How do I get to Silverdale? Look for a cab, I suppose. If there are any round here. There was no sign of any, no taxi rank or row of waiting vehicles. It looked as if she was in for a long wait, or else a long walk.

She went out to the station entrance: it was a dull grey evening in a dull grey town, barely seven-thirty but already getting dark, although she realized it couldn't possibly be, not yet, not in the middle of June. Just at that moment a minicab drew up and man got out, flung a five-pound note through the window at the driver, and dashed off into the station. Seizing her chance, Celia went up to the driver's side of the cab. The driver noticed her, and wound the window right down.

"Morgan?" he said.

Celia frowned. "Sorry?"

"Cab for Morgan?"

"Oh, no." She felt let down, disappointed. "No, my name's not Morgan."

The cab driver looked at his watch. "Was supposed to've been here quarter of an hour since, got held up in the bloody traffic. I s'pose Ms Morgan's got fed up waiting an' buggered off under her own steam, like." He gave a sudden, good-natured grin. "Oh, well. Not to worry. Where is it you want, flower?"

"Silverdale." It seemed peculiar to utter the name out loud. For so long it had existed only inside Celia's head, a mythical place – Camelot, Atlantis, Avalon. She half-expected the cabbie to scratch his head, puzzled: "Silverdale? Never heard of it, love. Sorry."

"Right you are," he said. "No problem. Hop in, then."

The sun came out from behind the lowering grey clouds as they drove along, a thin lemon-coloured sun that sent shafts of watery light across the fields. Celia vaguely noticed the prettiness of the countryside, low marshy meadows, a towering crag in the near distance, and glimpses of the glittering sea to her left. But only very vaguely. Her head was too full of the enormity of what she was about to do, the end of her journey in sight. The end of her quest, even. Was that too fanciful?

The cab turned left, and they drove along a narrow winding lane full of the scent of damp loam and wood garlic, and then all at once some houses came into sight: stone cottages, their gardens burgeoning with geraniums and fuchsias, and then larger more solid houses with neat, well-tended terracotta pots and hanging baskets.

"Silverdale," the cabbie announced. Celia's stomach gave a lurch of mixed anticipation and apprehension. "Whereabouts, love?"

"Hill House," she said. She knew the address by heart, had absorbed it into every fibre of herself. "Hill House, in Hesketh Road."

"The Cavendish place." He nodded, and Celia caught her breath.

"They're still there, then – the Cavendishes?" It was more than she could possibly have hoped for, that they still lived there. *Any minute now I'm going to knock on their door, and they're going to open it, and – what? What will I say? What will they say?*

28

Celia became aware that the cabbie was peering at her doubtfully in the driver's mirror.

"Who did you think lived there, then?"

"Oh, them. The Cavendishes. I knew they were still here – I mean, I hoped they were." Flustered, Celia began to babble. Then she checked herself. He was only a cab driver, for heaven's sake, not the police – what business was it of his, anyway? "We've lost touch recently, and I was coming through the area and thought I'd call in to see them," she extemporized, rapidly.

"Right." To her relief, he accepted her explanation. He pulled up outside a large, handsome house of pale stone, its front door painted the colour of egg yolk. "Here you go then, flower. Hill House."

She paid him, and he drove off. Celia stood at the kerb for a few moments, looking up at the gracious Georgian proportions of the house, and trying to calm herself. Her heart was beating like a steam hammer, threatening to burst right through her chest, and she felt faintly sick. She realized she had eaten nothing all day except that sausage roll on the train from Euston, and the recent bar of chocolate. The very thought of food made her heave slightly with nerves.

Come on, Duckenfield. It's do or die.

She hoisted her rucksack on to her back,

crunched up the gravel drive and, taking an enormously deep breath, rang the doorbell.

Nobody came to answer it. For several moments she stood there, finger poised over the bell, wondering whether to ring again or whether to just turn tail and flee, get back on to the main road and hitch a lift from some passing motorist, back to Carnforth and Lancaster and Euston and, eventually, home. She rang again; dithered, shifted her weight from foot to foot, close to tears of anti-climax and thwarted anticipation.

Then, just as she was about to give up and crunch down the drive again, the door opened with a creak worthy of a Hammer Horror film, and there stood a man in a faded blue cardigan. He had silver-grey hair and a pleasant, enquiring smile.

"Sorry I was so long," he said. "We were out in the garden, picking the raspberries. And the front door's swollen with all this flippin' rain we've been having."

Celia stared at him wordlessly, temporarily struck dumb. He seemed nice: amiable, even-tempered. Not the kind of man to throw his pregnant daughter out on to the streets, if you can tell that kind of thing from meeting someone on their doorstep for two seconds.

"Who is it, Stan?"

A woman's voice: broad Lancashire accent. She came into view behind her husband and smiled at Celia. They were both in their sixties, looked comfortably off judging by the tasteful prints on the walls behind them and the large kitchen Celia could just make out through the open door at the end of the passageway.

"Can we help you, love?" Her voice was warm. She had a large, motherly bosom and startlingly red hair.

It was the hair that did it. Conscious of her own, escaping from her beanie hat and hanging about her face in stringy ginger strands, Celia took a tentative step forward.

"Hello," she said. It came out as a meaningless squeak. She cleared her throat, and tried again. "Hello. My name's Celia. I'm your granddaughter."

CHAPTER 3

Celia was unused to provoking violent reactions. Irritation, yes; annoyance, exasperation, even. She'd got used to her parents looking at her with permanently irritated expressions on their faces of late. It seemed she only had to walk into a room these days and their looks of placid contentment would disappear as if wiped off with a damp cloth, to be replaced with ones of pained annoyance. God only knew what she looked like when watching them. The same, probably.

A response as mild as irritation, however, was not what she got now. The man – Mr Cavendish – took half a step back, a look of extreme dismay on his face, his left hand rising to cover his mouth. But his wife pushed violently past him, elbowing him aside, her face suffused a blotched damson colour.

"You're a wicked girl!" Her voice shook, thick and clotted with anger.

Celia stumbled, propelled backwards by the intensity of the woman's fury as if it were a physical force.

"But – but I. . ." she stuttered.

"A wicked, wicked girl!" She took a step forward, towards Celia. "You're disgusting, that's what you are! Is this some kind of a joke? Is it? Some kind of an evil, twisted joke?" A ball of spittle collected on her bottom lip, and Celia watched it with repelled fascination.

"*Well is it?*" she roared, and lunged suddenly at Celia, her eyes staring, her mouth contorted, the tendons in her neck standing out like ropes. She looked utterly mad. Celia could only stare at her, frozen to the spot with astonishment and bewilderment, and quite unable to move. Whatever reception she had anticipated, however she had expected these people to react to her turning up on their doorstep, it certainly hadn't been this.

Mr Cavendish caught his wife by the arm. "Now then, Freda," he murmured, gently. "Now then. That's enough. Calm down, now."

He put his arm about her shoulders and she subsided slightly, allowing herself to be led two or three steps back into the hallway, meekly, like a child.

Celia tried again. "Look," she began, warily. "I really do think there's been some—"

She broke off as Mrs Cavendish plunged towards her again. "You're evil!" she yelled, her mouth twisting again. "*Evil!*"

Her husband grabbed her once more. "That's enough," he said, his voice surprisingly tender. "I'm sure the lass don't mean any harm. I'll deal with this now. You go and put the kettle on. Make us a nice cup of tea."

Much to Celia's surprise she did as she was told, turning on her heel submissively, her head and shoulders drooping slightly. Her husband watched her go, then turned sharply back to Celia.

"I think you'd better leave," he said.

"But I – I mean, you don't –" She stopped, checked herself.

All the months of screwing myself up with shall-I-shan't-I; all the planning and secrecy. Then that bloody awful exam, and the endless train journey. I can't just give up and go now. Not without some kind of explanation.

"I don't think you understand," she said.

He sighed, and rubbed a weary hand across his eyes. "Aye, you're right there. I don't understand."

She took tentative step forward. "Then let me explain—"

"No." His voice was firm. He put a hand on the front door and began to close it. "You've got what you came for. You've seen what you came to see. You've had your fun. Now push off back to where you came from, lady, and leave us in peace."

And he shut the door squarely in Celia's face, leaving her standing on the doorstep and wondering what on earth was going on, and what she was going to do now.

Celia had been given the letter on her sixteenth birthday. Getting on for a year ago.

"It's what she wanted," Mum had said. "Your natural mother. The last thing. There'll be no more requests from her now."

Celia knew what the other things were, had always known: that she should be placed with a family of churchgoers ("God-fearing" was the phrase that always went through Celia's mind, though she didn't know why. Nobody else used it), and that she be given her birth certificate as soon as she asked to see it. She had been thirteen. Celia wondered if that made her a late developer, or just naturally incurious. It had been a bright spring day. Celia could remember the sun streaming through the kitchen window, and the blossom on the Japanese cherry tree in the garden.

"Where did I come from?" she had asked Mum, in the middle of a conversation about who-knows-what, and then blushed, aware of sounding as if she was asking about sex. That *would* have made her a late developer. "I mean, who was my real mother?"

Mum had gone upstairs, and handed her the birth certificate without a word. Celia remembered glancing at it without much interest, and then putting it away. Why should she have done differently? At thirteen, she was a Daddy's girl: loved, cosseted. Spoilt, even. She didn't mind admitting it. Her parents were who she lived with; quite simply, her real roots didn't impinge on her life at all. It was only relatively recently that things had changed, and her birth certificate had begun to take on such significance.

The letter, though, had been a total surprise. She had looked at it, still in Mum's hand. Mum twisted her lips, and handed her the envelope. It was very clean, pristine white, spotless and uncrumpled as if it had only just been written.

"Where's it been?" Celia asked. She turned it over: TO MY DAUGHTER, it said on the front, in bold black capitals.

"Inside Gran's bible. It kept it flat." Mum inclined her head towards the envelope. "Aren't you going to open it?"

"Yeah, sure." Celia traced the letters with her forefinger. "It feels dead peculiar. Like, it's for me, it's addressed to 'my daughter', but it's not from you or Dad."

Mum's face crumpled slightly. "It's been burning a hole in my heart," she confessed.

Celia glanced sharply at her; it wasn't like her

to talk like that, to use such flowery language. She was normally so pragmatic and down-to-earth.

Celia ripped the envelope open, pulled out the single sheet of paper it contained and quickly scanned the few lines. She gave a short laugh.

"There," she said, tossing the letter carelessly to Mum. It seemed somehow important to pretend she was unaffected by it, even found it slightly comic, this message from someone she didn't know and probably never would.

Mum took the letter gingerly, as if it might burn her fingers. "Are you sure?" she said, but it was a rhetorical question as she was already reading it avidly. Celia could hardly blame her: after all, it had been lying there temptingly, in the sitting-room bookcase inside Gran's bible, for sixteen years. How had she had the self-discipline, the will power, not to have read it before then? Nobody would have known. Except Dad, of course, but Celia suspected he wouldn't have cared much. Dad didn't really go in for agonizing over things.

"Well now," said Mum. She seemed at a loss for words. Not like her at all. "What do you make of that, then?"

Celia shrugged. "A bit odd."

"It smacks of post-natal depression to me,"

Mum said, briskly. That was more like her, wrapping things up in easy-to-explain terminology and thrusting them away, out of sight. "Let's go and see what Dad's done with your present, shall we?"

The present had been the mobile phone, which Celia was genuinely delighted with. She could see Mum and Dad exchanging pleased looks as she crowed over it. She remembered it particularly: there weren't very many looks like that between them after her birthday, that was for sure.

But the truth was, she had been deeply affected by the letter. If she were to be honest, the real desire to find her mother, the real yearning, had begun the moment she tore open the envelope. The contents were short, and to the point.

My darling,
You're now sixteen, and I hope you may be able to understand something of what made me go through with this. I know you will go to a good family who will be able to care for you and give you the things I cannot. Never doubt, though, that I love you. I always will.

Giving you up is the hardest thing I will ever do in my life. The second hardest thing is writing this letter. I hope you will find it in your heart to forgive me.

How could anybody not be moved? Even though Mum seemed not to be, Celia bet she was really, deep inside. Perhaps she just disapproved of the histrionic tones. Celia pondered it for days afterwards, going over and over the facts of her adoption in her mind.

There was the matter of her mother apparently having insisted on Celia going to a religious family, which seemed frankly odd in this day and age. It had been a thorn in her side her entire life, that much she knew; endless Sunday School as a kid, being teased about it at primary school ("Celia Duckenfield talks to Jesus!") The teasing stopped when she went to Lady Margaret's, but the downside was she had religion shoved down her throat there. It was enough to put anyone off, being taught by the likes of old Sykes-Jones, who banged on about Christian values and then went jack-booting round school like Attila the Hun. Then, as if that wasn't enough, Mum and Dad had a thing about cathedrals, and dragged Celia into them for Choral Evensong whenever they passed one on holiday. Edward, who somehow seemed to have escaped what he called the God-bothering after Sunday School days, always refused to go in and would sit in the car by himself, reading. All in all, Celia often felt she had a surfeit of religion, but also that she had no choice in the matter; her mother for whatever reason had wanted her brought up in a Christian household, and that was that.

Then there was the subject of her birth certificate, which was full of fascinating but apparently non-essential detail. All that was necessary on a birth certificate for an adopted child, Celia discovered later, was the name and place of birth, the sex and name of the child, and the mother's name. Celia's birth certificate, on the other hand, carried all her mother's particulars, although her father's details had been left blank: her mother's name, Genevieve Cavendish, and her address – Hill House, Hesketh Road, Silverdale. She had called her baby Simone: it seemed odd to Celia now, that for the first six weeks of her life she had been called something entirely different.

And finally, there was this letter. It was all very odd: the more Celia thought about it, the odder it became. Why had she been sent to her adoptive parents with such a detailed birth certificate, with instructions that she be allowed to see it as soon as she asked? Why had her mother written to her, a letter to be given her on her sixteenth birthday; a letter so touching it would be bound to ignite some spark of curiosity as to its author? She became convinced that her mother had intended her to be curious; that she had worded the letter to be as heart-rending and poignant as possible so that Celia would be moved to try to find her.

It was as if Genevieve had deliberately set out to lay a trail for Celia to follow, a trail that would lead to her. As time went by a picture of her mother began to form inside Celia's head, starting with the letter. It seemed to her that the age she was to be given it – sixteen – must have some special significance. Perhaps Genevieve was herself sixteen at the time of Celia's birth? She might have only been fifteen when she became pregnant. Under age. OK, she reasoned, but so what? Plenty of girls get pregnant under age. It might not be the best thing in the world, for anybody, but it happens. So why did Genevieve put her up for adoption? Why didn't she do what others in her position normally did – keep the baby, or just have an abortion? (At this point, Celia realized with a tingle of horror that the foetus she was calmly contemplating was, in fact, her.)

Celia knew it was rare for teenage girls to go through with pregnancy, only to give the baby up for adoption. Funnily enough, she had been reading an article about it only days previously, in a magazine in the dentist's waiting room. The author of the article had explained how the increase in abortion over the past thirty years had lead to a shortage of healthy, able-bodied babies available for adoption in the UK, forcing the childless abroad to places like Romania and China to adopt, always with some degree of hassle, and sometimes illegally. It had been the word "adoption" in the article's title that had caught Celia's eye, she remembered: "THE AGONY OF BRITAIN'S ADOPTION COUPLES!" it had shrieked, tabloid-style, and Celia had read it with a kind of detached interest but without in the least relating it to herself.

Now, though, she saw the connection. Why had Genevieve gone ahead with the birth? On balance Celia didn't find it especially strange that her father's details were not on the certificate. Perhaps Genevieve hadn't wanted to name him: maybe he was unsuitable in some way, much older than her perhaps, or married. Or maybe she hadn't even known who the father was. Maybe he hadn't been the first, or the only; maybe she was – what was the word the mags used, tight-lipped and censorious? Maybe she was *promiscuous*. Whatever: it was obvious he wasn't in the picture at all. Which meant there must have been some pressing reason to make her unable to contemplate an abortion, make her go through with the pregnancy.

Maybe her parents wouldn't let her – but that didn't make sense, Celia decided, because if her parents didn't want her to get rid of me (she shuddered), wouldn't they have helped her to bring me up and look after me? Surely, surely her parents would have supported her, if she wasn't to have an abortion? Unless they were monsters – *shades of Dickens and Josh's beloved Thomas Hardy*, she thought, *throwing her out on to the street in the snow*. . . There must have been something that motivated her, something that was big enough to justify and compensate for the unimaginably traumatic experience, if Genevieve's letter was anything to go by, of giving up her baby. Something like –

She stopped. *Religion. Something like religion.* It was so obvious she couldn't imagine why it hadn't occurred to her before. *She was religious – or her parents were – and that's why she didn't have an abortion, and why she wanted me adopted by churchgoers.* All the pieces of the jigsaw began to fit together. Poor Genevieve. Young, under age maybe, pregnant by someone she didn't want to name. Forced by religious parents to go ahead with her pregnancy, and then have her baby adopted. *But why didn't they let her keep me?* That's what she couldn't get her head around. What kind of religion was anti-abortion, but in favour of giving babies away?

She wondered again now, as the front door of Hill House was closed forcefully in her face. She hadn't really expected to find Genevieve still living with her parents. If she had been sixteen when Celia was born, she would now be thirty-two. Long past the age when what your parents said or thought held any sway, no matter how repressive or religious your upbringing. She would surely have left home long ago: Celia had been prepared for that. But the vehemence, the *ferocity* she had been met with had truly shocked her. It had literally taken her breath away. She stood there, gasping slightly. *What am I going to do now?*

She turned on her heel, utterly dejected, and began to trudge dispiritedly back the way she had come in the taxi, only minutes earlier. She was completely at a loss. She simply hadn't looked this far ahead. Her plans, such as they were, had only extended as far as getting to the address on her birth certificate. Starting out along the trail. She hadn't anticipated striking gold first time, so to speak, only to have it snatched away from under her nose.

She plodded along the road, sagging under the weight of her backpack, and found herself biting her lip to stop the tears brimming over. She had an almost overwhelming urge to sit down in the road, like a thwarted toddler, and have an enormous, sobbing, full-on tantrum.

Great forward planning, or what? No doubt old

Sykes-Jones would have something to say about it. The perils of impetuosity, probably. Lack of backbone. I can just hear her, patronizing old cow. Trouble is, she'd be right.

A tear spilled over her bottom eyelid, and she dashed it away with the back of her hand, suspecting she could add self-pity to the list. *Well, this is no use. What am I going to do? Come on, girl: think. Think!*

At that precise moment the skies opened again without warning, like some enormous heavenly bathplug being pulled. The rain tumbled down rushing away down the gutters and soaking Celia in the process. Cursing loudly, she wiped away the mingled rain and tears on her face and looked around. The road ended in a T-junction, and she could see a church about a hundred metres away. She put her hands up to the padded shoulder straps of the rucksack and, grabbing hold of them tightly, as if to a lifebelt, she made a run for it, the burden on her back jiggling around uncomfortably and making her feel rather like a drunken camel.

The gate to the churchyard stood open, and the porch was square, solid and doorless. Celia stumbled over the low step, pulled her arms from the backpack and, dropping it on the floor, sank gratefully down on to a stone bench inside the porch. It was at least dry in there. There was a large noticeboard on the opposite wall; Celia glanced idly at the notices, the usual lists of clergy duties, flower rotas and assorted appeals for Christian good causes, punctuated here and there by a selection of artwork clearly executed by the Sunday School. *JESUS SAVES!* proclaimed the largest of these, in rainbow-coloured, slightly wobbly letters ten centimetres high, underneath which someone had cynically scrawled *but Beckham gets it on the rebound* in scruffy blue biro. Celia sat there on the cold stone bench and explored her feelings, tentatively, like gingerly feeling a sore tooth with her tongue. She looked at the notices again.

Jesus saves, does he? OK then.

She stood up, picked up her backpack and turned the iron ring that was the handle on the church door. Slightly to her surprise the latch lifted, with a loud clunk. It was unlocked. She pushed open the door and stepped inside. The church was cold and dark, the gloom relieved only slightly by the dim evening light filtering in through the high ancient windows. There was a pervading smell of flowers, damp stone and polish. Celia could vaguely see two figures on the far side of the choir screen, putting armfuls of flowers in two huge vases either side of the altar and murmuring faintly to each other. Another extravagant floral arrangement filled the font: roses and outsized daisies and two enormous spears of salmon-pink gladiolus.

She slid into a pew, dumping the rucksack on the floor of the aisle. She sat there for a moment, not quite sure what she was doing or why she was doing it. Pulling a hassock out from beneath the seat she sank down on to her knees and rested her forehead on the smooth wood of the pew in front.

OK then, Jesus. Here I am. So save me.

Her mind was suddenly filled with memories of her childhood: Sunday School with Eddie, colouring in pictures of Old Testament stories, evangelical little choruses with plenty of enthusiastic actions, warm orange squash and custard creams (it was always custard creams, she remembered), and then all home for the Sunday roast that had been put in the oven on the timer, to cook itself while they were out. She could almost smell the lunch now, that wonderful welcoming roast-chicken-and-stuffing smell as Dad turned the key in the front door. . .

She was forcibly reminded of how little she had eaten during the day, and how hungry she was. Wriggling slightly on the lumpy hassock, she sighed and put her head in her hands. The words of one of the choruses came floating back to her: *Let Jesus into your heart, it's all he asks you to do, just open it unto the Lord, and he will see you through.* It was hardly Keats. She wriggled again, embarrassed at recalling the total conviction with which her eight-year-old self had bellowed the trite little verse.

She shut her eyes. *All right then. I'm opening my heart. I'm opening it, Jesus, I really am. Please see me through. Please. Please.*

"Are you all right, love?"

She opened her eyes. A middle-aged woman stood there, her arms full of flowers, peering anxiously down at Celia, who got up with a start, clattering out into the aisle and almost falling over her rucksack.

"Oh, yes, yes, I am, thanks."

"Only you were there for ever such a long time, motionless, like. I said to Edna, suppose she's ill? Suppose she's passed out? Only I said 'he'. We couldn't see you were a lass in this bad light, see."

"I'm not ill," Celia said. "Thanks," she added. *Tired, cold, hungry, and completely pissed off, but not ill. Yet.*

"You were praying," the woman said, nodding understandingly, "and I disturbed you."

"No, no, I wasn't," Celia said hurriedly, and then stopped. Praying, she realized, was just what she had been doing. *Celia Duckenfield talks to Jesus. . .* Which only went to show how useless it was; something she'd suspected for years but hadn't recently had the opportunity of putting to the test.

"I'll leave you in peace," the woman said. "Sorry to have disturbed you. I'll go and put the lights on, then we must get on with these flowers."

"They're very pretty," Celia said, politely. She felt she ought to say something nice, as she was in this woman's church under false pretences.

"It's the Flower Festival on Sunday." She beamed, full of pride, and indicated the blooms she held. "Edna and me are doing the altar. The Lilies of the Field."

"They're beautiful." Their heady scent filled Celia's nostrils, thick and exotic.

The woman smiled again. "Just keep your fingers crossed the weather brightens up, or it'll all be for nowt. They won't come out if it's raining, that's for sure."

Celia picked up her pack and, swinging it on to her back, started walking to the door. Then she had a sudden brainwave. She stopped, and turned round.

"Excuse me."

"Yes, love?"

"Could you tell me where I might find the vicar?"

"The vicar? Well, in the vicarage, my dear, I suppose. You could start there."

"And where's the vicarage?"

The woman turned and pointed towards the altar, as if the vicar might appear on top of it like a conjuring trick. "Round to the east side of the church, through the wicket gate and along the drive."

As Celia trudged along her second gravel drive of the day, she reflected that here, at least, the door wouldn't be slammed in her face. Nonetheless, the vicar took his time coming to the door; Celia stood there for a good three minutes, leaning against the jamb exhaustedly with her finger on the bell. The only reason she didn't give up was because she couldn't think where she might go instead.

At last, the door opened and the vicar stood there, a tall elegant figure all in black, wearing the requisite clerical collar and holding a white damask napkin to his lips. She had evidently disturbed his supper.

"Yes?" he said shortly, and wiped his mouth. "What is it?"

Celia blinked, taken aback. She hadn't expected him to be curt; weren't vicars meant to be good with people, have whatever the clergy equivalent was of a bedside manner? He was also quite young, and very good-looking. Celia wasn't used to handsome vicars; all the ones she had ever come across were old, or at least middle-aged, and somehow dusty-looking.

She stood there, on the vicarage doorstep, and blinked again.

"Well, come along," he said again, irritation in his voice. "What is it? What do you want?"

Celia swallowed. "I need help."

The vicar raised a perfectly shaped black eyebrow. "Oh, really? And would this help come in the form of cash, by any chance?"

"Cash?" Celia was puzzled.

"And once I've given you the help," he continued, "I daresay it would disappear up in smoke."

"What?" Then it dawned on her. He thought she was a druggie. Tears of frustration and helplessness pricked behind her eyelids. *To come all this way, for this response – first at Hill House, and now here, from a vicar of all people!*

She blinked away the tears and drew herself up to her full height. "I'm not a smackhead," she told him, with as much dignity she could manage. "I don't do drugs. I always thought priests were supposed to help people in need." She gulped slightly, emotion threatening to overwhelm her attempt to get across to the vicar that she was a genuinely needy case.

The vicar sighed, resignedly, and pushed back an immaculately laundered cuff to look at his watch.

"All right then. Shoot. I'm all ears. I can give you precisely one minute, then I must go off to the diocesan meeting for which I'm already twenty minutes late."

Celia stared at him. What kind of vicar treated his flock with such naked resentment? Or maybe he was charm personified with his flock, and had just taken against her for some reason.

She pressed her lips together, emotion suddenly overtaken by righteous indignation. "I'm sorry to be taking up so much of your precious time," she said. "But this won't take as long as a minute."

"What, then?" he frowned, puzzled. "What is it you want?"

"Sanctuary," Celia said, clearly, and lifted her chin. "I need sanctuary."

CHAPTER 4

Perhaps, Celia reflected, shovelling another mouthful of steak and kidney pie into her mouth as if she hadn't eaten for months, perhaps her praying, or whatever it was she'd been doing back there in the church, hadn't been pointless after all. Perhaps somebody – some higher being, some spiritual force for good – had recognized her genuine need, and heeded her petitions. Wasn't that how it went?

Oh yeah. Sure. She washed down the pie with a hefty slurp of Coke. *The only reason I'm here now is because of my own efforts. Because I insisted on that apology for a vicar helping me.*

"Feeling better, love?"

Celia looked up and smiled. The pub landlady stood before her, looking anxious.

"Fine, thanks."

"Food all right?"

"Delicious." Celia waved her knife and fork in appreciation. "Fantastic. Just what the doctor ordered."

"You're not still feeling ill, are you?" The anxious expression increased.

"No, no. I'm fine, honestly. It was just a whatsit – a figure of speech."

"Well, as long as you're sure. Would you like a sweet?" She consulted the typewritten list she held and reeled off a long list of alternatives, ending with sticky-toffee pudding. Celia's head reeled. She wasn't sure she felt up to making decisions, even simple ones like what pudding to have.

"That sounds great," she said.

"Which one?"

"Oh – er – the sticky toffee."

"Custard, cream or ice-cream?"

"Ice-cream, please."

While she waited for her pudding, Celia's mind returned to the vicarage doorstep. Her demand for sanctuary had dented the vicar's composure. There was no doubt about it. He had blinked, raised his eyebrows, put a hand to his throat – an elegant, manicured hand, she couldn't help noticing, with a gold ring of Celtic clasped hands on the little finger – and taken a sharp indrawn breath through his nostrils. It was worth having to resort to melodramatics, Celia thought, for the satisfaction of that response. *Pompous git!*

"Sanctuary?" he repeated, as if he had never heard the word before.

Celia said calmly, "Yes."

"Are you in trouble?"

"Yes," she said again, simply.

"What kind of trouble?"

She just looked at him, steadily.

He lifted an appeasing hand. "OK. Point taken. None of my business." He stepped back, into the hallway. "Look, come in a moment. While I think about what's the best thing to do."

"Won't I be keeping you from your meeting?" Sarcasm, to prevent the threatened tears from spilling over. He glanced at her sharply, and she felt herself blush.

"Can I stay here?" she asked, boldly, in an attempt to draw his attention away from her reddening face. *Pathetic – like a child, a silly, embarrassed little girl!*

He dismissed that suggestion with a wave of the napkin he still held.

"Of course not. This is a vicarage, not a hostel." Then he softened slightly. "I'm sorry. I don't have the facilities here for looking after the homeless."

"I'm not homeless!" Celia objected, lifting her chin.

"Then what's all this about needing sanctuary?

"I just do, OK? Stop asking all these questions!"

"But you can't just turn up on my doorstep, out of the blue, demanding sanctuary like a medieval martyr, and not expect me to ask *some* questions!"

"Please." Celia took a deep breath and shut her eyes.

Since the Cavendishes had declined even to speak to her, shutting the door in her face, she had felt as if she was losing control, as if something vital was slipping from her grasp. If she let this man gain the upper hand and decide her destiny she didn't think she could bear it.

"Please," she said again, imploringly. "Please help me. I'm in trouble, I need your help. I'm not asking for money. I've got money: I can pay. But I need a place to stay. Just for a few nights. Just to get my head straight."

She didn't know where the words came from, didn't think she was capable at that moment of being so articulate after all the traumatic events of the day, but it seemed to do the trick, because the vicar directed her back to the church.

"You'll find some women in there doing flowers for the Festival. Ask for Mary Thwaite. She's the landlady of the Eagle and Child, down the road; she should be able to put you up for a night or two. Tell her I sent you."

"Will it make a difference?" She wasn't being provocative this time, just asking.

"It will to the bill." Then he smiled at her. It transformed his face, turning him instantly from

Vlad the Impaler into the Good Shepherd. "Mary will look after you. Tell her I'll call round in the morning; if you're about I'll come and see how you're getting on."

Celia trudged back the way she'd come. She was reminded of a film she'd seen once, where the main character kept reliving the same events of the same day, over and over again, caught up on a bizarre exhausting treadmill from which there was no escape. The church-door latch clunked again as she lifted it, and the door creaked, just as before. There were the two women, trimming tall flower stems and pushing them into containers, murmuring quietly to each other. The only difference was that the lights were now on, and she could see more clearly.

"Hello, dear!" The woman who had spoken to her earlier, who had directed her to the vicarage, put down her secateurs and hurried briskly up the aisle towards Celia. "You're back again! Wasn't he in?"

"Who?" Tiredness fuddled Celia's brain, so that for a moment she didn't know who the woman was referring to, thought she meant the Cavendish man.

"Richard Daley. The vicar, love – I thought that was where you'd been, to the vicarage."

"Yes, he was in. He sent me back here. Are you Mary Thwaite?"

"That's right. What can I do for you?"

"He told me –" Celia swayed slightly, from the weight of her rucksack, and put out a hand on the back of a pew to steady herself. "He told me you might be able to put me up for a night or two. He said to tell you he'd sent me. He said he'd call round in the morning."

She was dimly aware of Mary Thwaite peering intently into her face. It was most odd, as if the other woman was at the end of a long black tunnel, receding further and further into the distance.

"Are you all right?" said Mary Thwaite, anxiously. Her voice echoed and boomed as if from a long way off. "You don't look very well."

"I'm fine," Celia assured her, and with that the end of the tunnel closed completely, and she keeled over on to the cold stone of the church floor in a dead faint.

It was lucky, Celia mused, swallowing the last mouthful of her pudding, that she had been wearing the backpack; she had slumped down on to it, it broke her fall and saved her from injuring herself. Ironic, too, as she'd been cursing the thing for its clumsiness and heaviness and downright *nuisanceness*, all day. All week, it felt like. All year. *My entire life has been spent heaving it around and having people send me away*. It was hard to believe she'd set out on her journey less than twelve hours previously.

She wiped her mouth with the napkin, stood up, and looked around for the landlady. Mary Thwaite materialized beside her as if by magic.

"This way then, love. I'll show you to your room."

The room, under the eaves at the top of three increasingly steep and narrow flights of stairs, was tiny and sparsely furnished, with just enough space for an iron-framed bed and a small chest of drawers. A washbasin was tucked into a corner under the window, and a curtained alcove did duty as a wardrobe. But it was large enough for Celia's needs, and pretty too, in a cosy cottagey way; the sloping ceiling was heavily beamed, the chest of drawers bore a large blue and white china dish of dried rose petals, the bed was covered with what looked like an antique patchwork bedspread in faded, lovingly hand-stitched blues and creams and greens. And the view from the window – Celia took two paces forward and peered out – was magical. She hadn't realized she was so close to the sea, having not taken much notice of her surroundings since stepping out of the cab at Hill House. Things other than the attractiveness of the place had somehow taken precedence.

It was twilight now; it had stopped raining, and the sky was daubed across with smeary clouds, their undersides reflecting pink and gold with the setting sun. To the right, lights from the town across a wide estuary twinkled and shimmered, against the dark navy-blue of the sky. Despite herself, Celia was impressed, moved by the beauty of the picture framed by the dormer window.

"Morecambe Bay," said Mrs Thwaite, with pride in her voice. "You can't beat it. I've done some travelling in my time, but I've always been glad to come home to good old Morecambe Bay."

It didn't sound very romantic. Celia smiled politely, dumping her backpack on the floor.

"This is great," she said, indicating the room, and sat down suddenly on the bed.

The older woman bent her neck and looked into Celia's face, clearly still concerned.

"Are you quite sure you're all right? You did faint, after all. People don't go around fainting for no reason, in my experience."

Celia smiled again, in what she hoped was a reassuring manner, and said: "Really, I'm fine. Honestly. I was just tired, and hungry – I hadn't eaten anything all day."

Mrs Thwaite nodded sagely. "A good night's sleep, that's what you need." She turned down the bedspread and pulled back the curtain concealing the alcove. "You can hang your things in here."

She glanced at Celia's rucksack, and Celia grinned.

"Haven't got many things. As you can see. Not stuff that needs hanging up, at any rate."

"Well, anyway." Mrs Thwaite busied herself around the room for a few moments, setting the china bowl on the chest into a more satisfactory position, giving the chintzy curtains a straightening twitch or two. It was as if she wanted to say something, to ask something, but lacked the nerve. Celia watched her, wondering when she would go and leave her in peace.

"When would you like breakfast?" she asked, eventually.

Celia shrugged. "I'm not really a breakfast person."

"But you must have breakfast!" Mrs Thwaite looked shocked, as if Celia had confessed to being a serial killer. "Most important meal of the day, breakfast! My full English is famous throughout the Lake District, even if I do say so myself."

Celia thought of bacon and mushrooms and sausages, glistening with grease, of runny-yolked fried eggs and pulpy grilled tomatoes sitting in their wrinkled leathery skins, and started to feel nauseous again.

"I'll see," she said, faintly, and turned to fiddle with the straps of her pack.

Mrs Thwaite went to the door. "Just come down in the morning when you're ready," she said. "I'll be around somewhere. Ask at Reception if you can't find me. Bathroom's along the corridor. And if you want anything in the night, there's a bureau with a bell on it on the middle landing. Give it a ring, and someone will come to help. Goodnight, then. Sleep well." She opened the door and went out, but almost immediately popped her head back round it. "Do you know, I don't even know what to call you. What's your name, my love?"

Celia felt a small panic, a momentary twinge of alarm. She put an involuntary hand on her backpack, as if the key to her identity lay within. Which in a way, she supposed it did. She thought of her birth certificate, lying snugly inside its velvet box.

"Simone," she said. "My name's Simone."

"Goodnight then, Simone."

Mary Thwaite closed the door behind her and Celia hefted her rucksack on to the floor, opened the drawstrings at the top and began taking things out in a half-hearted attempt at unpacking. After a very few moments, however, the comfort of the bed, the relief of a roof over her head for the night and the fact of not having to make any more decisions for at least another twelve hours proved too much. Bending, she pulled off her boots with a grunt, switched off the light, slid under the patchwork bedspread and was asleep almost before her eyes were properly closed.

A bell was ringing somewhere, insistently. Her alarm clock. It was time to get up and go to school. What exam was it today? *History 2, that's right. Oh God. Bloody History 2. No, that can't be right. That was yesterday.*

Celia opened one eye, completely disorientated, as the memory of yesterday's events swept over her. *If only that flaming bell would shut up, let me think straight.*

She opened both her eyes, and sat up. The ringing, she realized suddenly, was coming from her rucksack. It was her mobile. *Who on earth's ringing me at this time of night?* She peered at the luminous hands on her watch. Eleven-thirty. She could only have been asleep for an hour or so.

She plunged an arm down beside the bed and into the rucksack, feeling around frantically until she located the phone.

"Hello?"

"Thank Christ for that! Shit, Celia, where are you? Where've you *been*?" It was Phoebe. She sounded upset, to say the least.

"Until thirty seconds ago, in the Land of Nod," Celia mumbled.

"What?" Phoebe's voice rose several deci-bels. "You mean you were asleep? Your mother's got the entire Berkshire police force out looking for you, everyone's been imagining you murdered or raped or worse, and you were *asleep*?"

Phoebe's voice disappeared off the sound scale, and Celia held the phone away from her ear, wincing, and wondering vaguely what could be worse than being murdered or raped. Made to come back and finish History 2, perhaps.

"I'm OK," she assured her friend. "Honestly. Tell her I'm OK."

"You can tell her yourself," Phoebe said. "She's downstairs. I'll go and get her."

"No!" Whatever happened, she couldn't speak to Mum. No way. "Just tell her. Please, Feebs. It's important."

"But where are you?"

"I'm perfectly safe. There's no need to worry. I said so in my note."

"What note?"

"I left a note. At home. On the hall table. I said I was going away for a few days. I said not to worry."

"Nobody said anything about finding a note," said Phoebe, definitely.

"Well, what happened to it, then?"

"How do I know? Look, you're not with Josh,

64

are you? He said he hadn't seen you, but I thought he sounded a bit suss. Kind of evasive."

"I'm not with Josh. I'm not even in Ascot."

"So where are you, then? When you went belting out of that exam this afternoon, I thought – well, I didn't know what to think. And I've had your parents and mine bending my ear all evening as if I'm in cahoots with you, and must know where you are. . . What's going on, Celia?"

Celia tried vainly to collect her thoughts. All she could think of to say was: "I'm sorry."

"Sorry for what?"

"For getting you involved."

"I don't give a stuff about that. I just want to know you're OK, that's all."

"I'm OK. Like I said. I'm just – " She thought of something. "Why didn't you try phoning before? Why didn't Mum and Dad?"

Why didn't Josh, if he knew I'd gone off? Doesn't he care?

Back in Ascot, at the other end of the world, Phoebe sighed.

"Nobody knew you'd gone back to collect your phone and stuff. Nobody knew *anything*. Far as we were concerned," (Celia noted the "we"; so Phoebe was aligning herself with her parents now, was she?) "you'd run off, out of the exam, to God knows where. It was the police who suggested your mum check your room, see if anything was missing, although they told me to try ringing you. They thought there was a better chance of you talking to me than to her."

"So you weren't joking, then, about the police?"

"Celia, it's been hours! Your mum was *frantic*! If you could've seen her –" There was a tiny, guilt-laden silence.

"Sorry," Celia said again, softly. "I really am sorry. But I'm all right. You can hear I am, can't you? You will tell them, won't you?"

Another silence.

"OK," said Phoebe, doubtfully.

"And they'll tell the police? To stop looking for me?"

"I guess. Tell the truth, the cops were taking it with a sackful of salt anyway. They kept going on about boyfriends. Has she got a boyfriend, Mrs Duckenfield? It was obvious they thought you'd pushed off together somewhere."

"Where?" Celia couldn't imagine why any-body would have thought she and *Josh*. . .

"God knows. Gretna Green, probably."

"Yeah, right. As if."

Another pause. Then: "Celia?"

Here it comes. "Yeah?"

"You haven't gone looking for your mother, have you?"

This time the silence went on, grew and expanded until Celia could hear the echo of her own heartbeat, resounding in her head. How could she answer?

"Seal? Are you still there?"

"I'm still here."

"You have, haven't you? You've been and gone and done it."

Celia sighed, a heavy sigh of resignation. "Yeah."

"Well, look –" Phoebe lowered her voice, as if trying to prevent what she said from being over-heard, "you look after yourself. You hear me? Just – just be careful. There's people back here who care about what happens to you," she said, in a fierce whisper, "and I'm one of them. Understand? Look, gotta go. I can hear someone coming to check up on me. I'll tell them you're OK but didn't want to talk. Ring me soon, yeah? *Ring* me! Bye."

She rang off, and Celia was left holding her phone. She stared at the keypad, luminous green in the dark, and wondered what the morning was going to bring.

She woke again at seven, to her surprise, and was instantly awake, her mind alert and ready for action. The patch of sky framed by her window was blue and cloudless. Celia pushed back the bedcovers – she had gone to bed properly following Phoebe's phone call, even washing her face and brushing her teeth, like a good little Lady Margaret's girl – and swung her legs on to the floor.

Her clothes from the day before lay where she had dropped them, in a jumbled heap on the floor, still damp from when she was caught in the rain. She tugged out clean clothes from the rucksack and pulled them on hurriedly. Then she thrust her feet into her DMs, picked up her fleece from the end of the bed, and left the room, closing the door behind her with a soft click.

It was a stunningly beautiful day. There were already signs of life downstairs at the Eagle and Child: somebody was on duty at reception, a tall young woman in a trim dark blue suit, her fair hair pulled back in the kind of smart French pleat Celia's hair would never, in a million years, be tamed into. A dray was pulled up outside the front door, its rear doors open wide. Two men were unloading large aluminium barrels of beer and passing them beefily down to an unseen being in the cellar below. Celia peered down into the large gaping hole as she came out of the front door.

"Morning, flower." One of the draymen winked at her as she passed. "Mind that hole, now. Don't want you falling in there."

Celia followed the road around to her right, and found herself walking down to the seashore. She went through a kissing gate next to a cattle grid, and along a track which led to a car park. The salt marshes spread out before her, the sheep-nibbled turf washed clean by last night's tide. The grass was interspersed with irregularly shaped pools and channels, carved out by the sea; full of water now, they reflected the clear blue of the sky and glittered in the sunlight. It was as if, Celia thought, some mighty heavenly being had flung down a huge handful of mirror shards amongst the patches of green turf.

She walked right down to the sea, enjoying the feel of the wind on her face, and then turned left along the shore. There was a stiff breeze coming in directly off the sea, but unlike yesterday it felt warm and somehow tender. After a while, she scrambled on to a large boulder and sat there, looking out to sea, and listening to the plaintive cries of the seabirds. There were hordes of them searching for their breakfast out on the smooth vast expanse of sand exposed by the low tide. Despite the noise from the birds it was utterly peaceful. Celia felt both curiously calm and enormously strong, resolute, as if she could achieve anything. *Must be the sea air. Negative ions, Phoebe would say. . .* She closed her eyes and let her mind go blank, breathing in great draughts of it, enjoying the feeling of her diaphragm expanding, letting the negative ions – whatever they were – right down to the very bottom of her lungs. Faintly, in the distance, she was aware of a human voice added to that of the birds'. Someone, somewhere, was calling a dog.

It came closer. And closer still.

Go away, she thought, crossly. *You're disturbing all this lovely peace and quiet.*

But it impinged on her consciousness to such an extent that she couldn't blot it out any more. Reluctantly, she opened her eyes. She could see two figures a hundred metres or so in the distance – a black dog, galloping frantically around with something dangling down from its mouth, and a man. At least, she assumed it was a man.

He came closer. Tall; dark hair. Dark-blue shorts and lighter blue T-shirt. Dark-blue anorak thing. Yup. Definitely a man. No girl that Celia knew ever wore an anorak.

As Celia watched, the man lifted an arm and waved to her. Celia didn't wave back. It was either a case of mistaken identity, she reasoned – who knew her in Silverdale? – or a loony. But as the man drew closer, followed by the dog, still excited beyond belief by the presence of whatever it held in its mouth, Celia realized with a faint sense of foreboding that it was the vicar. Richard Daley.

"Morning," he said, as he reached her. "You're out early."

"So are you," Celia retorted.

"Walking the dog."

He waved a hand in its direction, and Celia could see that the object it was carrying was a dead rabbit in an almost final state of decomposition.

"Oh God!" she said, with a horrified giggle.

"Yeah, I know. Disgusting, isn't he? I try to ignore him. No, Tea!" he shouted, as the dog, spotting Celia, made a beeline for her, wagging from the shoulders down, and proudly showing her his present.

He threw a stick, and the dog went bounding after it, rabbit still in mouth.

"Fetch, Tea! Fetch!"

"Tea?" said Celia. "What kind of name is that?"

"Short for TFD," said the vicar. "Short, in its turn, for That – er," he glanced at her, "That Effing Dog."

"I see," Celia said, gravely.

"Didn't you hear me calling you?"

"I did," she said, "but I ignored you."

"Right." He nodded. "Can't say I blame you, after the reception I gave you last night. I wanted to apologize."

"Wanted?"

"OK. Want, then. I want to apologize."

71

Celia waited, and he grinned.

"You don't take any prisoners, do you? Simone, I apologize. I was rude and abrupt and – and various other things no vicar should ever be, and I apologize. Profusely. From the bottom of my heart." He placed a hand, gently mocking, on his chest, and bowed. "There. Will that do?"

"You forgot pompous."

"I did. It's a failing of mine."

"Forgetting, or being pompous?"

"Both."

Celia found herself looking at his legs. They were nice legs, tanned and muscular and with just the right amount of hair sprinkled on them.

"How do you know my name?" she said, suddenly.

He blinked. "Mary rang me. Last night."

"For a progress report?"

"Not exactly. Just to say you were OK, she'd fed you, you'd gone to bed. Why," he asked, leaning forward and looking into her face, "are you so prickly?"

Celia blushed. She felt it rise up her neck and face, a hot crimson tide.

"I'm not," she mumbled.

He sat down beside her, on her rock, and his shorts rose up his thighs. Celia averted her eyes, drew up her knees and wrapped her arms around them. She laid her head on her knees, right side down, away from him.

"I really am sorry," he said, softly. "Don't tell the bishop, will you?"

Despite herself, Celia giggled.

"In my defence, I'd had a pig of a day. And I really do get loads of druggies calling, asking for money. Thinking I'll be a soft touch."

"You should help them, too," Celia said, piously.

"I do. But I don't give them money."

A silence fell between them, but it was a silence Celia felt comfortable with.

"Mary's looking for kitchen staff," he said, at length.

Celia lifted her head. "Is she?"

"Casual work. Washing up, preparing veggies. That kind of thing. If you're interested."

"I might be." She was cautious, non-committal.

"Right then." He stood up. "Best be off, give the dog his breakfast. See you around, maybe? You know where I am if you need me. And Simone?"

"Yeah?"

"Good luck."

He whistled for his dog, and was gone, striding easily across the salt marsh.

CHAPTER 5

Celia came to an arrangement with Mary Thwaite that she would work two shifts a day in the kitchen in return for her food and room.

"I can pay," Celia objected, at first. "I told whatsisname – Richard Daley. The vicar. I'm not a charity case."

"No-one's suggesting you are," the landlady replied, mildly. "I just thought you might appreciate some help. Save your money. You might need it elsewhere."

"Elsewhere?"

The landlady smiled in a motherly way. "You do as you please, dear. You pay me if you want. I shan't take offence if you don't want the work. But the offer's there, just the same."

So Celia found herself working from eight until eleven in the mornings, and six until ten at night. There was a lot to do, but it wasn't hard work exactly. Not what Celia would call hard work, at any rate; revising for exams, that was hard work, not washing pots and pans, unloading the dishwasher, peeling vegetables, emptying bins and sweeping floors. The lack of mental effort needed for the work, the sheer mindlessness of it, Celia found curiously soothing. It could have meant she had time on her hands to think, to go over her situation endlessly in her mind, but she didn't let herself. She didn't permit herself to think of anything much as she went about her mundane little tasks, just let her mind drift lazily from this unimportant topic to that, like a piece of seaweed carried along willy-nilly by the tide, and never once allowed herself to dwell on thoughts of home, or anything connected with it. If any such ideas came into her mind she would cram them down into the lowermost recesses of her brain, and think vigorously of something else, something mundane, the slipperiness of the plates she was unloading, for example, or the bright colours of the peppers she was chopping.

Her off-duty time she spent walking along the seashore or sitting in her room reading or just daydreaming. It was as if part of her mental processes, the part responsible for decision-making and analytical thought, had short-circuited. She was quite content, nonetheless, in a sleepy, passive kind of way.

Mary Thwaite knocked on her door one day after lunch. Lunch had been leftover casserole of pork and cider and a jacket potato, followed by steamed ginger pudding, and Celia was lying on her bed, drowsy and heavy with food. They fed her well at the Eagle and Child, she had to admit. She had undone the waistband of her jeans, as it had been digging in to her middle.

"I wondered," Mrs Thwaite began, "if you'd consider helping out in the restaurant this evening? A spot of waitressing. We're short-staffed, you see, and as it's Saturday night—"

She gave an apologetic little grimace, spread her hands and shrugged, as if she alone were responsible for which day of the week it was.

Celia sat up, surprised. "Is it? Is it Saturday already?"

She had left the exam on Monday. Left school, left home. Left behind everything familiar and known.

"Well, yes. Is anything wrong?"

"Not really. I'd just lost track of time." Celia sat up. "I'll work in the restaurant if you want," she said, "but I haven't got the right clothes. I've only got these –" she indicated her jeans, "and a pair of combats. Nothing very waitressy."

"That's all right, dear. I'll have a word with Denise. I'm sure she'll be able to lend you something."

Denise was the head waitress; about ten years older than Celia, she was bossy with the rest of the staff and pert and flirty with the male customers. Celia had disliked her on sight.

Sure enough, twenty minutes later there was another knock at Celia's door. Denise had brought with her a voluminous black skirt with an elasticated waistband and a white polyester shirt, awful in its plainness, and three sizes too big. The whole ensemble was in such contrast to the Spandex pelmet skirts and stretchy little tops Denise wore at work that Celia wondered who on earth the clothes belonged to. Not Denise, that was for sure. Unless she'd lost around four stone since buying them, and had a taste transplant to boot.

"I'd have brought you something a bit more funky," said Denise, chattily, "but you're fatter than me, aren't you?"

Celia couldn't be bothered to react. Instead, she took the clothes from Denise and laid them on her bed.

"OK," she said. She was damned if she was going to thank the cow. "Oh, one problem. I've only got those –" she indicated her Doc Martens, lying blamelessly on the floor, "to wear on my feet."

"Oh my God." Denise eyed the boots as if they might contain a poisonous snake. "Oh well. You'll just have to wear them, I guess. Better than barefoot."

She somehow managed to imply from her tone that not only did Celia usually go around wearing no shoes, but that if she did so this evening all the customers in the restaurant would undoubtedly be gassed by the appalling stench coming from her feet.

After Denise had gone, Celia took two hangers from the rail in the alcove behind the curtain and carefully hung up the skirt and blouse. Then she sat back down on the bed, opened the top drawer of the chest, and took out her mobile. She sat looking at it for some time, turning it over in her hands and examining it from all angles. Eventually, she took a deep breath and started to punch in the familiar digits of Phoebe's number; but halfway through she changed her mind, and dialled another instead.

The ringing seemed to go on for ever. There was obviously nobody in. Celia could imagine the telephone at the other end, ringing insistently in the empty hall in the empty house. She was on the verge of pressing the End button when quite suddenly there was a voice in her ear.

"Hello?"

A breathless voice. Her brother.

"Eddie. It's me."

"Celia! Shit a brick! It's not really you, is it? Where are you? Mum and Dad have been going ape here, they're—"

"Never mind all that." She cut across him,

but gently. Their usual relationship was the normal one between a girl of her age and her younger brother, in other words, they rarely spoke to each other without some degree of either sarcasm or snarling. But for all that, she was absurdly glad to hear his voice. She could feel a small hard lump in her throat, as if she had swallowed a marble.

"Yes, but—"

"Eddie, just listen. Tell them," she said, slowly and carefully, "that I'm all right. I just needed to get away for a bit. But I'm safe, I've got a job, and somewhere to live. OK? Have you got that?"

"You're safe," he repeated, with abnormal obedience, "you've got a job, and somewhere to live. What sort of job?"

"In a hotel. Well, a pub, really. That's where I'm living, too."

"Living in a pub? Cool! When are you coming—"

There was an odd muffled noise at the other end of the line, as if Edward had dropped the receiver.

"Eddie! Hello? Are you still there?"

"Celia, what the hell do you think you're playing at?"

It was her father. Celia froze. She didn't answer. Couldn't answer.

"Celia!" he barked. "Are you there?"

She clutched the phone in dismay. She almost hung up, but a small part of her desperately didn't want to, wanted to retain that contact with home.

"Yes," she said. It came out as a croak. She cleared her throat. "I'm here."

"Just what game is it you're up to? You're to come home at once, do you hear? At *once!*"

"It's not a game," Celia muttered. She could feel all her new-found tranquillity and contentment drain away from her, like bathwater down a plughole. "And I'm not coming home," she added, in an attempt at defiance. It sounded hollow, even to her own ears.

"Of course you're coming home!" her father bellowed. "You've been gone for days! Your mother has been beside herself with worry, *beside* herself!"

"I'm sorry. I didn't mean to worry her." Useless to mention the note: according to Phoebe, they'd never found it.

"Well, you have worried her! What did you expect us to do, say 'oh well, that's her gone, then', and put your room up for rent? Of course we've been worried, you terminally self-centred child!"

I'm not self-centred, Celia wanted to shout, *and I'm certainly not a child.* But nothing came out.

"Have you run out of money?" he went on. "Have you got yourself stranded somewhere? Tell me where you are, and I'll come and fetch you. I'll come now, I don't care how far away you are."

"This isn't about *money*!" Celia yelled, galvanized suddenly into speech, furious tears springing to her eyes. "Why is everything always about money with you? What about people? Don't they matter?"

"Celia!" Her father's voice was suddenly replaced by that of her mother. "Celia, it's all right. Calm down. Just calm down."

"It's not me!" Celia roared, childishly. "It's him!" A tear spilled from her eye and rolled down the side of her nose and into her mouth, and she dashed it away with her hand, angrily.

"I know." Her mother spoke soothingly. "It's just such a relief to hear your voice, to know you're all right. Relief always comes out as anger with Dad: you know what he's like. He's been so worried about you. We both have."

Celia sniffed. She rooted around in her pocket for a tissue, and blew her nose.

"I only rang to let you know I was OK. I wasn't intending to have a slanging match with Dad."

"He doesn't mean it. Honestly."

Yeah, thought Celia cynically, *and I bet you'll*

make sure you tell him so, later. Dad might bluster around like a bear with a sore head – and did, frequently – but Mum had always been the one who made the decisions, the power behind the throne.

She sniffed again. "Well. Anyway. I'm all right. As you can hear."

"But where are you?"

"I can't tell you that"

"Can't? Or won't?"

"OK then. Won't." Celia felt another spurt of anger. She pushed it down. "I don't want you to know where I am. That do you?"

"Oh, darling." Her mother sighed.

Celia was astonished. Mum never called her darling, never. Theirs simply wasn't that kind of relationship.

"Look," she said, with some urgency. "I will come home, but not yet. There's just something I've got to do. And I've got to do it by myself. Please try and understand."

"Is it your mother?" Mum's voice sounded strained. "You haven't gone off on a wild goose chase looking for her, have you?"

Celia didn't understand how Mum could possibly have known. She had said nothing about wishing to trace Genevieve to anybody, apart from Phoebe, and she wouldn't have let on. On pain of death, she wouldn't. Feebs might have her faults – didn't everyone – but she wasn't a telltale, or a gossip either. Perhaps it was just a lucky guess on Mum's part.

"I can't tell you that," Celia responded, cautiously.

"Oh, Celia." Mum sighed again. "Please don't do anything stupid."

Celia's anger spilled over. "Why should I do anything stupid? Are you saying *I'm* stupid?"

"Of course not. But you're only sixteen—"

"Nearly seventeen."

"All right, nearly seventeen. But it's still very young."

"Young for what?"

"To be trailing round the countryside by yourself on a—"

"A wild goose chase, yeah. You said. What makes you so sure that's what I'm doing?"

A moment's silence. *That's got her. She can't answer that.*

Mum seemed to collect herself. Her tone changed to one of brisk efficiency.

"Well, you're a big girl now. If you won't tell us where you are and say you won't come home yet, that's that. We can't force you. Just promise me something?"

"Depends what it is."

"That you'll be careful. And that you'll ring, to let us know how you are?"

"That's two things."

"But you will, won't you? Promise?"

"I'll be careful. Of course I will."

"And you'll phone? Every day?"

"I'll try. But not every day. I can't promise that. But I'll do what I can."

"Then I suppose that must do."

"Mum, I've got to go now. I've got to work."

"You've got a job?" She sounded surprised.

"Yes. I told you I was all right, didn't I? Look, must go. Bye!"

"Celia!" Mum's voice sounded suddenly unsure, wobbly. Panicky.

"What? What is it?"

"I love you. *We* love you. Remember that, won't you?"

Celia rather enjoyed being a waitress, which surprised her mildly. When he was little, Edward had always called waiters servants: not from any precocious sense of superiority, but simply because he hadn't known the proper word for them. Celia had never seen herself in the role of serving others before, but now she was doing it, she quite liked it. She enjoyed carrying her little pad and pencil around, and trotting out all those well-worn phrases so familiar from countless meals out with Mum and Dad and Eddie: "Are you ready to order?"; "Can I get you the dessert menu?"; "Enjoy your meals!"

Nobody had told her to say these things. It all seemed to come quite naturally. It was as if she had been rehearsing a part for years – an undemanding part, with few lines to learn – and was now finally on stage doing it. The feeling of acting a role extended to the clothes she wore, those dreadful unflattering garments that had arrived courtesy of Denise. They were so outside the sphere of her normal choice of attire that putting them on had felt like dressing up. As she had suspected, the skirt was miles too big, so she had hitched it up round her waist with the belt from her jeans. She had then put on a white vest top, taken from her meagre and dwindling supply of clean clothes, and over it the shirt (which reminded her implacably of school uniform), unbuttoned, tied at the waist, and with sleeves rolled up to the elbows. Her Docs completed the ensemble, and she was quite pleased with the final result.

Until, that is, she caught sight of herself in the full-length mirror on the landing, on her way down to the restaurant. She stopped in her tracks, caught in a kind of horrified fascination. The vision that stared back at her looked like a cross between Little Orphan Annie and a bag lady.

"Bloody hell," she whispered, truly appalled.

There was nothing she could do about it now. She would have to go and present herself in those clothes, or not at all.

Downstairs, the kitchen was a hive of activity. Nobody else seemed to think she looked peculiar or inappropriately dressed, or if they did, they didn't comment. Apart from Denise.

"You'll have to tie your hair back," she threw over her shoulder to Celia, bustling in through the swing doors from the restaurant. "You can't wait on tables with that lot hanging round your face, it's unhygienic."

"Here." One of the other waitresses, a pale skinny girl with a long stringy dust-coloured ponytail and bad acne, passed Celia a small stretchy black towelling band. "I've got a spare – you can borrow it if you like."

"Thanks." Celia took it, gratefully, and forced her springy auburn tresses through it with difficulty.

"You've got such beautiful hair," the other girl said, dreamily. "Pre-Raphaelite."

Celia said "Thanks," again, and thought how much nicer Pre-Raphaelite sounded than ginger. She stuck out a hand. "I'm Simone."

"Karen. Pleased to meet you."

"Me too. What are we supposed to be doing?"

"Christ knows. Waiting for our orders from the Führer, I suppose. Tell you what though,

Simone." Karen lowered her voice, conspiratorially. "That Denise is a right cow."

Celia pulled a face, pretending to be shocked, and they exchanged grins.

"Tell you something else," Celia said, holding out the full folds of her skirt with a grimace. "This outfit is pants."

"I didn't like to say anything," said Karen. "I thought it might be *haute couture* down south, where you come from."

"Down south? Is it that obvious?"

"Obvious? Get off!" Karen smiled at her. "Steve and me thought you were a spy from Egon Ronay."

"Egon who?"

"Ronay. You know, the Good Food Guide lot. Come to check us out."

At eight o'clock, Celia and Karen took their short break together. The remark about Denise, Karen's recognition of Celia's opinion of her, had created some kind of bond between them. A fragile bond, but it was nonetheless there. It was good to have discovered a friendly face of her own age, somebody with some fellow feeling. Not that Celia told Karen anything about herself, or nothing of importance anyway. As far as Karen was concerned, Celia was Simone, a free spirit, just passing through in the process of getting her head sorted.

Just before the end of the shift, Denise sent Celia out into the restaurant.

"You can go and clear table twelve," she said, bossily. "And make sure you give it a good wipe. There's salt and spilt wine and all sorts on it. Just because there's only five minutes to go doesn't mean you can slack off, so don't think you can."

Celia, who had worked hard all evening and had thought no such thing, picked up a tray and pushed her way crossly through the swing doors. *Miserable cow! Just because she's having a bad hair day doesn't mean she has to take it out on us.*

She reached table twelve, pinned a professional waitressy smile on her face, and began loading the dirty dishes on to her tray.

"I hope you enjoyed your meal," she said to the elderly couple who sat there, chatting quietly and finishing their bottle of wine. "If I can just clear away these—"

She broke off, mid-sentence, as the man, helpfully passing her a plate, looked up and caught her eye, and Celia found herself looking into the face of Stanley Cavendish.

When Celia had first had the idea of trying to find her mother she had selected an adoption agency from the Yellow Pages, on an impulse and at random, and rung them for advice. It was when Celia had begun calling herself Simone, the name her birth mother had given her. When she started to ring the agency with more frequency, asking increasingly desperate questions, Kate Lane, one of the counsellors, had given Celia her home telephone number.

"I shouldn't really," Kate had said. "I shouldn't be helping you at all. I can't help you find your mother until you're over eighteen. It's the law."

"I am eighteen," Celia had lied.

Kate said, kindly, "Simone. We both know that's not true."

"So why are you doing it, then?"

"There's no law against being a friendly ear. I'm adopted, too. I understand what you're going through."

She thought of Kate now as she sat on her bed, still in the hated waitress clothes, with her mobile pressed painfully against her ear. Did she really understand? Celia somehow doubted it. And if she had started off understanding, she certainly wouldn't approve of—

"Hello?"

"It's me. Ce—" she stopped. "Simone."

"Simone, my love. Hi. How's things?"

"Pretty bloody awful, actually. Since you ask."

It had never crossed her mind that she might

bump into the Cavendishes, it had simply not occurred to her, despite the fact that they lived in Silverdale and so, for the time being at least, did she. The wonder was that it had taken until now for it to happen.

She had straightened up and walked away, just walked away from them and all their dirty dishes, and their table that needed wiping. Although she had remembered the tray. She was proud of that, now, of her professionalism. She hadn't left the tray behind.

She had walked into the kitchen, handed the tray to an open-mouthed Denise – she stood there with her mouth literally hanging open, like a startled fish – and said: "I'm not feeling very well. I'm going to bed."

Once in her room, she understood with a suddenness that hit her like a tonne of bricks that all her recent calmness and serenity and peace of mind had just been an illusion. Worse, an illusion she had created to avoid facing up to reality. All she was doing was running away: she had run away from Ascot, and she was still running away. She was no nearer finding her mother than when she had fled Lady Margaret's and History 2. *Sometime last century*.

It was time to face facts. She had to decide what to do: either get back on the trail to find her mother, or give up and go home.

"Oh dear," said Kate, calmly. "I'm sorry to hear that."

"Yeah, well," Celia mumbled. "Life's a bitch."

Kate laughed, tersely. "Tell me about it. Anything in particular?"

"Not really." She was suddenly embarrassed. "Look, I'm really sorry to have phoned you at home. On a Saturday night, and that."

"Don't worry about it. I don't mind a bit."

"I'd better go."

"If you're sure there's nothing I can help with?"

"There isn't." *Only I can do that.*

"And there's nothing you want to chat about?"

"No. See you, then."

"Bye. Take care."

"Actually," Celia said, casually. As an afterthought. "There is something. I think I'm pregnant."

CHAPTER 6

The ironic, the really *unfair* thing, was that they'd only slept together a handful of times – five or six at most. And they had been careful. Well, most of the time, at any rate. With Celia's family history she was keen on avoiding accidentally getting pregnant.

It wasn't even as if she had enjoyed it that much. The idea of it she liked – she fancied Josh like mad, thought of him frequently when they were apart, and cherished the fact of their sharing such a grown-up, mature relationship. The actuality of it, though, was disappointingly different. She felt bad for admitting it, even to herself, but there you go. It was the way it was. She wouldn't have dreamed of admitting it to Josh: she would have died rather than confess her real feelings. Wasn't everyone supposed to like sex? Particularly people their age. If the media were to be believed, all teenagers were at it like rabbits at every possible opportunity.

Josh enjoyed it very much indeed. That much Celia could tell. She was pretty sure it would have been his chosen activity every time they met; never mind going for a walk or to the cinema or out for a meal, he would prefer getting his kit off and getting right down to it, all evening every evening if possible. In fact, Celia thought it could quite easily feature on his CV: *NAME – Joshua Peters; AGE – 18; QUALIFICATIONS – 10 GCSEs, 3 A-levels; HOBBIES – cricket, drama, shagging.*

Not that he pressured her, especially. Not by anything he said or did. It was just there, in the air between them, the whole time they were together; Celia was constantly aware of what he wanted to do. She found herself perpetually trying to engineer their time so that they were always with other people, so that having sex would be impossible.

Of course, there were times when this strategy didn't work and Celia found herself feeling sorry for Josh's obvious bewilderment at her lack of enthusiasm. So she would end up acquiescing and feeling as if she was being somehow dishonest. Which she supposed she was, by pretending to be as keen as him. Not that Josh would have noticed if she just lay there motionless: he was far too bound up in his own pleasure to pay much attention to what Celia was doing.

All in all, she had found the whole thing sweaty and messy and rather tedious, and furthermore she had a sneaky suspicion that Josh wasn't actually very good at it. Sex, she decided, was a much overrated pastime. She supposed it must be one of those things that gets better with practise; it had to be, or else how could you account for the fact that the whole world appeared to be obsessed with it?

She calculated that she was now more than two weeks late, even given that she had never been particularly regular. Unlike Phoebe, who could practically set her watch by her periods. An irregular cycle, the doctor had called it. Celia had gone to see him once before when she had been late, six months or so ago, and she and Phoebe had later laughed at the clumsy phrase. She hadn't been as late as this, then. Of course, she hadn't started sleeping with Josh then, either. On that occasion there was no likelihood of her being pregnant, so she could afford to have a laugh about it.

She wasn't laughing now. Being pregnant wasn't only a possibility but almost a dead cert. As well as the obvious fact of her lateness, she had intermittent nausea and felt permanently tired. There was also the matter of her fainting in the church the day she had come to Silverdale, and she had also put on weight – not a lot, but enough to notice that her waistbands were tighter than usual. The signs, Celia thought, were unmistakable. She was pregnant: and just as it had been

94

with Genevieve before her, it was unintentional, unplanned, and most of all, unwanted.

Kate's advice had been simple: do a pregnancy test, or go to the doctor; do something, and do it *now*. It wasn't, of course, as easy as that. She didn't want to be pregnant, and all the while she put off finding out for sure, she didn't have to face up to the possible consequences. It was, she realized miserably, another example of her running away.

Am I that much of a coward? It was Sunday morning, early, and she was walking along the track to the seashore, her mind in turmoil. There were so many things to face up to, so many things she should do, that she scarcely had the strength to think about them all, far less do them. As well as the matter of whether or not she was pregnant, she knew she had to go back to the Cavendishes and find out once and for all why they had reacted to her appearance at their house in so extreme a fashion. Even if she didn't find her mother at the end of it, she knew she couldn't just leave things the way they were. It was unfinished business, and it was hanging round her neck like the proverbial millstone.

It was a spectacularly beautiful morning, the sun already warm on her face, the sky pearly with heat haze; very much like the first time she had walked here, her first morning in Silverdale.

Then, though, her state of mind had been quite different. She had felt calm and peaceful, capable of anything, of making the hardest decision, and sticking to it. Today, she had about as much resolution as a bowl of cold porridge.

"Hello there!"

It was, inevitably, Richard Daley, the vicar. He was standing at the water's edge, throwing a stick for his dog, who plunged ecstatically into the water to retrieve it. Celia had been trudging along so engrossed in her own thoughts she hadn't even seen him until she was practically upon him.

"Settling in?"

Celia shrugged. "Sure."

"I gather you were waitressing last night, quite a coup getting Denise to agree to that without putting you through the Spanish Inquisition first. A stickler for references, is our Denise."

"How do you know I was waitressing?"

"I've had MI6 trailing you. Joke," he added, seeing her gloomy sullen face.

"Ha ha."

She thrust her hands deeper into the pockets of her fleece. She felt chilly, despite the warmth of the sun's rays. The cold came from within her, a little nugget of ice deep inside.

Richard Daley whistled for his dog.

"C'mon, Tea! Fetch!" He turned to Celia. "Is everything all right?"

She shrugged again. "Yup. I'll be moving on soon."

"Yeah? Where are you going?"

"Not sure yet. Not sure when exactly, either. But soon. Tomorrow, or Tuesday."

He looked at his watch. "I've got to go and do the eight o'clock communion. Make sure you come and say goodbye before you leave, won't you? I shall miss our early morning trysts."

Celia shuffled her feet and looked down, and said, "Yeah, right," aware of being teased and suddenly shy. She watched him wend his long way back across the salt marshes, the dog gambolling friskily at his master's heels as if trying to round him up.

On an impulse, she decided to follow him to the church. It was her morning off, and she had nothing better to do. She had never been to church this early before in her life, although she had been to plenty of communion services, expected when younger to go with her parents, or more latterly required to attend by school. Choosing to go, making the decision of her own free will, was oddly liberating. It wasn't as if she actually had to participate in the service, have communion, take the bread and wine, pretend to believe in it all. There was no need to go that far. She would just sit quietly at the back. She suddenly felt enormously drawn to the thought of sitting in a cool peaceful church and letting her mind go blank while the familiar words and rituals of the service went on around her, as they had for hundreds of years.

There were about a dozen people in the congregation. Celia didn't know if that was average or not, had no idea how many would usually turn up to early communion. The flowers in the church were ravishing; she had quite forgotten that the Flower Festival started today. Was it really only last Monday that she had first gone there to shelter from the rain, and had come across Mary Thwaite and her friend arranging the altar flowers? *We're doing the Lilies of the Field.* It seemed much longer ago, an eternity.

She slipped quietly from her pew as the service drew to a close, meaning to leave quickly to avoid having to talk to anybody; but she was waylaid in the porch by an elderly member of the congregation keen to know whether Celia intended returning later to look at the flowers.

"They're so beautiful, dear, well worth a proper look. All the money will be going to charity, such worthy causes. Do say you'll come back."

Celia dithered, wanting to leave but not wishing to be rude. She turned away from the door and made to go, murmuring something bland

and non-committal, when she felt a heavy hand upon her shoulder.

"Not you again!" an angry voice said.

Celia spun round, and there before her stood Stanley Cavendish.

"What's your game? Following me around like this – bothering me on my doorstep, serving up food in my local, and now –" the rage bubbled over, he could hardly get the words out, "now, you're in my *church*!"

Stay calm, Celia instructed herself, *and for God's sake, don't run away this time.*

She took a deep breath and began: "I'm just—"

"Where've you come from?" he interrupted her, and took a belligerent step towards her. "Some kind of sick joke, is it, like Freda said? Trying to wind us up?"

Celia forced herself to speak quietly, placatingly. "Of course not."

"What, then? *What*?"

He took another step forwards, his face contorted, and she thought he was going to hit her. She flinched, half-lifted an arm, to shield herself.

"What in heaven's name is going on out here?"

It was Richard Daley, still in his white vestments. He hurried forward, the hem of his robe brushing the floor, the long embroidered stole swinging round his neck. Celia thought he was making for her, half-expected a protective arm around her shoulders, but to her surprise he looked past her and spoke instead to the older man.

"What's the matter, Stan? What's upset you?"

He pointed a wavering finger at Celia. "It's this – this –" He tried to find a suitable epithet, and failed. "This *lass*."

"Simone?" The vicar raised a baffled eyebrow.

Stanley Cavendish glared at her. "Simone? I thought you said your name was Celia!"

Celia, who had forgotten she had introduced herself thus on the Cavendish doorstep, was flustered.

"Oh yes. That's right. The thing is, I suppose I'm both. Celia and Simone, I mean." She was prattling, was aware of both men looking at her suspiciously.

"I think you'd better explain," the vicar began, but the other man cut across him.

"She turns up, out of the blue," he announced, wildly, "and tells us – me *and* Freda, mind – that she's our granddaughter. What d'you make of that, then? Eh?"

For the life of her, Celia couldn't understand what she had done that was so dreadful.

"I don't see," she said, shaking her head, "what you're so annoyed about."

"Annoyed!" Stanley Cavendish's face turned red, and the vicar put a soothing hand on his arm.

"It's all right, Stan," he murmured, placatingly. "I'm sure there's just been a simple misunderstanding." He turned to Celia. "Now then, Simone. Or Celia, or whatever your name is. I don't know what your reason is for thinking you're Stan and Freda's granddaughter, but the fact is, you can't be."

"But why can't I be?"

"Because they don't have any children."

"That's not strictly true, though, is it, Vicar?" All the anger had abruptly left Stanley Cavendish, all the bluster and the ranting. He stood there now with his head bowed, meek as a lamb. "We did have a child, a little lass. But she died."

"Died?" Celia felt something move under her, as if the ground had shifted beneath her feet. *Genevieve, dead? Surely not. . .*

"Aye." Stanley Cavendish's mouth twisted, and he put a hand up to it, his eyes bright with sudden tears. "Nineteen years ago it'll be, come Christmas. Beth, her name was. Apple of my eye. She had meningitis, and she died. She was three years old."

Richard Daley took them both to the vicarage. He sat them down in his gracefully furnished sitting room, brought them a large pot of coffee, and left them to it.

Stanley Cavendish continued where he had left off, as if there had been no break.

"Freda's hair turned white overnight. The shock, you see.'

Celia thought of the woman she had seen, that mass of bright Titian hair. It was what had made her convinced she was looking at her grandmother, the hair the same colour as her own. Dyed, of course.

"It must have been terrible for you," she murmured.

"Terrible doesn't even come close. Freda went quite mad, for months. I thought I'd lost both of them, my daughter and my wife." He shivered, and took a gulp of his coffee. It was good coffee, hot and strong and restorative. "She was our only one, Beth. And we'd waited years for her, years and years. Just when we'd both come to terms with never having children, Freda fell pregnant. We'd been away on holiday, a special one. A Caribbean cruise. Why not, we thought; no kids to spend our money on, why not treat ourselves. And then we come back, and Freda's expecting. It was like a miracle. I know folk talk of miracles, like – like life on Mars, and England winning the Ashes, but this was a real one." He smiled at the memory, fondly. "She was forty when Beth was born. I know it's commonplace nowadays, modern women having their babies later in life, but back then, it was unusual. And we'd been married seventeen years. Given up all hope."

"I bet you were thrilled."

"Aye. We were. Made up. Chuffed to little mint balls, as they say. And she was a right beautiful little lass. Perfect. The doctors had warned us she might not be, but she was. Perfect. In every way. And Freda – she was so proud of herself. But dignified, too. Stately, like a queen."

Celia thought back to the screaming harridan she'd met. It seemed hard to reconcile her with this picture of majestic maternal pride her husband painted.

He glanced at Celia. "I know what you're thinking," he said. "But how you saw her, on Monday – she's hardly ever like that, these days. She's fine now. Most of the time. Absolutely fine. But it was Beth's birthday, you see, last weekend. Twenty-two, she'd have been. It's always a difficult time for her, our Beth's birthday."

"God," said Celia, appalled. Of all the dreadful coincidences. "I'm so sorry."

He continued as if he hadn't heard her. "And then you turn up, announcing you're our granddaughter. It just set her off again, brought it all back. Momentarily. She'd had some stick, you see, at the time. After Beth. . . Kids, mostly, calling her names, saying she was mental, stuff like that. They can be cruel, can kids. She's OK now, though." He looked at Celia, hard, as if seeing her properly for the first time. "So tell me. What's your story? What are you doing here?"

Celia looked down at her hands, didn't know where to begin. Nothing made sense any more.

"I didn't know," she said, slowly. "If I'd known, I'd never have—"

"It's all right." He set his coffee mug down on the table, carefully. "I believe you. I can see you're a good lass, didn't mean any harm. But I want to know why you thought we were your grandparents."

Celia told him about herself, about looking for her mother. The truth. She felt a kind of debt, as if she owed him that much for being so candid with her. It was the first time she'd been completely honest about herself for days, and the relief was indescribable.

"And you say our address is on your birth certificate as being your mother's address?"

Celia nodded. "That's right. That's what I can't understand."

"What's your mother's name, on the certificate?"

"Genevieve Cavendish. I wish I'd brought it along, I could have showed—"

"Ginny!" he exclaimed.

"You know her?" Celia's astonishment was complete.

104

"We do, yes – that's to say, we *did* know her, years ago. But her name was Jones, Genevieve Jones. I can't imagine why she. . ." He tailed off, and looked at Celia again. "How old did you say you were?"

"Sixteen," Celia told him. "Nearly seventeen."

She could hardly believe he'd actually known her mother after all, that despite the confusion of her arrival in Silverdale, the awful false start and the misunderstandings, he might yet be able to provide her with some information.

"So you were born in which year?"

She told him.

"Good grief," he said, slowly. "So she must have been pregnant when she was here. That explains why she left in such a hurry. And to think we never knew. . . Actually –" He looked at her face, studying it for some seconds. "You do look a bit like her."

"Do I?"

She was avid for more details, desperate to build up a mental picture of her mother, but rather to her disappointment Stanley Cavendish began to reminisce again about the time following his daughter's death.

"Freda was in hospital for some time," he said. "Six months or more, I can't remember exactly. It was a hard time, for both of us."

When his wife eventually came home, he

told Celia, she wasn't at all herself. She didn't want to do anything, would sit around all day in her nightdress if he let her. He was a builder, a successful one, with a business to run; he simply couldn't be with her night and day, he couldn't afford the time, even if he'd wanted to.

"Which I didn't," he said, bluntly. "Every time I looked at Freda's empty face I was reminded of what had happened to Beth, and I didn't want to be reminded. I just wanted to work, get on with life, get through as best I could. I daresay you'll think me hard-hearted," he said, picking up his empty mug and putting it down again, distractedly, "but it was how I felt. I couldn't help it, any more than Freda could help the way she was."

After a few weeks of this, he told Celia, he advertised for a live-in companion for Freda; somebody to be with her, keep an eye on her, keep her company.

"As soon as she arrived," he said, "Freda began to get better. I don't know what it was about her, but she had some kind of knack; she got people to open up, talk about themselves. The magic touch, Freda used to say. Ginny's got the magic touch."

"*She* was Ginny?" Celia exclaimed, in surprise. "Your wife's companion?"

"That's right. Freda became very fond of her. We both did, if truth be told."

"But surely she wasn't old enough!" How could somebody of her own age, a teenager, be able to take on a job like that, looking after a woman who was, face facts, mentally ill? She knew that she, Celia, wouldn't be capable of that kind of work, that kind of responsibility. "And wouldn't she need references, or something?"

"She had references, very good ones." He looked at her, oddly. "Why do you say she wasn't old enough? She must have been well into her twenties when she came here."

For the second time that day, Celia felt something change; a movement in the air around her, as if the world had tilted slightly on its axis.

"Her *twenties*?" she whispered.

"She certainly looked it. Are you all right, lass?"

Everything had changed, every single preconceived idea she'd had of her mother. Her name, her circumstances, her background – even her age was different. It was as if the image of Genevieve she had built up had been knocked down, destroyed, and she had to start again from scratch.

"I'm OK. I just kind of assumed that she was younger, that's all."

"A teenager, you mean? A schoolgirl mother, as they used to be called?"

"I guess so."

"Well, she wasn't. She was a mature woman, very capable. So why on earth she should want. . ."

He tailed off, and glanced at Celia, briefly. She knew what he was about to say. *Why on earth should she want to give her baby up for adoption?*

"It's what I've asked myself," she said, slowly, "over and over again."

"I daresay you have, aye. One of life's perpetual mysteries, isn't it? Why these ruddy awful things happen to us?" He reached forward, and put a hand over Celia's, gently. "I'm sorry. It's all been a shock for you, too. I can see that. Thinking you were going to be reunited with your grandparents, and finding us two mad old biddies instead."

Celia swallowed. She was suddenly near to tears, perversely wishing he wasn't being so nice to her. Handling her emotions when he was yelling and angry had been easier to cope with.

"Can you tell me anything else about Ginny?" She brought the unfamiliar name out with some difficulty.

He frowned, trying to remember. "It was a long time ago. What is it you want to know?"

What she looked like — what she was like. Where she came from, where she went. Why she used your name and address on my birth certificate. Who she was, so I can know who I am. Just everything, really.

"I don't know," she said, lamely.

Stanley Cavendish looked at his watch. "Great Scott, is that the time? Freda will be wondering where I've got to." He stood up and looked down at Celia, still sitting on the sofa in a dishevelled heap. "Why don't you give me a little while to brief Freda, and then come round and have a chat with her? She'll be able to tell you about Ginny. She was the one who spent the most time with the lass, after all."

Celia thought of the reception she'd had at Hill House the previous week, of the picture Stanley Cavendish had painted of his wife following their daughter's death, literally maddened with grief.

"I don't know," she said, doubtfully. "Are you sure it won't –" What was the phrase he had used? "Set her off again?"

"Not if I explain. It's true she thought you were sent by the devil, last week." He smiled, but it was a kindly smile. "We both did, truth be told. But I'll tell her. I'll tell her you're Ginny's daughter. She'll be glad to talk to you. She was fond of Ginny, like I said."

It was with some trepidation that Celia walked up the Cavendishes drive again and rang the doorbell, but she was greeted in a perfectly civil way.

"Do come in," Freda Cavendish said. "I hope

you don't mind talking in the kitchen. I'm getting lunch ready."

Celia followed her into a large bright kitchen. The aroma of roast lamb hung deliciously in the air, along with hints of garlic and rosemary.

"Would you like coffee?"

She busied herself with the coffee pot, milk and mugs, and then turned to Celia suddenly. "Stan tells me you're Ginny's daughter."

Celia was a little taken aback by the lack of preamble. "That's right. I'm adopted now, but she's my natural mother."

"And you're trying to find her?"

Celia nodded. "She gave your address as hers, you see, on my birth certificate, and I—"

"Do your parents know you're here? They must be terribly worried about you."

Celia was even more taken aback. "It's OK," she reassured her. "They know I'm safe."

"And how does your mother feel about it all?"

"My *mother*?" Celia thought she meant Genevieve. "Well, nothing. She doesn't know. That's the whole point."

"Not Ginny." Freda Cavendish pushed a plate of biscuits towards Celia. "Your adopted mother. The one who looked after you when you were a baby, brought you up. What you might call your proper mother."

As Celia bit into a biscuit she thought of all

that had happened to this woman, and realized that her views on motherhood must necessarily be coloured by losing her own daughter in such an abrupt and tragic way.

"I don't really know," she confessed. "I hadn't really thought about what Mum might feel."

Freda Cavendish pressed her lips together and gave a little nod, as if her opinion had been confirmed.

"Well, think on. So," she said, "what was it you wanted to know about Ginny?"

It was obvious that the two women had been close. It was written all over Freda Cavendish's face, which grew soft as she spoke, telling Celia how Ginny had come into Freda's life and home and worked wonders, made her face up to things and, eventually, feel life was worth living again. Which made it all the more odd when she disappeared, went off one day without giving notice but instead leaving a brief note telling her employers she had left.

"No explanation, nothing. We hadn't a clue where she'd gone, or why. It was upsetting, I'll make no bones. I'd thought we'd been closer than that. I thought she'd have been able to confide in me if she was in any kind of trouble."

"D'you think she might have been pregnant?"

"It's possible, aye. It never occurred to us at the time. Well, it wouldn't do, would it? It wasn't as if she had boyfriends calling here, or anything. Not once. It was one of the things that made Stan and me realize how lucky we'd been that it was her we'd engaged, and not somebody less responsible or reliable."

"How long was she here?"

"Six or seven months. I can't recall exactly. I can tell you when she left, though. It was February, seventeen years ago. Valentine's Day. I remember that, all right. Stan always buys me red roses; one for each year we've been married. He came home that year with the roses, and found Ginny gone."

"And I was born the following September," Celia said slowly. "So she must have been pregnant, mustn't she, in February?"

The two women looked at each other, silently.

"It wasn't Stan, you know," said Freda suddenly. She turned to the hob, vigorously stirred something in a pan. "That's not why she used our name and address. I don't know why she did that, but it wasn't for that reason. Stan wasn't interested in other women, he's never looked at anyone else, never, not even when I –" She turned back to face Celia, and there were tears in her eyes. "He's not your dad, I'll stake my life on that."

The idea had never occurred to Celia. She was shocked.

112

"Oh, no," she assured the older woman. "I never thought that. Honestly."

The fact was, she had barely given her father a thought, never wondered at his identity. All her energies had been centred on finding her mother; it was as if she was Celia's only parent, which Celia knew was untrue, quite apart from being a biological impossibility. Wondering why this was the case, why it was only her mother who had provoked Celia's curiosity to such a degree, she could only conclude that it was something to do with the blank space on her birth certificate. It was truly as if she had no father.

"She might have gone back to Devon, of course."

Freda Cavendish spoke casually, so that Celia at first wondered if she had heard correctly.

"Why Devon?"

"It's where she came from. Where she was brought up. Where her parents still lived – she spoke about them, often. They were a close family, I could tell. I liked that."

A spark of excitement stirred within Celia. "You don't happen to know whereabouts in Devon, do you?"

"I do, yes. Exeter, it was. In fact, the more I think about it, the more sense it makes. If she was pregnant, she probably went back to her mum. For some home comforts, like."

Genevieve Jones, from Exeter. Celia could feel the trail getting warm again. "Do you have her parents' address, by any chance?"

Freda laughed shortly. "No. That would be useful, wouldn't it? But you could start with the church."

"The church?" Celia didn't understand, thought she meant the church there in Silverdale, Richard Daley's church. "Why?"

"Because her father was a clergyman. A vicar. I suppose that's why her being pregnant never entered our heads. She was nicely brought up, you see. Came from ever such a respectable family."

A God-fearing family. . .

Suddenly, all kinds of things began to add up in Celia's head. She leaned forward, urgently.

"You don't happen to remember the name of the church – her father's church?" It was too much to hope for.

But astonishingly, Freda nodded. "As a matter of fact, I do. I remember her telling me; it was one of those coincidences that strike you at the time, and stick in your mind. It had the same name as our daughter, you see. Elizabeth." She smiled at Celia. "It was St Elizabeth's."

CHAPTER 7

"Josh. It's me."

"Celia?" She could hear noises in the background. "Just a sec – I'll shut the door." His voice, when it returned, sounded different from how she remembered it. Deeper, somehow. Sexier. "Celia, where the hell are you?"

"In a phone box."

"Where?"

"It doesn't matter."

"Yes, it bloody does. Shit, Seal, the police have been round here and everything! They thought you and I—"

"I know."

"You know? How do you know?"

"Phoebe told me."

"*Phoebe?*" He sounded suspicious. "OK, so what're you two up to?"

"We're not *up to* anything." She took a deep breath, to quell her impatience. "This isn't about Phoebe, Josh. It's about me. I just rang to let you know I'm OK." *Pregnant, but OK.* "I thought you might be worried."

"Too right I've been worried! The cops have

been round here twice, my parents are constantly on my case, your dad's been on the phone non-stop – I'm sure he still doesn't believe I've got nothing to do with all this."

"I meant, worried about me."

"Well, of course I'm worried about you! But it hasn't exactly been a picnic here for me, you know. My father is a solicitor."

"Meaning?"

"Meaning he's not going to want his son involved in any scandal, is he?"

Celia let the words resonate inside her head.

"Well, excuse me," she began, slowly. "Pardon me for being scandalous. I certainly wouldn't want—"

'No, look, I'm sorry." He was instantly contrite. "I have been worried about you. Of course I have. But once my dad gets going about something he won't leave it alone, he's like a dog with a sodding bone. Anyway." He made a huge attempt to collect himself. Celia could actually sense the physical effort it took him coming down the line. "You're all right, then?"

"Yeah."

"So where is it you've gone?"

Celia struggled with herself for a long moment. *To tell, or not to tell.*

"If I tell you," she said, "you're to keep it secret. I don't want to run the risk of anyone catching up with me and forcing me to go home."

"But what if the police—"

"Oh, *bugger* the police! I've rung home, they know I'm all right. The police aren't going to bother you any more, they know you're not involved."

"OK. Tell me, then. I shan't let on."

"Promise?"

"Yeah, sure. Where are you?"

"I'm looking for my mother."

"Your mother?" He was baffled. "But I only saw her the other day."

"Not *Mum*," she said crossly, "my birth mother. I'm adopted, remember?"

"Right." He whistled, impressed. "And you've gone off looking for her, by yourself? Cool! So have you found her yet?"

"Of course I haven't! I've barely been gone a week!"

"Christ, Celia, chill! I don't know, do I? I don't know what you've been doing."

"I've just got a new lead."

"Well, that's good, isn't it?" His tone changed, became cajoling and intimate. "Don't let's argue. I've really missed you. When am I going to see you? When are you coming back?"

His voice was a warm, sexy brown. It was one of the things about him that had attracted her in the first place, consolidated by seeing him in *King Lear*, and it still had the power to make her toes curl.

"I don't know yet. Not for a little while." She changed the subject, not wanting to go into details. "So what's new with you, then?"

"Nothing much. Getting ready to go away tomorrow, packing and stuff."

"You're going away? You never told me!"

He sighed, patiently. "Yes, I did. A post-A-level beano with the lads – remember?"

"Oh yes." She did remember now, remembered how her heart had sunk when he'd told her about it, weeks ago, thinking he and his hormone-overladen mates were bound to go off and get as drunk and as laid as possible, and where would that leave her? It seemed so long ago now, and so inconsequential. "Where is it you're going?"

"Torquay. The English Riviera." He drawled the phrase ironically.

"Torquay?" As he said the word, her eyes settled on a brightly coloured poster a few metres away, on a billboard on the station concourse where she stood. FRIENDLY TORQUAY, it announced. THE HEART OF THE ENGLISH RIVIERA!

"Yes. It's in Devon. I know it sounds a bit naff, but – "

"I know where it is." She suddenly wanted to see him, achingly and desperately, in much the same way as she had been moved to ring him, to hear his voice. There were things she needed to tell him; seeing him would be much better than telling him over the phone. "You're not going to believe this, it's a massive coincidence, but I'm actually quite near there at the moment."

"Yeah? Near Torquay?"

"That's right."

"Hey, we could meet up!"

"We could, yeah. I wouldn't want to cramp your style, though."

"Don't be daft! You'd never do that. When shall we meet, then?" He sounded keen, she had to give him that. Perhaps he really had missed her.

They made a date for two days' time, as Celia felt sure she would still be around then.

"So will you come to me?" Josh asked her.

She didn't want there to be any likelihood of bumping into any of his loud leery mates; not with what she had to tell him. On the other hand, she also didn't want him turning up at her lodgings. She somehow felt it would be better if nobody knew her exact whereabouts. Not even Josh. If he didn't know, there would be no danger of him letting it slip.

"Difficult. I haven't got transport. Why don't we meet –" she peered through the glass of the telephone booth to the bustle of the station around her. "Somewhere neutral. Somewhere we can both get to easily."

He swallowed the bait. "How about a railway station?"

"Yeah, why not. Say, Exeter St David's? Main concourse?"

"Right. I'll look forward to it. And you take care until then, yeah?"

When Celia had got back to her room after talking to Freda Cavendish, the first thing she did was telephone Phoebe on her mobile. There were several things she wanted her friend to do for her, most of which involved looking things up on the Net. Some time later, Phoebe rang back.

"Right. There's good news and there's bad news."

Celia sighed. "Better give me the bad news first."

"OK. The bad news is, I couldn't find a St Elizabeth's church in Exeter."

"You're joking!"

She had been so sure of the next step – follow Freda Cavendish's advice, start with the church. Now she would have to think again. What was she supposed to do now, wander round Exeter asking if anybody knew a vicar called Jones?

"Hang on a tick. I couldn't track down the church, but I did find a St Elizabeth's Road, and – um – a St Elizabeth's Place." Phoebe's voice grew fainter, as if she was consulting something away from the telephone. "Both in the same area; according to the map it's a suburb to the north of Exeter called Stoke Barton."

Celia's disappointment was acute. "I see."

"Well, it sounds quite promising, doesn't it? It's the only St Elizabeth's anything in the whole city. Tell you what, though: it's as well it's quite an unusual name. You want to be grateful it's not St Mary's; there's about ten churches called St Mary's listed here. Or St Michael's – there's – hang about – twelve of those!"

"So that's the good news, is it?"

"Part of it. The rest of it is that I've found out your train details, and I've booked you into a B&B in Exeter starting the day after tomorrow, for three nights."

"Feebs, you're brilliant."

"Told you there was good news too, didn't I?"

"Thanks for everything," Celia said to Mary Thwaite the next morning. It was the day of her departure, and she was breaking the habit of a lifetime and eating breakfast, scrambled eggs and toast, at the landlady's insistence. "It was really kind of you."

"You're all right, love. It was a pleasure." Mrs Thwaite sat down at the table, next to Celia, and minutely straightened the butter dish and salt and pepper pots. "We'll miss you. You're a right hard worker, and no mistake. I've told Denise, we won't stumble across another like you in a hurry. Are you sure you won't change your mind and stay?"

"Can't," Celia mumbled, through a mouthful of toast, and shook her head. "I have to move on. There's something I have to do."

"Well." Mrs Thwaite stood up. "Like I say, we'll miss you. All the best, love. I hope you find whatever it is you're searching for."

After talking to Phoebe for so long the previous evening her mobile had needed recharging, so Celia had plugged it into the single electric socket in her room, set inconveniently into the skirting board behind the bed. Both phone and charger lay there still, hidden by the bed. In her haste to set off on the next leg of her quest she completely forgot about them, which is why she was obliged to telephone Josh from a phone box on her arrival at Exeter. She was furious with herself. It wasn't like her to be forgetful.

Celia bought a street plan of Exeter from a newsagent's stall at the station. When she opened it out, straightening its pristine crackling folds, she could see Stoke Barton immediately, in large red letters up at the top. The north side, as Phoebe had said. There was St Elizabeth's Road, quite plainly marked, and there, at right angles to it, St Elizabeth's Place. Nowhere near either of them could she see the black cross that indicated a church; although further down, almost in the middle of the map, she noticed the name of the street that harboured the bed and breakfast Phoebe had booked her into. According to the map, it was close to where she stood at the moment, outside the railway station. Easily within walking distance, she judged.

Feeling a strong sense of *déja vu*, she hefted her rucksack on to her back with a gusty sigh. It was very hot, the rain of the previous week completely gone now, a distant memory. The sky was a sullen leaden grey, the air clotted and with the threat of thunder. Consulting the map again, she turned right and began walking along the pavement, her boots kicking up small clouds of dust from the dry pavement.

Then, on a sudden impulse, she stopped, turned, and started back the way she had come. There was a taxi rank outside the station, with a few mini-cabs lined up in the marked bays. Celia approached the first in the line, a grubby-looking red Vauxhall Cavalier. Somebody had written "Clean me!" with a finger in the dust on its boot. The driver was smoking, and reading a newspaper propped up on the steering wheel. Celia could hear the loud blare of the radio as she bent and tapped on the window, which despite the heat was firmly closed.

The driver glanced at her, and wound the window down.

"Yes, m'dear. Where to?"

"St Elizabeth's Road, please."

The driver furrowed his brow. "St Elizabeth's Road. Now where would that be, then?"

"It's in, er –" Celia unfolded the map, with difficulty, and brandished it at him through the open window. "In Stoke Barton – here, look."

"Right you are. Hop in."

Celia duly hopped, throwing her rucksack in first. Inside, the fug of cigarette smoke almost overwhelmed her. She opened the window as wide as it would go, and was glad when the cab pulled up beside the kerb of a long, tree-lined road a few minutes later. Once the cab had gone, she rather regretted the rashness of her behaviour. She wasn't at all sure why she was here, what she was going to do now she was here, or how she was going to get back to the B&B, her home for the next three days.

Standing on the pavement, she looked

around. The place was deserted, the road quite empty. No sign of life at any of the large bay-windowed Edwardian semis that lined the road to the left and the right, as far as she could see. Then she saw it, along the road on the left. A squat church tower, unmistakable in its sombre grey solidity. Celia felt a surge inside her, a wonderful rising of hope. She hurried along the pavement with winged feet, barely noticing the weight of the pack on her back.

The church was surrounded by a fence of white palings, what Americans call a picket fence, enclosing a small untidy garden bursting with untamed flowers of every colour imaginable. Stone urns spilled lobelia and ivy across the path, and by the door stood an old white china sink crammed with pansies like little upturned faces.

Celia wondered why a church should have such an elaborate garden; it seemed odd, inappropriate. She opened the gate and took a tentative step along the path (crazy paving, with healthy weed growth in the gaps). There was a large dormer window set into the church's slate roof, bedecked with Austrian blinds, the kind of frilly curtains Eddie always scornfully said looked like tart's knickers. Celia's suspicions, her doubtfulness as to the kind of church that would possess a cottage garden and dress its windows with Austrian blinds, culminated when she reached the front door, which was painted pillar-box red. Next to it, nailed to the irreproachable grey stone church wall, was a black cast-iron sign, decorated with painted poppies and announcing that this was Elizabeth Lodge.

Celia realized, with a sinking of her heart she was becoming used to, that St Elizabeth's Church was a church no longer; it was now lived in, it had been converted into somebody's home, which was presumably why it no longer appeared on any map.

She dithered halfway up the path, not sure whether to go and ring the doorbell or retire to her B&B and consider her next move, when the front door was thrown open and a small yapping dog of indeterminate breed hurled itself along the crazy paving towards her legs.

"Hello," said a male voice. "You're early, we weren't expecting you until the morning. Did you catch an earlier train? I'm afraid Sally and the kids aren't back yet, but I daresay you won't mind being here by yourself for a bit until they get home."

Blinking, against the sun in her eyes and with surprise at this apparent anticipation of her arrival, Celia shielded her eyes with her hand and squinted at the owner of the voice and, she assumed, the dog.

He was thirtyish, Celia guessed, trendily

dressed in grey suit and black polo shirt buttoned to the neck, wearing Jarvis Cocker horn-rimmed specs, carrying a briefcase, and apparently in a hurry. She opened her mouth to say something, to say whoever it was he was expecting wasn't her, but before she had the chance he spoke again.

"I've got to go to a meeting now, I'm frightfully sorry. I'm sure you'll be OK though, won't you? Sally shouldn't be long. I'll show you your room and you can settle in, get to see the lie of the land, as it were. Spike, get down!"

He looked at his watch, and Celia was suddenly, sharply, reminded of Richard Daley and her arrival on his doorstep. The difference, though, was that Richard Daley wouldn't let her stay when she asked, whereas this man was inviting her in to his home when she didn't have the first clue who he was, or perhaps more importantly, who he imagined her to be.

"Will that be all right?" He looked at his watch again. "Spike, for God's sake!"

The dog was still yapping, and leaping up ineffectually against Celia's jeans-clad legs. Celia's curiosity got the better of her. She pushed the dog away and made a rapid decision, hoping she wouldn't regret it later.

"OK," she said, and followed the unknown man into Elizabeth Lodge.

CHAPTER 8

Afterwards, she wondered what on earth had possessed her, what had made her silently concur that she was who he thought she was, and follow him wordlessly into the house. What she should have done, she later realized, was tell him he was mistaken, and that if she were to go with him into his home she would be doing so under false pretences. But she didn't. Instead, she trailed meekly along behind him, and from that moment it was too late to say anything. She simply became more and more embroiled in a mesh of deceit that, if not entirely of her own making, became increasingly impossible to extricate herself from.

Inside, Elizabeth Lodge looked exactly what it was: a converted church, cleverly executed, its various rooms still proclaiming their origins with their multi-paned, high ecclesiastical windows, pitched roof and multiplicity of beams. He showed her the entire house in two minutes flat, throwing open doors with an introductory flourish of his arm – "this is the drawing room; this is the kitchen" – until at last he reached a large room at the top of the house.

"This is your bedroom," he declared. He opened another door. "En suite here. Telly, video, etc. etc., under here." He took her rucksack and flung it into a large built-in wardrobe. "Plenty of storage space. Sal will show you the kids' rooms once she's back, go through everything with you, that kind of thing. OK?"

He turned to her, enquiringly, and she pinned a bright smile on her face as if she understood exactly what he was talking about, wishing he would just go.

"Fine."

"Splendid." He looked at his watch again and gave a little gasp. "Heavens, the time! I'm going to be so late. I'm desperately sorry about this, Jessica – I was sure Sally's mother said you were arriving tomorrow. I'll give Sal a call from the car, tell her you're here. Anyway, must dash. Just make yourself at home. Ignore the mess, the cleaning woman's off sick. See you later."

After he had gone, Celia felt breathless, as if she had run up several flights of stairs very quickly. At least she now knew what her name was supposed to be. *Funny, I've never thought of myself as being a Jessica. Jessicas are blonde, fluffy, girly. Not like me at all.*

She couldn't stay there. Of course she couldn't – she knew that perfectly well, although looking round the room she was in, she was tempted. It was large, airy and spacious, with what Edward called "all mod cons". Like the rest of the house, it was decorated in cool creams and whites. This room, however, was clearly a guest room; it was ordered and neat, whereas the attempts at pristine minimalism in the rest of the house were spoilt rather by drifts and piles of jumbled belongings on every surface and floor – books and papers, dirty cups and glasses, discarded items of clothing, abandoned toys. Celia couldn't resist creeping out of her room (*no, not my room; Jessica's room*) once she heard the front door slam, to have a snoop around the rest of the house. The opportunity for an insight into these strangers' lives, for seeing how they lived, for being deeply, unashamedly *nosy*, was quite irresistible.

She walked tentatively along the landing, stumbling over a Lego model which crunched underfoot. Ahead of her was the large dormer window she had seen from the front garden, the Austrian blinds at careful half-mast. She pushed open the first door on her right: a boy's bedroom, judging by the posters of footballers on the walls. The walls had been carefully rag-rolled in palest blue and the duvet cover, lying on the floor, was printed with bright jolly jungle pictures, but the room itself looked as if a small explosion had taken place within. There were so many things lying on the floor Celia was unable to see the carpet.

The next two rooms, a girl's bedroom and a baby or toddler's, were in a similar state of cluttered chaos. The one at the end was the children's bathroom, Celia guessed, from the littering of oozing tubes of strawberry-flavoured toothpaste, bottles of exotically scented bubble-bath, and damp floor-strewn towels, and the two on the left another bathroom and bedroom; more guest ones, probably, as they were as spruce and uncluttered as her own (*Jessica's*.)

Down to a mezzanine floor – edging past, on various stairs, a gardening magazine, a plate holding half a piece of cold buttered toast, a bar of soap still in its wrapper and one small red wellington bearing a picture of Postman Pat – with another door, firmly closed. Celia opened it, cautiously. The master bedroom, obviously: an enormous wooden bed, its head swathed in muslin drapes suspended from a gilded coronet fixed high on the wall above; a low armless chair covered in pink brocade; several large dusty pieces of mahogany furniture; and a huge oval sculpted Chinese rug at the foot of the bed. The wardrobes were hung about their outsides with shirts and dresses and suits on hangers, and there was more detritus scattered around, on the bed, the floor, the chair, the chest of drawers. At the end of the room stood open a door leading to what was visibly another en suite bathroom. Downstairs, the picture was the same – expensive-looking furnishings, tastefully decorated, but everywhere with this haphazard scattering of belongings. The whole place looked as if it had been inexpertly burgled.

Time to go, Celia decided. Turning on her heel, she was in the process of re-tracing her steps and retrieving her rucksack from the room on the top floor where Unknown Man had tossed it, when she heard the unmistakable sound of a key in the lock of the front door. The door was flung open, and in came a very thin blonde woman with hair in a boyish crop, followed by a flock of children, all talking at once. Celia froze where she was, in the hallway at the foot of the stairs.

"Where's Spike?" demanded the largest of the children, looking aggressively at Celia. "What have you done with him?"

Celia dimly remembered that Spike was the dog.

"Um, he's shut in the kitchen," she managed to say, trying to sound as if she was discovered in the houses of total strangers on a regular basis, and that it was no big deal.

"What's he doing in there?" the child wanted to know.

"Er, I think your daddy put him in there."

"Darling, don't quiz poor Jessica. She's only just arrived. She must be exhausted." The woman strode towards Celia, hand outstretched. "I'm Sally Armstrong. I'm so pleased you're here early, I simply can't tell you how tiresome it's been." She gave a weary little grimace. "Magnus rang to alert me, I hope you haven't been too bored here by yourself?"

"Oh no," Celia said, truthfully, shaking her hand. "I haven't been bored."

"Super. Oh heavens, I haven't introduced you to the children yet. I'm sure you've been looking forward to meeting them: they've been simply dying to give you the once-over!" She clapped her hands. "Come here, children!"

Celia found herself confronted by the children, of whom there were actually only five. A small flock, then.

"This is Cinnamon."

Cinnamon was the one who had interrogated Celia about the dog. She clasped him now to her chest, like a shield; both child and dog eyed Celia with a beady mistrustful gaze. Celia wondered when she would get the opportunity to correct this misapprehension that she was the anticipated Jessica, and make her getaway. Nonetheless, she felt she ought to say something to the little girl. It seemed rude not to.

"Hello Cinnamon," she said gravely. "And how old are you?"

The child completely ignored Celia, turning dismissively on her heel instead and marching back into the kitchen.

"She's nine," her mother informed Celia, with a quick, social smile. She put a hand on the little boy's shoulder, proprietorially. "And this is Storm. He's seven. And this –" she turned to the smallest of the children, a toddler of two or three, who was squatting on the floor and pushing a headless Barbie doll around in an absorbed way – "is Pixie. Say hello to Jessica, Pixie."

Pixie didn't even glance up, but carried on with her game. "Brm brm," she said.

"Pixie is fascinated with cars at the moment," her mother explained, fondly.

Celia nodded. "And what are their names?"

She indicated the final two children. Identical pairs of pale blue, slightly vacant eyes stared at her from under identical light-brown fringes.

"Oh," said Sally Armstrong, dismissively, "they're just the twins. They're in Storm's class. They've come for tea, haven't you, twinnies?" The twins nodded wordlessly, in unison. "Run along now, all of you, while I fill Jessica in on her duties. Go up to the playroom for half an hour before tea."

Duties? Alarmed, Celia started edging towards

the door, thinking she might be able to slide out and make a run for it, and then stopped when she realized her rucksack with all her possessions was still upstairs. *Shit! How'm I going to get out of this one?*

Sally Armstrong strode imperiously into the drawing room, and Celia found herself haplessly following her, drawn along in her wake.

"Sit down," the older woman said, sweeping a large dozing tabby cat off the sofa, sitting down herself and patting the cushion beside her.

Celia perched uncomfortably on the edge of a large armchair containing a pile of National Geographic magazines and a toy revolver. At least, she hoped it was a toy. At the moment, she wasn't certain of anything.

"Now then," Sally Armstrong began. She spoke very fast, clipping her words, as if they were forming inside her head quicker than she was able to articulate them. "As my mother told you when she interviewed you, we basically want you just to look after the children – get them up for school, cook their meals, supervise bedtime, etc. etc. Pixie goes to nursery three mornings a week, so you'll take her and collect her. There's no housework as such – Mrs Carter comes in to do that, Tuesdays and Fridays, she's off sick at the moment, that's why everything is in a bit of a mess." Celia vaguely wondered how long Mrs

Carter had been ill. About ten years, judging by the state the place was in. "Oh, and you'll wash the children's clothes, of course, but no ironing. Mrs Khan comes to collect the ironing on Wednesday mornings. You'll only have to shop for the children's meals and other bits and pieces. Then there's the extra-curricular activities." She began marking on her fingers, as if crossing items off a list. "Cinnamon has Brownies on Mondays, tap Tuesdays, French Club Thursdays, Pony Club Saturday mornings. Storm has his flugelhorn lesson on Wednesdays, Tai Chi Thursdays, Cubs Fridays, junior band Saturday afternoons. And Pixie goes to TumbleTots and Baby Band on the two mornings she's not at nursery."

Celia listened, fascinated. She felt quite breathless at this catalogue of social activity. *Poor Jessica*, she thought, *having to keep up with that lot*.

"They're very bright children," their mother went on, matter-of-factly. "Storm is actually borderline-gifted, we have to be so careful to keep them stimulated at all times or they get so terribly bored. Between you and me," she leaned forward conspiratorially, "that was the problem with the other *au pairs*. They weren't really up to the job. Now then." She leaned back again, comfortably, against the cushions. "Do you have any questions so far?"

"Yes. I'm not an *au pair*. I'm not Jessica. There's been some kind of misunderstanding. So do you mind if I just leave now?"

The words were all lined up on her tongue, ready to be uttered. She opened her mouth to say them, but they didn't come out. Instead, like an idiot, she found herself shaking her head and saying: "No."

"Good. Mummy said you seemed very capable, keen to take everything on. I must apologize again for not being able to interview you myself, but as I think you know, we were on holiday when that dreadful Gabriella left us in the lurch, and when Mummy offered to do it instead. . ." She leaned forward again, looking slightly puzzled. "Are you quite sure you're twenty? You look very young. And you don't sound very Scottish, either."

This was her chance, the moment for her to explain. But how could she account for what she had done? What was she to say – that she had followed this woman's husband into their house, let him leave her there, unsupervised, while she poked around their home, allowed herself to be introduced to their three children whom she was apparently to be looking after, listened to the details of what her supposed job entailed, and all the while she was too gormless to say a word? The fact that this was the absolute truth would not, she knew, convince Sally Armstrong. It didn't even convince her, Celia – it seemed far too implausible.

Then, into her mind came a brilliant plan. Why not just go along with things for a bit, pretend she actually *was* Jessica? What harm could it do? Surely there was no law against it. It would give her some time in Stoke Barton, to try and find someone who remembered Genevieve and her family. To put out some feelers. She would surely have plenty of time during the day. The two eldest children would be out at school, and she could always put the little one in a pushchair if necessary and take her along with her. If she played her cards right, she should be gone long before they began to suspect a thing. And after all, just how difficult could looking after three children be?

She arranged her features into what she hoped was an expression of intelligent subservience.

"I know," she said solemnly. "People often remark on how English I sound."

"Now, how about your references?" said Sally Armstrong, standing up briskly. "Have you brought them along?"

Celia panicked. *Oh God! Don't say I'm going to fall at the first hurdle!* She'd totally forgotten about references – of course this woman wasn't going to let a total stranger look after her precious children without any references! How *could* she have been so stupid?

"Oh, don't worry if you haven't brought them," the older woman went on, misinterpreting Celia's worried look. "Mummy said they were impeccable. I would like to take a peek at them some time, though. Perhaps you could get someone to put them in the post for me?"

Reprieved, Celia managed a smile. "Sure, no problem."

"And look, as you're here earlier than expected, you needn't worry about seeing to the children this evening. I'm sure I'll be able to manage." She spoke, Celia thought, as if the prospect of looking after her own children for one evening was totally alien – uncharted territory. "You take the evening to settle in, and start in the morning. How does that sound?"

"That's fine. Thank you," she added, as Sally Armstrong was looking at her expectantly. She allowed herself a small inner self-congratulatory smile – yet again, she had managed to get a free roof over her head, this time being paid into the bargain. At least, she assumed she was to be paid. She had no idea what the usual convention was when it came to *au pairs*' financial arrangements.

"There is one other tiny thing, before you go

and unpack." Sally Armstrong looked sombre, as if she was about to say something distasteful. "I particularly specified I wanted a non-smoker, and I can definitely smell cigarette smoke on you."

Celia opened her mouth to explain that the cab driver had been smoking like a train, but Sally Armstrong lifted a restraining hand.

"No, don't say anything. I can smell it, Jessica; it's pointless for you to try and deny it. I have to say I'm disappointed, but as your references are so glowing and as I can't be certain whether the error lies with you or with the agency, I'm prepared to overlook it. However I must stress I don't want you smoking in the house, or anywhere near the children. They are all extremely sensitive, and Cinnamon is liable to have one of her attacks of breathlessness if anyone smokes near her."

She was obviously convinced that Celia was a closet smoker. It seemed prudent to just let it go.

"Oh dear," Celia said, trying to sound sympathetic. "Does she have asthma?"

"The doctors say not." This was said with pressed lips, as if to imply that medical opinion was not to be trusted. "Now, is there anything you need?"

There was. There was something she needed

very urgently. She didn't want it, on the contrary, but she quite definitely needed it.

"There is, actually," Celia said. "I've just got to pop out and do a bit of shopping. Is there a chemist's round here?"

CHAPTER 9

It was hot. Celia, half-waking from a disturbed and fitful sleep, kicked the duvet off and rearranged the pillows, damp with perspiration, into a more comfortable position. Twenty seconds later, she threw herself on to her other side and punched at the pillows again. So comfortable and welcoming when she had fallen gratefully into bed last night, they were now clumped solidly beneath her head.

It was no use. She was awake. She sat up, and looked at the bright-red digits of the clock radio placed beside her bed. *4:05*, they proclaimed, the colon between the first and second numbers winking on and off to mark the seconds. *Bloody great. It'll be light soon. Why can't I sleep properly any more? It's not as if I'm not tired when I get to bed; I'm always knackered.* She was thirsty, and had an unpleasant pain in her stomach caused, she thought, by the pork pie she'd eaten for supper. She thought it smelt a bit dodgy when she found it in the fridge, but couldn't be bothered to cook herself anything.

Swinging her legs over the edge of the bed,

she padded into the small en suite shower room. She turned on the cold tap, and ran some water into the glass that sat on the white tiled surround of the handbasin. She took a long swallow. The water was lukewarm; she shuddered with distaste. Running the tap again, until the water was properly cold, she refilled the glass and drank until it was empty. Then she held her wrists under the still-running water for several long seconds, turning her hands this way and that until her blood cooled and she felt calmer and less on edge.

Her sleep had also been disturbed by her dreams. She couldn't recall them exactly, but had a vague sense of having been busy all night, of arguing fervently with some person or persons, trying to persuade them of something she had or hadn't done. She gave her head a shake, trying to clear the faint fragments of dream that still clung damply about her, like cobwebs. *It was only dreams. It's not important.* What was important now was that she should get back to bed, and try and get some more sleep. She turned off the tap, dried her hands, and went back into the bedroom. She opened the window to its fullest extent, picked up the duvet from where it lay on the floor in a puddled heap, and arranged it neatly on the bed. She shook the pillows once more, lay down, and closed her eyes, willing sleep to overtake her. *I'm calm now. Really I am. Look how calm I am. My mind is empty, I'm not thinking of anything at all. . .*

Despite her best efforts at fostering a state of Zen-like serenity her mind insisted on wandering off by itself, revisiting the events of the previous day. Her first night at the Armstrongs' had also been ruptured by disturbing dreams, nightmares in which she was discovered as the imposter she was and marched, in handcuffs and nightdress, to the police station to account for her actions. Her first thoughts on waking had been ones of severe doubt that she was doing the right thing, and incredulity that she could have considered she might get away with it. She was sorely tempted to just grab her stuff and make a run for it, but once her brain was more in gear she soon realized it wasn't going to be as easy as that. The household was already awake – there were definite signs of life, noises of squabbling children and running water as someone flushed the lavatory and switched on a shower somewhere close by. What was she to do – stroll downstairs and calmly announce that she wasn't Jessica after all? Hardly. It was no use: she would just have to brazen it out somehow, hope the two adult Armstrongs would soon be off to work for the day (why else, she reasoned, would they need an *au pair*?) and let her get her head around her self-inflicted problem of caring for their children.

Her blithe assumptions of the previous day, that looking after three children surely couldn't be that difficult, had been swept aside by the growing suspicion that these particular three children might just be a nightmare waiting to happen. These thoughts were not helped by the realization, accompanied by a lurch of horror, that the real Jessica was due to arrive today. She would have to concoct some story to present to her when she turned up, and hope to God she swallowed it.

The hassles began as soon as Celia appeared downstairs, freshly showered and dressed. She sidled into the kitchen sheepishly, half-expecting one of them to look up and say: "What! But you're not Jessica!' as if she had a sign on her forehead proclaiming THIS IS A FAKE! That hadn't happened – of course it hadn't, she reasoned with herself later – but Sally Armstrong immediately began hurling instructions at her about a car.

"You can take the Volvo today, but do make sure you clear the edge of the wall at the bottom of the drive as you back out," she flung over her shoulder, en route to the dishwasher with a half-empty coffee mug. "It's a very tight turn on to the road, and I don't want you scraping the paintwork off. You wouldn't be the first."

Celia stared at her dumbly as she rattled on. At sixteen, she hadn't even begun to learn to drive, let alone passed her test. There was no way she could get out of this one. With a sinking feeling in the pit of her stomach, she took a deep breath.

"I'm afraid I can't drive," she confessed, cutting Sally Armstrong off in the middle of explaining the vagaries of the car's clutch.

Sally Armstrong looked at Celia as if she had just told her that she didn't wash. "What?"

"I said, I'm afraid—"

"Yes, yes, I heard what you said. I simply don't believe what I'm hearing, that's all. It's most inconvenient. I thought you told Mummy you were taking your test, and you were certain you'd pass?"

Celia seized on this straw. "That's right. I'm afraid I failed after all. When I said I can't drive, I meant I'm not allowed to. Because I failed," she added, aware she was rambling.

Sally Armstrong had sighed, down her nose, and pressed her lips together. Celia was beginning to recognize this combination. It meant she was being strongly disapproved of.

Luckily, Magnus Armstrong had intervened. He shook his newspaper with a rattle.

"Not to worry," he said, cheerfully. "They can start walking, won't do them any harm. You've got no problems with walking, have you?"

Celia, clearly hearing an edge of sarcasm in his voice, shook her head.

"No," she said. "I enjoy walking."

"That's good," said her employer, "because they don't."

"You'll have to walk to all their other things, too," his wife put in, irritably. "They won't like it. Brownies is a good kilometre away."

She said it as if getting to Brownies involved a fifteen kilometre hike through a crocodile-infested swamp. Celia smiled, brightly.

"That's OK. I love walking. I'm sure the children will enjoy it too."

Eventually, the children had gone off to school, duly breakfasted and packed-lunched by Celia, their parents to their various employment, and she had just got Pixie settled down in front of a video with a mug of milk and a biscuit (all, apart from the milk, strictly prohibited by her mother except at prescribed times, but Celia was past caring) when there was a ring on the doorbell. Celia's nerves, already on edge, jangled anew.

She scuttled guiltily into the hallway and peered out of the spyhole set into the front door. An unknown face stared back, unaware of being observed, in that curiously fish-like, enormous-eyed way such devices bestow on people. Celia could see enough to ascertain that the fish's face was young, and female. Her heart thudded beneath her ribs. *Shit! It's her – the real Jessica! She's arrived!* She wiped her suddenly sweating hands down her legs, ran hastily through the speech she'd improvised while in the shower earlier, took a deep breath, and opened the door.

A plump, jolly-looking girl stood there holding a battered suitcase in each hand, her hair scraped back from her face in an unbecoming manner.

"Hello," she said, putting one of the cases down and holding out her hand. "I'm Jessica McLean." She had a strong Scottish accent.

Celia's stomach gave a guilty lurch. She forced a smile on to her face.

"Oh, hi," she said. She passed a hand through her fringe, distractedly, wondering how to proceed. Perhaps a smile wasn't appropriate? She changed her expression to one of apology. "I'm glad to see you. Or rather, I should say I'm not glad to see you, because I've been—"

"And you are –?" the real Jessica interrupted, politely.

"Oh, I'm, er, Sally's cousin," Celia stammered. "Look, I'm terribly sorry, but there's no easy way to tell you this. There's been a crisis – a family crisis. A death, in fact. Suddenly. Abroad."

The real Jessica gave a small frown of incomprehension. "What?"

148

"Abroad," Celia repeated, firmly. "Magnus's, um, father," she improvised. "The whole family's off to the funeral. They're going to be away for the rest of the summer, and – well – the fact is, they won't be needing you after all."

"What?" The real Jessica put down her other suitcase, dismayed. "But the agency never told me!"

Celia added regret to the apology already on her face. Just as well she'd already thought there might be an agency involved. . . She nodded understandingly.

"I know. I've been trying to get hold of you – it all happened really suddenly, you see – but the agency said you'd already left. The only thing I could do was wait for you to turn up. I'm really terribly sorry," she added.

The real Jessica bit her top lip, her eyes filling with tears. "So where are Mr and Mrs Armstrong? Why aren't they telling me this – why are you doing their dirty work for them?" she demanded.

Celia spread her hands appeasingly. "Getting flights and things. There's so much to organize, it's been just dreadful for them – I'm sure you can imagine," she said, ignoring the comment about dirty work and praying she wouldn't insist on coming in and waiting for the Armstrongs to come home to have it out with them.

"So I'm really sorry," Celia went on, as firmly as she could manage, "but it looks as if you've had a wasted journey."

"But I've come all the way from Glasgow, on the sleeper!" the real Jessica wailed. One of the tears spilled over and ran down her cheek.

"I know. It's a bummer." Celia made a deeply sympathetic face. "Would you like to come in and have a coffee or something? As you're here?" It was a risk, but one she was prepared to take if it meant getting her to go quietly.

The real Jessica bent to pick up her cases. "Well, OK then." Then she straightened up decisively. "Actually, no. I'll use the phone, if I may. I'm going to ring the agency and complain. I hope the Armstrongs are going to reimburse my train fare, at least."

"Oh God, no! Don't do that!" Celia burst out, horrified.

Jessica stared at her. "Why the devil shouldn't I? I've been looking forward to this job."

"Oh, please. . ." Celia searched frantically around in her mind for a plausible explanation. "Poor Magnus has been so upset. It's been just awful for him, you've no idea. Between you and me, I think he's that far away from a nervous breakdown –" she held her thumb and forefinger a few centimetres apart, "and if he has any more stress to cope with I reckon it'll just push him over the edge." Her own stress stood out as beads of perspiration on her brow. She wiped them away with the back of her hand. "Please don't complain to the agency," she whispered.

"But what about my train fare?" the real Jessica persisted, stubbornly.

Oh, bugger your train fare! Celia took another deep breath. "Can't you just leave it for a couple of weeks?" Surely she would be safely away from Stoke Barton and any possible repercussions by then. "Until things have died down a bit? Please?"

Jessica pressed her lips together, clearly battling between doing the decent thing and seeing justice being done. Luckily for Celia, the decent thing won.

"Oh, all right then," she muttered ungraciously, picking up her cases at last. Relief flooded through Celia like an actual physical force.

"Oh, thank you!" she gasped, gratefully.

Jessica glared at her suspiciously. "Yeah, well, you can tell them I'm not best pleased. And you can tell them this isn't the last of it," she added, and stumped off down the path, not bothering to close the gate behind her so Celia had to go running after the dog to prevent him from following her, yapping, all the way down the road. She felt sorry for Jessica, but not sorry enough to tell her the truth and make way for her. Her, Celia's, need was undoubtedly greater than Jessica's. She walked up the path, her arms full of Spike. Pixie stood in the doorway regarding her gravely. Her mouth was rimmed white with milk.

"Who were that?" she asked. It was the first words she had uttered to Celia.

"Oh, just a girl," Celia replied, falsely cheerful.

"She were Jessica," Pixie declared.

Celia laughed, a bogus tinkling little laugh. "Don't be silly! I'm Jessica; how could she be?"

"She was," Pixie insisted, staunchly. "I did hear her say her name."

"Oh well," Celia said, determinedly jolly. "I'm sure there's more Jessicas in the world than just me. Now, let's go indoors and see what Postman Pat's up to, shall we?"

Eventually, Celia fell into a sporadic doze, from which she awoke again just after six o'clock. The stomach ache was still there, changed from a sharp persistent grumble to a dull pain. Her heart sank at the recollection of all she had to do before eight-thirty. She had the children to get up and breakfasted and chivvied into clothes, and packed lunches made before walking them to school. No wonder she had a stomach ache. She could feel her head beginning to throb, coming out in sympathy, the result no doubt of too little sleep in a too stuffy a room.

Making a herculean effort, she sat up and got out of bed. This afternoon was when she was to meet Josh, at the railway station, although with Pixie in tow and the children to meet from school she would have to cut it shorter than she would have liked. Before she met him, though, there was something vital she had to do. She could put it off no longer.

She retrieved something from deep within her rucksack and looked at it intently. A rectangular cardboard packet, measuring roughly fifteen centimetres by seven. It was a very small thing to have been weighing so heavily on her mind. After purchasing it she had thrust it away in her rucksack, out of sight, but far from out of mind; the knowledge of it lying there, waiting to impart its inescapable but unwished-for message was, she knew, at least partly responsible for her wakeful night and the oddness of her dreams. And probably, she reflected, her headache too.

She went into the small bathroom and sat down heavily on the lid of the toilet. *Right. This is it. I can't prat around any longer. I've got to know for certain before I see Josh this afternoon.* Sighing, she unwrapped the pregnancy test from its cellophane wrapper and read the instructions on

the box. *Hold in stream of urine for five seconds –*
results show in approximately one minute – at least
99% accurate.

She spent a few anxious and uncomfortable
moments, attempting to do what the test
instructed without peeing on either her hand
or, probably worse, the carpet. That done, and
still sitting on the loo, she reached around for
the handle and flushed it. Then, somehow,
whether due to apprehension or worry or just
plain clumsiness, she dropped the test wand.
Worse, she dropped it into the toilet; its flimsy
plastic shape submerged momentarily under the
flow of water. Startled, and furious with herself,
Celia leapt up and peered down. It was still
there – thankfully, it hadn't been flushed away.
She grabbed the toilet brush and managed, with
some effort, to retrieve it, snatching it up and
staring anxiously at it. *Damn! DAMN! Why can't*
I even manage to do something simple like this
without messing it up?

For what seemed the longest minute of her
life, she watched as the blue stripe slowly
climbed up the wand. It bypassed the window
which proved pregnancy (with reputed ninety-
nine per cent accuracy) and reappeared in a
small window above. According to the test, this
meant she wasn't pregnant.

Celia cursed herself for not having taken

more care, for not paying proper attention to what she was doing. *Bugger! All that screwing myself up to do it, not to mention the expense of buying the thing, and I've cocked it up. Now I'll have to go and buy another one, and somehow find the time to do it before this afternoon.*

She threw the whole lot into the bin in disgust, and then thought better of it. *Better not leave any evidence lying around. I don't want the cleaner to find it.* Retrieving it, she wrapped it all in a plastic supermarket carrier bag and stuffed the package into her rucksack, which she pushed under the bed. Then, feeling hot and sticky and somehow grubby, she ran the shower.

She stood under the shower for a long time, her eyes closed, letting the warm water run soothingly through her hair and over her body. She would have to start giving some thought to how she was going to get back on the Genevieve trail, and soon. She must not repeat the Silverdale experience, she told herself, letting herself stay there indefinitely, away from all the hassles of home and lulled by the unaccustomed benefits of a job and a temporary home and the freedom of reinventing herself, taking on the persona of somebody else – Simone in Silverdale, and now Jessica. Anyway, there was no telling how long this little scam might last. She was not at all certain that the real Jessica had been wholly convinced by her invented story. It would only take one call from her to the *au pair* agency, one complaining call demanding that the Armstrongs explain themselves personally and reimburse her train fare – or, God forbid, a visit from Sally Armstrong's mother (who, having interviewed The Real Jessica, Celia realized with a twinge of panic, would certainly recognize her as not being the girl she had engaged). Tomorrow, she promised herself, tomorrow I'll start making proper enquiries.

Celia reached for the soap, and as she did so she felt a sharp tweak in her abdomen. Looking down, she saw blood mixed with the water swirling in the shower tray. It was running down the insides of her legs. At the sight of the blood she was alarmed, and then, with a gradually dawning realization that was like a mist lifting, she understood what it was. She hadn't messed up the pregnancy test after all; it hadn't lied. Here, at last, was the indisputable evidence, the reason for her stomach pains earlier. She wasn't pregnant. There was to be no baby.

In celebratory mood, Celia caught a bus into the centre of Exeter. Her feelings of light-heartedness were caused by a mixture of thankfulness and indescribable relief. She felt so good that she didn't mind having to take

Pixie along with her, having to cope with both her and the pushchair on the bus. She felt like spending some money.

Once in Exeter, Celia went to the building society to make a withdrawal from her savings account. The account wasn't as healthy as she would have liked – she had treated herself to a new mini hi-fi a few weeks earlier in anticipation of finishing her GCSEs, and under the circumstances she rather wished that she'd hung on to her cash. Still, she reasoned, she shouldn't have too many expenses whilst staying at the Armstrongs'. She told herself she must summon the nerve to ask them what arrangements had been made regarding paying her. She could always plead loss of memory, or even terminal stupidity – what did she care if they thought her thick?

She withdrew a hundred and twenty pounds, leaving her account fifty pounds in the black, and spent almost all of it within the hour, on some new CDs and some clothes much more suited to the current sweltering temperature, including a swirling peasanty skirt in bright Indian cotton, a pair of trendy designer flip-flops and a particularly fetching pair of dungaree shorts. Crushing down the feelings of guilt that rose within her on spending that much money in so short a space of time, she hastily bundled

Pixie, pushchair and assorted carrier bags on to another bus, and went to St David's station to meet Josh.

She was five minutes late and he was already there, standing on the concourse as arranged and looking in the opposite direction, idly scanning the milling crowds. She called his name and he turned, just as she came up to him. He was suntanned, wearing faded Levi's and a blue chambray shirt with rolled-up sleeves. His hair had grown since she last saw him; it curled deliciously over his brown neck and on to the collar of his shirt. He looked clean and wholesome and wonderfully, reassuringly familiar.

He smiled when he saw her, his mouth curving slowly upwards to show his white, even teeth in the way that always made her stomach contract.

"Hi!" he said.

Ridiculously glad to see him, she launched herself at him and kissed him soundly.

"God!" he said, kissing her back with enthusiasm. He sounded pleased. "What a welcome! What have I done to deserve this?"

Not got me pregnant, Celia thought. She didn't say it aloud, although she thought she might tell him, some time. Some more appropriate time. *Not now, though. Not with all these people around, and Pixie sitting earwigging in her pushchair.* The child looked the picture of innocence but Celia was unsure just how much she understood, how much went in. She didn't want things, private things, being repeated back to Sally Armstrong.

Josh noticed Pixie for the first time.

"Who's this?" he asked Celia, wrinkling his brow. "Surely she can't be –"

A kind of light went on behind his eyes, and Celia knew what he was thinking, could tell as surely as if the words were scrolling across his forehead – *surely she can't be yours? Surely she's not the reason you ran away?*

She snorted with a mixture of amusement and scorn. "Yeah, right! I've got a secret kid I've kept hidden away all this time!"

Josh smiled, sheepishly. "Right. Of course. I didn't really think she was yours. It was just the surprise, of seeing you with a baby. What's she doing with you, then?"

"I'm looking after her," Celia told him. "And her brother and sister. I'm living in their house – I'm the *au pair*."

"Yeah?" Josh looked at her with respect. "Good for you. You have got yourself sorted, haven't you? Funny; I've never pictured you looking after little kids."

If only you knew. . . Celia forbore from telling him she'd never imagined herself in that role either, and that she was only doing it now because of a fortuitous case of mistaken identity. She bent, and straightened Pixie's T-shirt in an unconsciously maternal gesture. The child had fallen asleep, her face flushed from the afternoon sun, her wispy blonde hair sticking to her forehead, her mouth slightly ajar.

"Yeah, well, it's only for a little while. Until I get some more leads about my mother."

"What's her name?"

"Pixie."

"*Pixie?*" He grimaced. "Christ. Poor kid. What're the others, Gnome and Leprechaun?"

"Almost as bad. Cinnamon and Storm." She looked at him, affectionately. "Oh Josh. I'm so pleased to see you."

They walked and made small talk, and eventually found themselves back in the city centre, near the cathedral.

"Shall we go and have tea somewhere?" Celia said, on an impulse. "Real afternoon tea? We can pretend we're a proper couple, and she's our baby."

She indicated Pixie, who was beginning to stir in her pushchair. She felt a sudden rush of fondness for the child, for Josh, for the entire world. She was so glad she wasn't pregnant, so enormously relieved and grateful, that she felt able to cope with anything.

Josh was staring at her. "Why would we want to pretend that? I can't think of anything worse."

"Oh, cheers!"

"I don't mean us as a couple. I mean having a kid."

This was getting rather too close to home. Celia shrugged, attempting nonchalance.

"Oh, I don't know. Worse things could happen."

"Yeah? Like what?" He stopped walking, looked intently into Celia's face. "There's a bloke in my year whose kid sister's pregnant. I mean *really* pregnant – out here, she is. Due next month. There's no ignoring it. Only fifteen, and she's up the duff. Will says his parents are carrying on as if her life has ended – in fact, he reckons they'd be happier if she had died."

"That's a terrible thing to say!" Celia was shocked, truly shocked.

"Yeah. I know. But it's how they are, Will says. The shame, what will the neighbours say – you can imagine."

"Yeah." She could; only too well.

"Thing is –" He sighed, put his hands in his jeans' pockets, and carried on walking. "Thing is, they've got a point. I mean, her life has virtually ended, hasn't it? Her life as it's been. As her mates' lives still are, probably. What kind of life is she going to have with a kid hanging round her neck?"

161

Celia carried on pushing the pushchair, her head bowed over the handle, silently and fervently thanking her lucky stars that she hadn't, after all, had to tell Josh today that she was pregnant; that it had all been a false alarm.

"Wanna drink!" said Pixie suddenly, from the pushchair. "Wanna drink!"

"Oh God, Seal!" Josh stopped again, suddenly. "I'm really sorry. I totally forgot."

"What about?" She was genuinely perplexed.

"About –" He gestured, embarrassed. "About you. About your mother. It's what happened to her, isn't it? It's why you're adopted." She had told him, months ago, told him about her birth certificate and Genevieve's letter, and her theories about everything. "Your mum was young, wasn't she? Under age? That's why she had you adopted, you said. Trust me to go and put my foot in it and upset you."

It seemed easier to let him think that was the reason for her sudden withdrawal. She didn't feel up to explaining what she was really thinking about. She stooped, and wiped a string of drool from Pixie's mouth.

"That's what I thought," she said, slowly. "Originally. For months, actually. Since Mum gave me that letter on my sixteenth birthday. Or perhaps even before that – perhaps it was brewing in my mind since I first saw my birth certificate, years ago. I don't know. But everything's different now."

She told him, briefly, what she had learned in Silverdale, about Genevieve Cavendish turning out instead to be Ginny Jones, a totally different person.

"But isn't that good?" Josh queried. "That she wasn't a teenager when she had you?"

"Is it? Why?"

"Hasn't it stopped you torturing yourself with thoughts of how awful it must have been for her? You know, young and pregnant, like Will's sister?"

"No," Celia said, shortly. "She still gave me away, didn't she? However old she was at the time, she still didn't want to keep me." She stopped walking, and turned her head to look at him. "The fact is, Josh, I don't really know anything any more. Everything I thought about my mother – all the reasons I came up with for her having me adopted, everything I've been carrying round inside me for what feels like my entire life, turns out not to be true after all. And that makes me feel –"

"What? How does it make you feel?"

"It makes me feel as if I'm not really me, either."

"Of course you're you!" She could tell by his face he didn't understand. He put out a hand and touched her shoulder. "You're lovely!"

"Wanna *drink*!" said Pixie again, and began drumming her feet on the pushchair's footrest.

Celia carried on walking, and Josh's hand fell away from her shoulder.

"It's nothing to do with being lovely," she said sharply. "It's not about that kind of thing. Look, you live with your mum and dad, don't you? And your little brother and sister. And there's photos all round your sitting room, photos of you all when you were small, and ones of you with your grandparents and stuff?"

"Ye-es."

He didn't know what Celia was getting at, she could tell. She felt herself growing hot with frustration, the heat rising from the inside, as if she had swallowed a pan of boiling milk.

"Well, it's your history, isn't it? Your family history."

"But your family's got a history, too."

"But I'm not part of it! Can't you see? Don't you understand?" she cried.

Josh touched her arm again, helplessly, not knowing what to say that might help. "I'm sorry. Don't be upset."

"Drink!" Pixie wailed. "Drink drink DRINK!"

"Look, let's go in here," said Josh. They were in the cathedral close, standing outside a large white Georgian building whose sign, hanging over the front door, proclaimed it the Queen

Adelaide Hotel. "Let's go and have your famous afternoon tea, shall we?"

They went in, but Celia's holiday mood was spoilt. She felt uncomfortable, out of place amid the starched damask table cloths and napkins, the formal flower arrangements and elegant bone china and silver cutlery, the genteel hubbub of the largely elderly clientele as they sipped their Earl Grey and nibbled their cucumber sandwiches and looked forward to hearing the cathedral choir later at Choral Evensong.

Josh ordered two Devonshire cream teas, but Celia could barely touch hers. She felt restless, on edge. Pixie whined and fidgeted and spilt her orange juice on the tablecloth, and then kicked the supercilious waiter who came hurrying with a cloth to clean it up.

"Pixie!" Celia scolded her. "That's very naughty!"

"Piss off!" Pixie roared, heaving against the restraining straps of the pushchair and red in the face with rage.

Mortified, Celia could feel the scandalized eyes of the other customers upon her back. She's not mine, she wanted to say. I'm not her mother. I'm only looking after her. She felt a sudden, overwhelming urge to stand up and face the room and tell them that she was quite used to coming to places like this for tea, more appropriately dressed, with her family. She'd even been to a few Choral Evensongs in her time. This wasn't really her, this was an anomaly.

She couldn't, of course. Instead, she stood up to leave, thrusting a ten-pound note on to the table and trying to manoeuvre the pushchair around to face the exit.

"I'll pay," Josh said, hastily standing up too, swallowing the last of his tea and wiping his mouth on his napkin. He picked up Celia's uneaten scone from her plate and, not knowing what to do with it, held it on the palm of his hand as if it were a cricket ball he was about to bowl.

"No need. It was my idea. Come on, let's go."

They stood on the pavement outside the hotel, ill at ease and not knowing what to say to each other. It was still very hot, the air completely windless, the sky a dull hazy silver grey.

"I think it's going to thunder," Josh observed. He bent, and handed the dry scone to Pixie, who hurled it to the ground in disgust. A small flock of pigeons immediately swooped down on to it, stalking around and pecking it to crumbs.

"Maybe." *Is this what we're reduced to,* Celia thought in desperation, *talking about the bloody weather?* "Look, I'm going to have to go. I've got to pick the other two up from school."

"Cinnamon and Storm?" Sarcastically.

"That's right."

"Where did you say you're staying, exactly?"

"I didn't."

"Oh." He looked surprised. "Aren't you going to tell me, then?"

"I don't think so. I think it's best if nobody knows. Nobody can trace me then, you see."

"Oh," he said again. He raised an eyebrow, and gave a small, faintly patronizing smile. "You're on the run, then, are you?"

"You know I'm not. It's just – this is something I need to do. By myself. I don't want there to be any chance of my dad coming charging in to fetch me back home."

"Right." He sighed, a sigh of tolerant resignation that got right up Celia's nose. "Well, good luck, then. I guess I'll see you around. When you're back."

On the bus, Pixie fell asleep again. Celia sat her on her lap, and tried to work out why she was feeling so irritated and out of sorts. It was Josh's lack of understanding, she realized, his utter inability to comprehend what was driving her. *But he did try to understand*, she reflected. *It's not his fault he doesn't know how being adopted makes me feel, how important it is for me to find my mother and to learn the story. How can he possibly know? I didn't explain it very well. He did try to help. I do care about him.* She just wondered why, in that case, she felt so let down and exasperated with him. Try as she might, she couldn't manage to conjure up any of her old feelings for Josh – they seemed to have gone, vanished, melted away in the summer heat.

CHAPTER 10

The trouble with a school like Lady Margaret's, Celia reflected, was that it didn't prepare you for the really important things in life. It seemed to her that the only thing an LM girl was encouraged to do was pass exams and behave in a generally meek, humble and accepting way. Meekness and humility were all very well, but they didn't get things done.

Take her current situation. When she had followed Magnus Armstrong into his house, meekly (that word again), too wet, too curious or too stupid to put him straight as to her identity, she had had no conception of what was actually going to happen. It had seemed like a splendid idea at the time, but the fact was, now she was there, Celia simply didn't know what to do. She had fully intended to go knocking on doors in Stoke Barton, asking questions, but she very quickly realized it wasn't as easy as that. She was supposed to be Jessica, the *au pair*, from Glasgow – how could she possibly explain away her interest in a former vicar and his family without drawing attention to herself and arousing suspicion? Quite apart from which, it soon became apparent that, like the Armstrongs, most of the neighbours were out at work during the day – the safe time, Celia realized, the time Sally and Magnus were also securely out of the area – and there were therefore very few people around that she could actually question.

But on the other hand, Celia knew with a crushing certainty that she could not stay in Stoke Barton for long. Her fear of imminent exposure as an imposter – she jumped every time the telephone rang, certain it would be the *au pair* agency; hid away behind the curtains, wild-eyed and sweaty-palmed, at every innocent ring of the doorbell – was only matched by her frustration at the inadequacy of her child-minding skills, and her impatience with the impossibility of asking anyone for help or advice. Difficult though it undoubtedly would be, she would have to get a new lead soon.

The problem was, thwarted in her original plan to doorstep the neighbours, she didn't have the first clue how she should now proceed. Freda Cavendish's suggestion, of starting with the church, hadn't reckoned with the church in question now being someone's home. She had a vague notion that, having failed with the church building, she might now try the establishment, the administrative side of the organization. Records must be kept of this kind of thing, of the movements of clergy; surely there would be somebody, somewhere, who would know what had happened to Genevieve's family? The trouble was, she didn't have the foggiest idea how to find out who that somebody was. After all, you could hardly look up Vicar Tracing Services in the Yellow Pages. All in all, even though she had only been at Elizabeth Lodge for a short time, she felt perpetually on edge, trapped and frustrated: unable to settle to her job, unable to progress with her search, unable to move on (unless it was to give up and go home, and that was no option at all).

Even the financial side of things turned out to be a big let-down. Buoyed up by the thought that, whatever she had to suffer at the Armstrongs' she was, at least, being paid for her pains, she had eventually summoned the courage to ask Sally Armstrong what was happening about her money. The older woman had eyed her with suspicion.

"How d'you mean?"

Celia swallowed, nervously. "I – I've forgotten what we agreed."

"You've *forgotten?*" Her voice rose theatrically, incredulous that anybody could be so ineptly absent-minded.

Celia could only nod. Sally Armstrong sighed, and made a you-silly-little-girl gesture of impatience.

"We're paying you fifty pounds a week."

Fifty? Celia's face must have reflected her disappointment, because Sally Armstrong hurried on defensively: "It's only supposed to be pocket money. You do get all your living expenses paid for. I'm not prepared to negotiate; I'm sure Mummy made all the arrangements quite plain at your interview."

It would have to do. She was in any case hardly in a position to argue the toss.

"It's just," Celia said apologetically, "I was wondering when I might be paid?"

Sally Armstrong regarded her in the same way she might have looked at a stain on the carpet.

"All in good time," she sniffed disapprovingly, as if Celia had asked her something intimate. "I do hope you're not planning to take the money and run, Jessica."

Celia blushed with mortification. *I wish. Anyway, what's wrong with wanting to be paid?* she wanted to yell. *God knows I'm working bloody hard enough for it!*

But she couldn't, of course. Completely unable to demur, she felt the shutters clanging down around her. What she needed was a few lessons in assertiveness. But if you had never

172

been assertive, if your instinct and upbringing was always to be polite, to avoid upsetting or offending others, it was far from easy to begin. Aggressive – now that was another matter; she could do aggressive, oh yes indeedy. In fact, according to her parents, aggression was Celia's most often displayed attribute, along with belligerence ("Don't be aggressive, Celia" "Celia, is there really any need to be quite so belligerent?"). But experience had taught her that aggression and assertiveness were not at all the same thing. Besides, her aggression usually sprang from anger or frustration, or from feeling backed into a corner. To be assertive, you couldn't just allow yourself to respond willy-nilly to events, a knee-jerk reaction to things not going your way. You had to be in control. And Celia knew, with a sinking of her heart that seemed to increase daily, that control of her current situation was something she simply did not possess.

And quite apart from all of this, there were the children. Any idea she may have had that masquerading as the unfortunate Jessica would be a cushy little number, any notion of herself as a Mary Poppins figure, happily singing about her favourite things to a bunch of bright-faced, eager, lovable children, disappeared after she had spent about five minutes in their company.

They were without doubt the worst children Celia had ever had the misfortune to come across, or at least the worst-behaved, which amounted to much the same thing. Not that she'd had a great deal to do with children up to now; and they were certainly doing their damnedest to put her off having anything much to do with children in the future.

They were like cartoon kids from a film – rude, stroppy and unco-operative. Communication with them swiftly degenerated into a battle of wills. She spent one entire morning tidying Cinnamon and Storm's bedrooms; ten minutes after they returned home from school, she went upstairs to find both children in Storm's bedroom, sitting on the floor and determinedly emptying the bookcases on to the floor. Wordlessly, she went into Cinnamon's room. A scene of chaos greeted her, even worse, if that were possible, than how it had been before she had tidied. Every drawer in the prettily stencilled pine chest of drawers was open, the wardrobe doors were flung wide. Both were empty, and all Cinnamon's clothes were strewn across the floor and every available surface.

Celia felt her blood pressure rise. She marched back to Storm's room.

"Cinnamon," she said, forcing herself to speak calmly and at least pretend to some measure of control. "Why are your clothes lying around everywhere? I put them all away this morning."

The child shrugged, carelessly. "I like them like that."

"You can't possibly."

"I do. Ask Sally." Another thing they did, which irritated Celia beyond reasonable measure, was to call their parents by their first names.

"I'm sure your mother would be very cross at seeing all your things lying around like that. Expensive things," she added.

For answer, Cinnamon just shrugged again. Storm, casting a provocative glance at Celia, pulled out the two last paperbacks from the bookcase and flung them half-heartedly at her. Celia was incensed.

"Storm!" she hissed, all pretence at control evaporated in the face of this blatant disobedience. "Don't you dare do that! Now just you put all those books back on the shelves *at once*!"

Left to himself, Celia believed he probably would have done so, but his sister quelled him with a look.

"He doesn't have to. He likes his books on the floor, don't you, Stormy?"

"He does have to," Celia roared, "because I'm telling him to. And you, miss, can go and put all your clothes away!"

A look of unutterable boredom crossed

Cinnamon's pretty, sulky little face. She manufactured a yawn, opening her pink mouth wide to show Celia just how tedious she found her. Then she looked her full in the face, and smiled seraphically.

'Fuck off,' she said, sweetly.

In a rare moment of confidence, Storm told her once that no other *au pair* had lasted longer than two weeks.

"We don't like *au pairs*," he said. He was playing Donkey Kong on a Gameboy, his head bent over it intently, his thumbs busily working as if they had lives of their own.

"Don't you?" Celia asked. She wondered if Storm would give some insight as to why.

"No way."

"Why's that, then?"

"Too bossy," he declared. "Granny says they've got to be bossy, but we don't see why." The Gameboy let out a series of urgent electronic bleeps. "What's a toy boy?" Storm asked, without looking up.

Celia's face flamed. What answer were you supposed to give a seven year old to *that* question? She dissembled. "Why?"

" 'Cos Granny's got one. She's on holiday with him. She's gone to –" he frowned at the Gameboy disapprovingly, "to Rio di Something with him, for the whole summer. He's called Hugo. Magnus calls him Granny's filthy-rich toy boy. So d'you know what a toy boy is or not?"

He fiddled with the game again, and Celia realized that he didn't really expect her to answer, he just wanted to shock her. Instead, though, she felt relief. At least with her safely tucked away in Rio di Something, toy boy in tow, she wouldn't have to worry about the Granny factor for a little while.

The Gameboy bleeped again, triumphantly, and Storm threw it petulantly across the room.

"Cinna an' me," he said, after a moment, "we have bets on how long the *au pairs* stay until we get rid of them."

"Oh?" She knew she shouldn't, but it was irresistible. "So how long did you have me down for, then?"

"A week. Cinna said three days. That's how long the last one stayed. Gabriella. Gabri-smeller."

"Well," Celia said gloomily. "I reckon I'll still be here at Christmas."

At this rate, it was far from impossible. The thought filled her with horror.

One evening, Magnus Armstrong made a pass at her. Although Celia didn't think of it in those terms: "making a pass" sounded tame, twee, old-fashioned. (*"Gosh, Miss Duckenfield, but*

*you're jolly pretty. Would you mind awfully if I
kissed you?")*

There had been nothing old-fashioned about
what Magnus had done. Short of actually raping
her, it could hardly have been more full-on. She
had been in the kitchen, desultorily cooking the
children's tea. He came in, throwing his briefcase on to the table with a gusty sigh, and took
a bottle of Beck's from the fridge.

"Bloody clients." He flopped down on to one
of the artfully mismatched spoonback chairs,
kicking off his spotless Italian leather loafers
and pulling another chair towards him to rest
his feet on. The chair scraped along the terracotta tiles with a noise that set Celia's teeth on
edge. She flipped over the beefburgers in the
frying pan and peered under the grill to check
the progress of the chips. Sally didn't like con-
venience foods, but it was too bad – Celia was
blowed if she was going to spend ages concoct-
ing some wholemeal pasta dish to Sally's
specifications, only to have the children leave it
after two mouthfuls. They could leave beef-
burgers, and their mother could lump it.

She smiled politely at her boss. "Hard day?"
she enquired.

She was only being civil, but the effect on him
was galvanizing. He leapt to his feet, waving the
beer bottle excitedly. Celia had the distinct

impression it wasn't his first of the evening.

"Yes!" he cried. "Yes, I have, and do you know what, Jessica?"

Dumbly, she shook her head. She had never seen him this animated before. It was rather disturbing.

"You're the first person who's asked me that in Christ knows how long. It makes a nice change, Jessie. It makes a very nice change."

She wanted to say *don't call me Jessie*, but felt she couldn't very well be proprietorial with what wasn't even her name. She took three plates from the drainer, and set them in the bottom oven to warm. Magnus prowled around in his socks, getting in her way and burbling distractedly.

"Sally never seems to have time for me any more. This house has been warmer since you came, you know? More alive."

Celia felt like laughing. She, who felt half-dead most of the time, making the place feel alive? *Oh, puh-lease. . .*

But he was in deadly earnest. He took another slug of beer, and a step towards her. He lifted a strand of her hair; she had washed it earlier, and it was hanging loose around her shoulders.

"This is so beautiful," he murmured. "My father always said that hair was a woman's crowning glory, and he was right." Moving closer, he took a handful and buried his face in

179

it, sniffing appreciatively. "Mmm. Beautiful."

Embarrassed, and boxed in between him and the counter, Celia half turned and reached up to the cupboard above her head for a tin of baked beans. Quick as a flash Magnus had her turned right round with her back to him, grabbing at her breasts with both his hands.

"Mmm," he said again, in her ear. "Nice tits, too."

He squeezed her breasts, hard, and tweaked her nipples through the thin fabric of her T-shirt. Celia froze, horrified and repulsed, and still clutching the fish-slice she'd turned the burgers with. He pushed her down further over the counter, and she could feel his erection pressing against her buttocks; the only thing standing between it and her, it seemed, was her shorts – her beautiful funky dungaree shorts she'd been so proud of. If only she'd worn something different, something less provocative. . . Certain he was going to rape her, she could hear the words of the defending counsel now: "*the defendant was enflamed beyond reason, m'lud, by the wantonness of the witness's clothing. Basically, she's just a filthy little slapper. . .*"

"You're a dirty girl," Magnus panted. "I know you want it too."

Somehow, Celia summoned the strength to free herself. Twisting frantically from his grasp, she ducked under his restraining arm and, flinging the fish-slice at him, she flew gasping and terrified from the kitchen, leaving the beef-burgers and chips to fend for themselves.

Barricaded up in her room, and still in mild shock, Celia sat on her bed with her arms wrapped around her knees and thought what a cliché it was: the boss having it off with the *au pair*. Or in her case, attempting to have it off. Utterly appalled – he'd seemed so respectable and, up until then, wholly uninterested in her apart from her child-minding capabilities – she wondered how many of her predecessors had been less lucky, how many of them had left because of it, succumbing to the twin onslaughts of Magnus's brutal and tacky seduction technique and his children's insupportably awful behaviour.

She knew two things for certain: that Sally Armstrong wouldn't believe her if she were to tell her what her husband had done, and that she couldn't stay there any longer. She had to leave, and soon; she couldn't stand the suspense any longer, of hanging around waiting either for Magnus to try it on again (probably full-scale rape next time) or to be arrested (lurid Bogus-Nanny-from-Hell type newspaper headlines filled her mind). Leads to Genevieve or no leads, she would have to make other arrangements.

181

CHAPTER 11

That evening, after the children had gone to bed with their usual strenuous reluctance and deafening catalogue of demands – drinks of water, more pillows, fewer bedclothes – Celia went back downstairs to the kitchen. Her employers were sitting at opposite ends of the scarred pine farmhouse table, eating couscous and bickering mildly across the usual heap of detritus that covered the table's surface about whose turn it was to put the dustbin out. Something loud and stridently brassy was blaring from the radio – Radio Three, Celia guessed, although she knew for a fact that Sally had been watching *EastEnders* while preparing the meal, on the miniature TV that occupied a shelf above the sink. She had heard the signature tune quite clearly from upstairs. Sally tried to hide her more populist tastes when Celia was around, and Celia despised her for it. What was wrong with admitting to liking *EastEnders*, for heavens' sake? She and all her friends adored it.

The Armstrongs didn't invite Celia to share

their meal. She was expected to eat with the children, and then spend the evening in her room doing quiet inoffensive *au-pairy* things. This evening, because of the *contretemps* with Magnus, she had no appetite and had eaten nothing. Whether his children had, she neither knew nor cared. Avoiding his eye, she mumbled something about going for a walk.

"Good idea," approved Sally, brightly. "Get a breath of fresh air."

For an uneasy moment, Celia thought she was going to offer to come too. She didn't, merely asked Celia to go via the postbox outside the newsagent and post a couple of letters for her. Celia, who wasn't intending to go in that direction at all, found herself agreeing, and then cursed herself once more for her inability to say no. *I'm not her slave*, she fumed inwardly. *Why can't she post her own bloody letters? Why can't I stand up for myself?*

"Could you be a darling and take Spike?" Magnus asked. "I really don't feel up to walking him tonight. I've had a sod of a day, and it's still far too hot." He stretched his arms above his head, lazily, and took another mouthful of Valpolicella from the huge vase-like glass he clutched.

Take him yourself, you drunken lecherous git!
"OK," she muttered.

"That's my girl." He winked at her roguishly, behind Sally's back, as if they shared a delicious secret. "Have fun."

Celia, walking along the pavement five minutes later with the little dog straining excitedly at the lead, remembered the feel of Magnus's hands on her, and shuddered. He'd been straining pretty excitedly, too. She went over in her mind, for the hundredth time, whether she had ever done or said anything that he could possibly have construed as a come-on. She felt soiled, contaminated; she would have a shower when she got back, a good long shower with some of Sally's CK One stuff she'd nicked from her bathroom last week, the end of a tube thrown casually, carelessly away in the bin. Although she doubted it would make her feel much better. The feeling of pollution was inside her, and no amount of scrubbing with upmarket shower gel would eradicate that.

She went into the telephone box three streets away, tethering Spike to some railings outside. The little dog sat down obediently. He was quite well-behaved for her. It was when the children were around that he racketed about, yapping excitedly and generally behaving like a wind-up toy on speed. It was nice to know she was a good influence on somebody, even if that somebody was just a dog.

"Feebs, listen. I'm in a phone box. I've only got ten p left – you'll have to call me back."

She read out the number, and Phoebe duly rang back within seconds.

"How come you're in a box? What happened to your mobile? I've been trying to ring you for ages."

"I lost it. Well, forgot it, really. Left it behind."

"You didn't! Bummer."

It was clear from her tone that Phoebe, who was surgically attached to her own mobile, considered this a tragedy on a par with the sinking of the Titanic.

"Yeah. I feel kind of cut off. It's been a real pain."

"So where are you?"

"Devon."

"Yeah? You're still there? Josh said he'd seen you when he was on his lad fest – said you had a little kid in tow."

"He told you? The pig!"

Celia was filled with righteous indignation. If he'd told Phoebe after he'd promised he would keep it secret, who else might he have told?

Phoebe was baffled. "Why's he a pig? He knew I was worried about you."

"He said he wouldn't tell anybody. Anyway, I was going to tell you myself. I wasn't keeping

185

you in the dark on purpose; it's just been really, really difficult to get to a phone."

Celia told her about working for the Armstrongs, leaving out the bit about being mistaken for the real *au pair*. Phoebe was impressed.

"Sounds fab. Are they paying you megabucks?"

"Er, not exactly. And the kids are a nightmare, she's a control freak and he's a sleaze bucket. He's been coming on to me. Like, a full-on grope attack."

Phoebe gasped with shocked delight. "He didn't! Jesus H! When?"

"This evening."

"No! God, that is just so. . . D'you remember that time at Anna Berry's party, when her big brother was all over me like a rash? I couldn't get rid of him. When I got undressed that night I thought my skin was going to be indented with his hand prints, like that film-stars' pavement in Hollywood."

Celia remembered the party in question. As she recalled, Phoebe had rather enjoyed the encounter with Chris Berry at first. It was only later, when he wouldn't leave her alone, that she had become annoyed with him. Fighting off the not wholly unwelcome advances of Anna's drunk eighteen-year-old brother in a room full of people was hardly the same as her brush with

Magnus Armstrong. She could feel his hard body against her now, groping her, breathing goatishly into her ear. *You're a dirty girl*... A shiver of revulsion passed through her.

"So what did you do?" Phoebe went on, breathlessly. "I'd have kicked him in the fundamentals and told him I was suing him for sexual harassment."

"I managed to escape from his evil clutches," Celia said, attempting light-heartedness. "I keep asking myself, was it my fault? I was wearing these dinky little shorts, you see..."

"So?" Phoebe's voice rang out assuredly. "Celia, you could have been wearing nothing at all. It still didn't give him the right to assault you. He's your boss, for crying out loud! Or did your contract give him – what's it called? – *droit de seigneur*?"

Celia said, dully: "There is no contract. Basically, I'm up shit creek. I've got no money, no more leads for my mother, and my boss has got the hots for me."

Phoebe whistled. "Yeah. I can see you've got problems."

"I thought I might ring home, see how the land lies there."

"Are you sure?"

"Why wouldn't I be?"

"Your parents ring me now and then, to see if

187

I've heard anything. I've had the distinct impression you haven't been keeping them up to date."

"And they're pissed off about it?"

"Celia, they're worried. They're your *parents*." There was a note of pleading in her voice.

"Well, I'll ring now, OK? Actually," she said, rather sheepishly, "I can't. I've run out of money. Could you ring them and ask them to call me back?"

Seconds later, the phone rang again. It was her father, his voice throbbing with a whole range of emotions, chief amongst which was anger.

"Celia, what on earth are you up to now? Where are you? Are you in some kind of trouble?"

Celia, not knowing which question to reply to first, answered none of them.

"Where's Mum?" she said, instead, playing for time.

"Out," her father replied, shortly. "The first time she's torn herself away from the phone in weeks, and you choose now to ring."

'Sor-*ry*," said Celia, sulkily. Why was it Dad always had this effect on her now, made her feel about ten years old and permanently in the wrong? It never used to be like this, not when she'd actually been ten years old; she'd adored him, he'd been her absolute hero, her role model for maleness.

"You promised her you'd ring," Dad went on, "you promised faithfully you'd ring every day, and we haven't heard from you for God alone knows how long!"

"It hasn't been that long," Celia protested. "Anyway, I didn't promise every day – I said I'd ring when I could."

"Well, it certainly feels like it to your mother, I can assure you!"

He'd been worried. Relief always made him angry, Mum had said so. Celia tried to hang on to that.

"Sorry. I lost my mobile, just after I rang last time."

"You lost your. . ." He ran out of words. Celia could just picture him at the other end, head bowed, hand clasped to his forehead in exasperation. "And it's taken until now to discover a phone box? Just where have you been? Have you any idea, any *conception*, of how concerned your mother's been?"

A flash of temper passed through Celia.

"You don't seem to be, though," she muttered. "You haven't even asked how I am." Not the right thing to say. It just wound him up even tighter.

"Don't be ridiculous! You're my daughter, of course I care how you are – of course I've been worried!" he bellowed. "You *are* our daughter, whatever ideas you might have to the contrary!"

"What's that supposed to mean?"

"I mean, you go racing across the country-side on some hare-brained scheme with no thought of how it might affect your mother, and even less thought for your future."

'My future?" She was genuinely baffled. "What's my future got to do with it?"

"I'm talking about your education. Do you really think Lady Margaret's is going to want you back to do A-levels after your little display in the History exam?"

"Oh. You heard about that, then."

"Of course we heard about it! What on earth were you thinking of?"

Genevieve. . .

"Dad," Celia said, summoning every ounce of assertion she possessed, "I really couldn't give a monkey's about Lady Margaret's. There are more important things in life than A-levels."

Her father's voice was tight with suppressed rage. "Oh, really. Well, what I want to know is, when are you going to get your priorities sorted and come home, you silly, selfish child?"

"Stop *calling* me that!" she snapped, any pretence at self-control gone. "I'm *not* a child!"

"No? That's how you're behaving – like a spoilt child who wants to do what *she* wants to do, and hang everybody else!"

"That's not true!" She was wounded, all the

more so because she recognized a grain of truth in what Dad was saying – she hadn't given much thought, if any, to how her parents would feel about her search for Genevieve. She hadn't even considered it an issue that affected them. It was her problem, not theirs. But she could see, albeit grudgingly, that Mum might be upset about it, about Celia going off looking for Genevieve when it was she who'd brought her up and cared for her. It was what Freda Cavendish had meant, back in her kitchen in Silverdale.

Dad, however, didn't have a leg to stand on as far as she could see. He just seemed to view the whole thing as an exercise designed by Celia to cause him as much hassle as possible. The problem was, he couldn't cope with her making decisions of her own. All the recent friction between them at home stemmed from him wanting to control her life in the same way as he had when she was small, and it wouldn't wash. Not any more.

"I'm not a child any more, Dad," she went on. "You've got to stop thinking of me like that. I'm grown up now – I've got a life of my own. You've got to let go of me."

He snorted down the line with scorn. "Oh Celia, please! Enough of the psychobabble! You're sixteen years old; I'm still responsible for you, whether you like it or not."

All of a sudden, Celia had had enough.

"Yes!" she cried heatedly. "I'm sixteen, not six! When will you stop thinking of me as your blue-eyed little girl? I thought I was pregnant a couple of weeks ago – just how childish is that?"

As soon as the words left her lips she knew it was a mistake. In her fervent wish to make her point, to get him to understand, she had let slip the one thing she should, at all costs, have kept to herself.

To say her father was angry would be an understatement. Celia practically dropped the phone at the bellow of rage that issued from it, after a second of utter, incredulous silence.

"I knew it!" he roared, beside himself. "I just knew that Joshua Peters had something to do with all this, the feckless, shifty little toerag! My God, when I get my hands on him, that young man will wish. . ."

Just what Josh would wish Celia never found out, although she could take a pretty good guess. She laid the receiver carefully on the empty shelf intended for the directories and tip-toed from the booth, leaving Dad ranting tinnily at the other end. She felt shaky, shivery; washed-out, as if she was going down with flu. This wasn't what she'd intended, not at all. She had wanted a quiet comforting word with Mum, to confide in her about her experience with

Magnus Armstrong maybe, perhaps even to suggest that she come back and sensibly make more enquiries from the safe, comfortable haven of home. She had even been prepared to admit it was possibly what she should have done in the first place, instead of taking off armed only with her birth certificate and a few false assumptions.

All of that was out of the question now. She couldn't go home, couldn't even countenance it after Dad's rabidly extreme reaction to what she'd just let slip. He would be unbearable; her life simply wouldn't be worth living. She had burnt her boats well and truly. Like it or not, she would just have to find some way out of this mess by herself.

CHAPTER 12

Very few people at school knew Celia was adopted. She had known Phoebe for two years before she told even her. Phoebe was bemused by why she had kept it a secret all this time: she also, when Celia told her, thought it was unbearably romantic. She couldn't understand why Celia swore her to secrecy.

They were both thirteen at the time, and Phoebe was clearly captivated by the whole notion. For Celia, though, being adopted wasn't glamorous or exotic, it was just normal, the way things were. The only thing she rather liked about it was thinking of her surname, very occasionally and privately, as Cavendish rather than Duckenfield. Celia Cavendish as a name had a certain raffish sophistication, whereas Celia Duckenfield on the other hand was wholly unglamorous, with definite overtones of middle-aged women in hair curlers and beige cardigans.

She wasn't altogether sure why she didn't want the world at large to know the details of her birth. It was difficult to explain that even to herself: just why did she want to keep it private? It wasn't as if she was ashamed of the fact. She could only put it down to her experiences at primary school, when she was picked on and teased for going to church. Being adopted made her different, and being different ensured you got stick at school. She had frequently observed girls at Lady Mags being tormented for being fat, or acne-ridden, or even just for living in the wrong bit of town. Above all things, she wanted to fit in. She didn't want to give anybody the slightest reason for turning their jibes in her direction.

"And after all," she'd told Phoebe, at age thirteen, "you don't introduce yourself by saying "Hi, I'm Phoebe, and I live with my natural parents," do you?"

Phoebe hadn't got it. "Course not!"

"Then why should I tell them I'm adopted? It's none of their business."

Now, aged nearly seventeen, she realized what she'd been trying to say. There was more to her than simply being adopted; she wasn't defined merely by her parentage. That being said, the matter of her parentage, or more specifically her mother's identity, had started to impinge more and more on her consciousness. It had changed from being so much an integral part of her that she barely gave it a thought – like the mole on her neck, say, or the infuriating frizziness of her hair – to something that began to take over her thoughts to such a degree that it coloured everything she said and did.

It had come to an almost unbearable head around the time she'd first suspected she was pregnant, that fated History exam and her precipitous, improperly planned escape from home. It was as if the prospect of being a mother herself was forcing her to examine her own identity: her roots, her background, all the little family connections and intertwinings in everybody's lives that give one a history and a sense of self. It had been the catalyst, what had finally impelled her to turn her yearning to find her mother into reality, to leave the examination room in such haste and get on the train to Silverdale.

She had told Josh about being adopted after they had first slept together: it had seemed somehow fitting, appropriate – romantic even – to entrust him with her precious secret in a moment of post-coital bliss. In the event, the bliss was purely on Josh's part, and his reaction to her revelation was merely to blink lazily, say "Are you?", and turn from her in the most uninterested way imaginable. She told herself later that it was a reassuring reaction: it meant he didn't find anything odd in it, he considered her exactly the same person as before. However, it also brought it home to her with crashing finality that nobody, absolutely nobody within her sphere understood what it meant to be her, how being adopted made her feel, all the questions it raised in her mind and why she felt this overwhelming and growing need – more than a need, it was now a compulsion – to track Genevieve down. She was on her own.

It was the day after Celia's encounter with Magnus Armstrong, and she was taking Pixie home for lunch after TumbleTots, her mind whirling with thoughts of the mess she was in and what on earth she could do to extricate herself from it. The heatwave continued – it was still stiflingly hot and sultry, the air thick and clotted and without even a hint of a breeze to move and freshen it. As Celia pushed Pixie along in her pushchair, the tarmac of the pavement felt melted and sticky under the thin soles of her flip-flops.

"What do you want for lunch?"

Pixie squirmed mutinously. "Not hungry."

She was hot and overtired. Janet Newsome, who ran the group, had told Celia when she arrived that Pixie had started a fight. Although she hadn't put it quite as bluntly as that.

"I'm afraid there's been a bit of a scrap." Her broad kindly face looked anxious.

"Oh, God. What's she been up to now?"

"It was Petroc's turn with the Indian clubs, but Pixie wanted to hang on to them. I'm afraid she hit him over the head with one, and he retaliated. It was very naughty of them both."

The Indian clubs in question were brightly coloured polystyrene, as light as cardboard, but Petroc was sporting a bruised eye and Pixie had a livid scratch across her cheek.

"Pixie!" Celia exclaimed. "Why are you such a pain? What's your mother going to say?"

"Don't care." Pixie shrugged nonchalantly, three going on fourteen.

"She can be rather a handful." Janet Newsome looked nervously around as Petroc's mother entered the hall. "Still, it's what TumbleTots is all about – expending all that excess energy in a positive, directional kind of way."

Celia, hurrying out of the hall with Pixie clamped wailing and heaving in the pushchair before Petroc's mother could buttonhole her, privately thought a couple of hours alone in a padded cell was what Pixie really needed.

"Want Smarties for lunch," Pixie said now, eyeing Celia sideways to watch her reaction.

"I don't think so. Your mother said scrambled egg or mushroom pâté on toast."

"Yeeugh!" Pixie wriggled frantically and made

vomiting noises. "Horrid! Want Smarties an' Coke!"

Celia sighed wearily. She didn't have the energy for yet another fight about food.

"If I buy you Smarties and Coke for your lunch," she leaned forward, across the pushchair handle, "will you be good for me this afternoon?"

Pixie tilted her head backwards and looked up at Celia, her blue eyes round and innocent.

"Yes," she said.

"Promise? You'll go down for a nap without any fuss?"

"Yes."

"And what will you say you had for lunch, if Mummy asks?"

Their eyes met in a moment of silent complicity.

"Scampered egg," said Pixie, confidently.

"Right. It's a deal."

Celia pushed the pushchair resignedly into the newsagent. The woman behind the counter smiled indulgently at Pixie.

"Hello, my little duck! And what can we do for you?"

"Smarties an' Coke," Pixie demanded.

"Oh, you are a lucky girl! Treat time, is it?"

"Lunch time," Pixie corrected her.

"Bribery," said Celia, at the same time.

The woman smiled again. "Worked with my lot, every time. How are you getting on?" she asked Celia, in a friendly way.

Celia frowned, her mind full of random and impatient thoughts of escape. "How d'you mean?"

"At Elizabeth Lodge – with the Armstrongs? You're their latest *au pair*, aren't you?"

Celia nodded. "That's right."

The shopkeeper turned and took a bottle of cola from the chilled cabinet. "I only ask," she went on, "because their *au-pairs* usually come in here at some time or another. Loads, they've had." She lowered her voice. "Children a bit S-P-O-I-L-T, are they?" Pixie watched in fascination as the woman spelt out the word, and Celia nodded again.

"You could say that, yeah."

The shopkeeper smiled in sympathy. "Hardest job in the world, looking after children. I should know, I've had four of my own."

Celia handed over a five-pound note; then, impulsively, she decided to risk asking a question or two. Swayed by her new and increased urgency to get out of the Armstrongs' house, she didn't care any more if people thought it strange for her to want to know about erstwhile locals; she had nothing to lose any more. Encouraged by the other woman's friendliness, she found herself asking about Elizabeth Lodge.

"How long ago was it converted from the church?"

"Let me see." The shopkeeper counted out the change into Celia's hand. "It was a good few years ago now; ten, maybe. Handsome job, isn't it? It must be beautiful inside."

"Do you remember a vicar who was there when it was still St Elizabeth's? Jones, his name was. He had a grown-up daughter called Genevieve – Ginny."

But to her disappointment the woman shook her head. "Afraid not, m'dear. I haven't been round here very long. Last vicar I remember, his name was Wetherspoon. He never had any daughter – he was what you might call a confirmed bachelor."

Disheartened, Celia pocketed the change, thanked the woman, and tried to turn the pushchair around in the confined space by the counter.

"Oh, let me help you. I keep telling Harry not to dump those boxes in the customers' way." She bustled from behind the counter and manoeuvred the pushchair in a practised fashion. "It's my mother-in-law you want to ask, if you want to know anything about what goes on round here," she went on. "Regular mine of information, she is – knows everything about everybody. In fact –" she lowered her voice again, "between you and me, she's a proper nosy old B-A-G."

Rose Yelverton had lived in Stoke Barton for all of her eighty-two years, and had been what she called "living over the shop" for sixty of them. Fifteen years ago, when her husband died, she had handed everything over to her son Harry and his wife Pauline, who moved down from the Midlands with their family; but having nowhere else to go, she had continued living with them in the flat above the shop.

Celia was told all this within five minutes of being shown by the younger Mrs Yelverton into the cluttered, airless upstairs room where her mother-in-law sat and held court by the window behind a yellowed net curtain, watching the world go by. Celia also learnt that the two Mrs Yelvertons didn't get on: "Harry won't hear a word against her, but Pauline's heart's not in this shop. It was our life's work, mine and Cedric's, but she's going to sell up just as soon as I pop my clogs. She doesn't think I know, but I do – I've heard her and Harry discuss it, when they think I'm asleep. Deaf *and* daft, they think I am. All kinds of things I learn about sitting here, I tell you, girl – all kinds of things."

Celia tried to steer the conversation on to less

contentious issues, such as the Reverend Jones and his daughter, but Mrs Yelverton had begun telling her about the time Pauline and Harry had tried unsuccessfully to get her to move to an old people's home.

"All my life I've lived here," she said, her voice quavering indignantly, "and they want to ship me off to one of them awful institutions. I've heard what goes on in them places; I told them, you'll not catch me going there. This is my home, this is where I live, and this is where I stay until I'm taken out in my wooden box."

The old lady grumbled on, but when she paused for breath, Celia seized her chance.

"You must have seen a lot of comings and goings in your years here."

"I have that." Mrs Yelverton's face changed, became avid and eager. "I could tell you some stories, girl, I could indeed. Where did Pauline say you were from – the papers, was it?"

"No." Jessica and Simone were one thing, impersonating a member of the press quite another. Not with Pixie downstairs in the shop, being fed Smarties and entertained by Pauline Yelverton. "I'm looking after the Armstrong children at the moment, at Elizabeth Lodge – the old converted church, you know?"

Mrs Yelverton nodded sagely. "I know the

place. Waste of a good building, you ask me. Sacrilege, that's what it is, mucking around with a house of God like that."

"I just wondered," Celia said, casually, "if you happened to know the history of the place."

"History?" She narrowed her eyes and looked suspiciously at Celia. "Why would you be interested in history?"

"It's what you said, about the building." Celia marvelled, not for the first time, how she could tell lies so convincingly while her stomach churned frantically with adrenalin. "I'm off to university soon to learn how to be an architect."

"Part of your training, is it?"

Mrs Yelverton still regarded her doubtfully, and Celia gave a little, oh-shucks-you've-found-me-out type of laugh.

"Not exactly. I suppose I'm just being nosy."

To her surprise, Mrs Yelverton smiled approvingly.

"Nothing wrong with that, girl. It shows you're interested in your fellow members of the human race."

"That's what I've always thought." Playing her advantage, Celia leant forward confidingly. "To be honest, it's the people connected with these old places I'm fascinated by. I think they're as interesting as the buildings themselves."

Mrs Yelverton nodded again in agreement,

and Celia, encouraged, plunged into the question she so desperately needed answering.

"Do you remember a vicar at St Elizabeth's called Jones? He had a daughter called Genevieve, a grown-up daughter who went to Lancashire to be a live-in companion for a lady? It would have been about seventeen years ago."

The old lady's face screwed up with concentration.

"Old Gethin Jones? I do remember him, yes. I used to go to St Elizabeth's, once upon a time. Folk round here were suspicious when he first came here, you know – thought he'd bring a whiff of the Chapel with him, coming from Welsh Wales, but he didn't, oh no, not him. Higher than the Papists, he was, all smells and bells and Stations of the Cross, although his sermons did have a touch of the Lloyd George about them. Rhetoric, my Cedric used to call it, though where he got hold of such a word, the Lord alone knows."

Celia, who had only the vaguest idea what Mrs Yelverton was talking about, nodded amenably.

"Did you like him?"

"I did, yes. So did a lot of other folk. He was very popular. Things weren't the same when he moved on, it was the beginning of the end for that poor old church. The next one brought in guitars and tambourines, and wanted everyone hugging everyone else during the service. It had them leaving in droves."

"Was that the one called –" What was it Pauline Yelverton had said his name was? "Witherspoon, or something?"

"Wetherspoon. Frank Wetherspoon. No, he was the last, before the authorities called it a day and sold off the church. He was only here a year or two, but it was a lost cause by then. The congregation was down to half a dozen or so."

"And were you still going there?"

Mrs Yelverton laughed derisively. "Not me, girl. I stopped once the happy-clappies moved in, and never went back. Not my cup of tea at all. No, give me a good old-fashioned minister like old Gethin Jones; you knew where you were with him. Proper hymns, proper services; none of this new-fangled twangy nonsense and changing the words of the Lord's Prayer, and suchlike."

Celia felt a tide of excitement rising up inside her; it had to be him, Genevieve's father, it simply had to be. Jones was a common enough name, but it would surely be too much of a coincidence for there to have been more than one vicar called Jones during the right time, when the church was functioning and within Rose Yelverton's memory.

Celia had to make sure. She pressed the old lady.

"And he was the only Reverend Jones you remember?"

"Oh yes. There was only one Jones, right enough. We always got to know the clergy families, Cedric and me – the vicarage used to be just down the road, they were our neighbours. They knocked it down, of course, once the church was sold. Too old and draughty for modern families, I daresay. They built a whole road of modern houses where it stood. St Elizabeth's Place, they called it."

"So you remember his daughter, too? Genevieve?"

Again the screwed-up face, the concentration. "Genevieve. Yes, that's right. That was her name. Fancy you knowing that. Jenny, they called her, for short. Always Jenny, she was. Pretty little thing. So solemn, and with such lovely hair." She looked at Celia, really looked at her for the first time. "A bit like yours, it was. Same colour. But she always wore hers in pigtails."

"Pigtails?" It seemed an odd way for a grown woman to wear her hair.

"That's right. Plaits, I suppose you'd call them now."

"And she used to come and visit her parents, quite often?" Celia prompted her.

The old lady looked puzzled. "Visit them? Why ever would she visit them, a little girl like her? They were her parents – she lived with them!"

"When she was little, yes. But when she was older, she moved away to live in Lancashire, didn't she?"

Mrs Yelverton shook her head, quite definitely. "Oh no. No, you've got that wrong. I thought you said something about her going off to Lancashire. I don't know where you got hold of that from. Jenny Jones was just a little tacker. She could only have been about ten when they moved away. That was when the long-haired guitar player came along – Robert Foxley. I told you about him, remember? Call Me Bob, we used to call him; he was always saying it, standing there in his sandals with his guitar slung round his scrawny neck. Call Me Bob."

She was moving away from the topic. Celia didn't want to hear about Call Me Bob, or anybody else for that matter. She felt sure Mrs Yelverton must have got it wrong. Eighty-two years was a long time to hold information in your brain; she must have muddled this particular vicar and his family with another. Hadn't Freda Cavendish said that Ginny went to visit her parents in Devon, spoke of them often? *They were a close family, I could tell – I liked that. . .*

Why would Ginny have told Freda her parents lived in Devon, even told her the name of the church where her father was the vicar, if they had moved away when she was ten?

Celia put a hand on top of one the old lady's. It was thin, the skin papery as parchment and speckled here and there with brown liver spots, the veins and tendons like twisted string beneath.

"Are you quite sure?" she said, gently. "Are you sure Jenny was only a little girl when they moved away?"

Mrs Yelverton snatched away her hand, offended. "Of course I'm sure," she snapped. "I may be old, girl, but there's nothing wrong with my mind. No, nor my memory, neither."

"Of course not," Celia muttered. "I only thought –"

"You youngsters, you're all the same. Think you rule the world."

"I'm sorry. I didn't mean to upset you."

"I've got reason to remember, see. She was around the same age as my granddaughter, Anne, Jenny was. They moved up to the Midlands, near where Harry and Pauline were at the time, and I thought they might be play-mates. I was fond of Jenny. She was a pretty little thing, like I said, and so well-mannered. I felt sorry for her, moving away from all her friends.

She came in to buy sweets, just before they left, and she told me she was sad and would miss everyone. Fair broke my heart, it did. So you see —" she glared at Celia, balefully, "I do remember. I remember perfectly well, thank you, madam. It's you who's got it wrong."

Celia felt a sharp stab of disappointment mingled with another emotion, harder to name. Once again, everything she had formed in her mind about Genevieve had to be re-thought. The calm, capable woman in her mid-twenties had somehow turned into somebody quite different — a ten-year-old girl, moving away with her family and sad at leaving all her friends behind. Where had they gone? Where did *she* go, later? And why had she lied to Freda Cavendish?

"So how long ago was this?" she asked.

"It must be — oh, thirty-odd years ago. Yes, that would be right." She nodded vigorously, glad of the renewed opportunity to display her superior powers of recall. "You said about seventeen years, didn't you, but it was much longer than that. Our Annie will be forty next birthday."

"And did she and Jenny ever get to play together?"

"Not that I know of. They did end up living quite close, but of course Jenny would have gone to the cathedral school so they wouldn't have had the chance to get to know each other after all."

"The cathedral school?" Celia wrinkled her brow, not understanding. "What cathedral school?"

"At Lichfield," the old lady said, with exaggerated patience. "On account of her father being at the cathedral himself. I thought I told you. It was why they moved – he got this post at Lichfield Cathedral, some canon or another. I never did find out what the official title was."

Her face creased with dissatisfaction at having missed out on this vital piece of information, so long in the past there was no chance now of getting to learn it.

Celia, however, jumped to her feet, and planted a kiss on the top of the astonished old lady's head.

"Mrs Yelverton," she declared, fervently, "you are a star."

Positively flying along the road on winged feet, Pixie squealing with delight in the pushchair, Celia couldn't believe how simple it had been to get started again. She felt weak, positively boneless with relief at the thought of getting away from Elizabeth Lodge, of being able to stop keeping tabs on everything she said to avoid giving away her true identity, of no longer having to keep Magnus Armstrong at arm's length.

Right – time for action! I can't faff around any longer – I'll tell them tonight that I'm going, and I'll leave in the morning.

As she walked into the kitchen, Sally Armstrong loomed up from one of the chairs. It was unusual for her to be home at that time of day. She looked unwell, her thin face pinched and white.

"Hello," said Celia, in surprise. "Are you OK?"

Sally pursed her lips together. "No," she said forbiddingly. "I'm not OK. In fact, I'm really – "

She stopped and looked at Pixie, the scratch livid across her cheek, strapped into the pushchair with chocolate smeared around her mouth and clutching the by now empty bottle of cola.

"What's happened to her face? And what have you been giving her? You know perfectly well I don't like her having chocolate in the week, and as for Coke. . ."

"Not Smarties an' Coke," Pixie said obediently. "Scampered egg."

Her mother ignored her. She clearly had other, more pressing things on her mind than the forbidden items her daughter had been eating.

"I think it's time," she said to Celia, "that you and I had a little chat. I don't appear to have had your references yet, despite asking for them to be sent when you first arrived here."

Caught out, Celia blushed. "Ah, yes. I can explain about that," she stammered, playing for time. *Any moment now,* she thought frantically, *she's going to tell me she's had a call from the agency and she knows I'm not Jessica. I know I wanted to leave, but not like this — not being done for fraud, or impersonating an* au pair, *or something!*

"Never mind," Sally went on, with a dismissive wave of her hand, as if the references were after all unimportant. "There's another matter I want to ask you about."

"Oh?"

"I came home from work," Sally said, "with a foul headache and no painkillers in the house. When I went to the chemist to buy some, I was asked by the assistant — in front of a shopful of customers, mind — how my *au pair* was keeping, as she was in the other day buying a pregnancy testing kit. Now what," she said grimly, "do you have to say to that?"

"It was negative," Celia said, aware as she did so how lame it sounded.

"Negative!" her employer screeched, her eyebrows flying into her hairline. "I should damn well think it *was* negative!"

"I'm sorry," Celia said politely, "but I don't understand the problem."

Sally Armstrong collected herself with a enormous, visible effort of will.

"The problem," she said, through gritted teeth, "is that you had the need to buy and use a pregnancy test in the first place. The problem is that you're in my house, caring for my children, and you clearly have the morals of an alley-cat, as the entire clientele of the chemist's now knows and is doubtless busy spreading around Stoke Barton at this very moment. The problem, Jessica, is that I have absolutely no intention of allowing my children to be looked after a moment longer by a little *tart* like you, and under the circumstances I think it's best if you leave immediately!" Her voice trailed upwards, shrilly.

Celia took a deep, calming, liberating breath.

"OK," she said, reasonably. "OK. I was going to go anyway. I've had more than enough of your horrible spoilt children, and if you want to know the real reason why all your other *au pairs* have only stayed for five minutes, you ought to look at your kids' behaviour. Oh, and your husband is a lech who can't keep his hands to himself – it might have had something to do with that, too."

"What!" Sally Armstrong's face was magenta

with rage. These home truths clearly weren't doing her headache any good at all. "How dare you – just pack and go, will you!"

"Don't worry, I'm going," Celia said, astonishing herself by still being as cool as a cucumber. "But there is just one other thing. Was it the possibility of my being pregnant that bothered you most, or the fact that everybody else in the shop knew about it too, and might spread gossip?"

She left the question hanging in the air and turned to leave the kitchen, and at that precise moment Pixie leaned over the side of the pushchair and was immensely, extravagantly sick on to the expensive French terracotta tiles.

CHAPTER 13

It was a long way from Exeter to Lichfield. Especially by coach, which was the only means of transport Celia could now afford. Before boarding at Exeter, she had gone into the building society and withdrawn the rest of the money in her account, which meant she now had the princely sum of fifty-seven pounds left to her name. That was all; her entire assets, to pay for everything she would need from now on. She was shocked at how quickly the money had vanished since starting out, and was beginning to regret having been so free and easy with her cash, buying all those new clothes, and taking taxis as if they were going out of fashion. She especially regretted the clothes; she had been unable to fit them all into her rucksack and she'd had to leave things behind, her jeans and thick sweater and towel, as well as all those brand new, scarcely-played CDs which took up far too much space. *Tess of the d'Urbervilles* got the chop, too: she never had got around to finishing it, either. Too depressing, she decided. And too many memories of Josh.

She had been unbelievably glad to leave the Armstrongs', a huge weight of anxiety lifting from her shoulders as she stuffed everything she could into the backpack. She had been so certain, standing there in the kitchen, that her deception had been uncovered, that the enormous relief she felt went a long way to make up for the fact that she hadn't, after all, been paid a penny. *Who needs money, anyway? Something will turn up. I'll have to get another job, if necessary. And who needs jeans in this weather? It won't take much longer to find Genevieve now, surely it won't.*

She had learnt an important lesson: that secrecy was unnecessary, a waste of both time and effort. Nobody was going to come looking for her now, demand her return, drag her back home. She just had to get on with things, swallow her reticence and ask around. At least she had more idea now of the kind of people to ask: people like Rose Yelverton, who had lived in the same place for years and knew, as her daughter-in-law had so succinctly put it, everything about everybody.

The coach was packed and overheated and smelt sourly of dusty upholstery and unwashed bodies. As Celia sat on the cramped prickly plush of her allotted window seat, she took out from her rucksack the velvet-lined box containing her birth certificate and the letter from her mother. She crammed the rucksack into the corner between her legs and the seat in front, spread out the documents on her knees, smoothed out the creases as she had done hundreds of times before, and gazed at the papers as if they were some kind of talisman.

She felt no nearer her mother than when she had set out. She had learnt certain things about Genevieve, it was true, but at the end of the day, what did she really know about her? That, despite writing this emotional, heartstring-tugging letter to be given symbolically to her daughter on her sixteenth birthday, she wasn't after all a teenager herself when her child was born, forced by hard uncaring parents to have the baby adopted, but a mature independent woman in her twenties. That her Welsh father was a clergyman; that she had lived in Devon as a child, but had then moved to the Midlands when her father took up a cathedral post. That she was Genevieve, Jenny and Ginny; Jones and, inexplicably, Cavendish. That she had lied, on Celia's birth certificate about her name and address, and to the Cavendishes about visiting her parents in Devon when they had moved away years ago. Where had she gone when she had told Freda Cavendish she was visiting them, and where had she gone after Celia's birth? Above all, what was the story surrounding

Celia's birth – just why had she given her baby daughter up for adoption?

Oh, Genevieve, Celia whispered to herself. *Where are you? Who are you? Am I ever going to find you, find answers to all my questions?*

She stared at the documents for a long time as the coach swayed and bumped its long way eastwards, as if she could burn the imprint of the words they contained on to her brain and thereby, by osmosis, gain some insight into their background, the circumstances under which they were written. Then, with a sigh, she folded the papers away, tucked them back into their box, rested her head against the greasy seat, and tried to sleep.

It was late when she arrived at Lichfield, which was small as cities went, and dominated by the floodlit Gothic triple-spired cathedral. Celia had a vague impression of narrow medieval streets and Georgian buildings – a sign proudly proclaimed: "Lichfield, Birthplace of Dr Johnson" – before the coach turned into the bus station in a decidedly less attractive part of the city, next to a modern shopping centre. She found a room for the night in a pub within a stone's throw of a twenty-four-hour Tesco; after being shown to her room – cheap and not very cheerful, with no lock, a stained carpet, a chipped porcelain sink in the corner and a kilometre trek along creaking corridors to the shared bathroom – she visited the supermarket and bought two cut-price packets of egg-and-cress sandwiches at the end of their sell-by dates and a can of Fanta, which she carried back to her room and consumed hungrily, having had neither lunch nor breakfast that day.

She wedged the single wooden chair under the door handle in lieu of locking the door, and despite a lumpy mattress, continuing hunger pangs and a nagging suspicion that she really should have visited the loo again before getting into bed, she slept like a log, waking at quarter to eight as refreshed as if she had spent the night in her own bed with nothing of any importance pressing on her mind. It was far too early for breakfast. She didn't feel at all hungry yet, despite her rumbling stomach of the night before. She decided to go and check out the cathedral before anybody else was up and about.

It was easy enough to find, its impressive red sandstone bulk towering above everything else for kilometres around. It was encompassed by a close of quaint half-timbered houses and large elegant Georgian buildings, obviously built to house both the ordinary citizens of the time and those whom Eddie would scathingly call the Rich Gits. Celia walked slowly around the close, breathing in the balmy warmth of the July air and savouring the peace and solitude of the early morning. An avenue of horse chestnuts in full leaf on the north side of the cathedral rustled in the soft breeze, and a handsome grey cat strolled across the road and then stopped halfway, stretched luxuriously, yawned, and sat to wash its whiskers with delicate thoroughness. Celia could hear music, very faintly in the distance. She had reached the front of the cathedral; the great west door was firmly closed, locked and bolted, but rather to her surprise – it was barely quarter past eight – a smaller one to its side was unlocked and standing open. She walked in.

The choir were practising at the far end of the building, their sweet notes rising in the air to the vaulted roof, dizzily high above, and min-gling with the dust motes that swirled lazily in the shafts of sunlight streaming through the clerestory windows. Not wishing to disturb them, Celia tiptoed carefully along a side aisle, over the ancient stone flags which were overlaid here and there with coloured lozenges of light from the stained glass, until she reached the front of the nave. There were the singers, in the choir stalls beyond a heavily gilded and angel-encrusted screen. The choristers only: she counted them – eighteen small boys, some so small their heads could barely be seen over the stalls. Mum and Dad had often exclaimed over choristers in other cathedrals during the deadly Evensong visits, how sweet they were, how musical, how dedicated. They would secretly have liked Edward to have been a cathedral chorister somewhere, Celia suspected, have him dressed in a cassock and ruff with all the old ladies clucking and fussing over him, but unfortunately he turned out to be utterly unmusical and loathed going to church to boot. Not the ideal credentials for a choirboy, clearly. It was just as well, really. Edward shunned the limelight with a passion, and would sooner have died than be thought of as sweet.

Now, though, she could see Mum and Dad's point of view. These choirboys were dressed for their practice not in cassocks but school uniform, the usual small boy assortment of untucked shirts, unbrushed hair and askew ties. The very ordinariness of their appearance was misleading; not one of them was even as old as Edward, judging by their size, but the sound they made was phenomenal, strong and focussed. They were singing a setting of the evening service, the Magnificat.

My soul doth magnify the Lord. . .

A solo treble took up the melody, his voice rising effortlessly and purely, and as the familiar words soared to the heavens Celia thought she had never before heard anything quite so beautiful.

For he hath regarded the lowliness of his handmaiden. . .

Celia sat and listened until the practice was over, her mind emptied of everything except the music flowing around and above and beneath her.

"Good, aren't they?"

She turned, startled, to find a man standing beside her, a priest dressed in his working uniform of long black-belted robe and white dog collar.

"Er – yes." She stood up clumsily, dazed and disorientated, and was embarrassed to discover her face was wet with tears. "Yes, they are. They're amazing."

The boys were clumping down the aisle towards her now, off-duty in dark blazers, carrying yellow caps and school bags and instrument cases, and bickering mildly amongst themselves.

"The really amazing thing," the priest continued, "is that they do all this so unselfconsciously. They don't consider themselves in the least bit amazing. Do you, Cary?"

"Sorry, sir?" A small untidy boy at the end of the straggling line, carrying a violin case.

"You don't think you're amazing, do you?"

"I do, sir," he objected. "I got four wickets in the House match yesterday."

"Did you? Wow! That's terrific."

"Cool, or what?" He shot the priest a cheeky grin, and galloped off to join his mates.

"And don't run in the cathedral!" the priest called after him, affectionately. He turned back to Celia. "Are you visiting? Why not come back for Evensong, hear it all again for real, as it were?"

"I don't know." Celia brushed her wet face with her hand, quickly.

"I'm sorry. I'm intruding – how tactless of me. Let me leave you in peace." He gave her a gentle smile and turned to go.

He hath filled the hungry with good things, and the rich he hath sent empty away.

The words of the Magnificat still rang in Celia's ears.

Celia Duckenfield talks to Jesus. . .

Yeah, and? So what? Why shouldn't I talk to whoever I want?

She put out an urgent hand and touched his sleeve. "Please," she said, "don't go. You're not disturbing me. You might be able to help me."

The priest smiled again, and spread his hands. "That's what I'm here for."

"Not in a soul-saving sort of way, I mean," she said, hastily. Best to get that clear.

"Oh dear. What a shame. I haven't saved any souls yet today. You'd have been my first." He was teasing her. Celia was almost certain.

"I'm looking for somebody. Another priest here. A canon, would it be?"

He nodded. "What's his name?"

"Gethin Jones. He came here from Devon, probably about thirty years ago?"

"Ah." He pulled a rueful face. "In that case, I'm afraid I can't help after all. There's no canons here now who've been here that long. I've only been here myself for two years."

Again the lurch of disappointment, the sharp stab of let-down. "Oh. Oh well, never mind then."

"No," he went on, "it's Jeffrey you want to talk to. The head verger. He'll be in the ducket this time of the morning, having his early-morning cuppa. He's been here for donkey's years. In fact," he inclined his head towards her, conspiratorially, "between you and me, I reckon he's older than God himself."

"Gethin Jones?" The head verger took a long swallow of his tea and nodded his head knowledgeably. "Course I remember him. Proper star turn, he was; place was always packed out when he was preaching. Course, that were back in the days when folk appreciated a proper sermon –

none of this three-minute fix rubbish everyone demands these days. I blame all those computer games, myself."

Celia, who couldn't see the connection, was reminded of Rose Yelverton the previous day. How these old fogies did love to rabbit on. Grateful though she was to the verger, and to Mrs Yelverton too, she couldn't afford to let him get off the point.

"But he's not still here, of course."

"Get away! He'd be well into his seventies by now. Not that that stops some clergymen, mind – look at the Pope. He gets any older, they'll have to dig him up before wheeling him round on his next tour. When are they going to let him retire, that's what I want to know."

"So when did Mr Jones retire, then?"

"I don't rightly know." His brow furrowed with concentration; he clearly didn't share Mrs Yelverton's powers of recall. "Nope. Sorry. Can't remember at all. Must be a good few years ago now, though. He went back to the Land of his Fathers, that much I do remember."

"Back to where?"

"The Land of –" He stopped, clicking his tongue in mock disapproval. "Don't they teach you youngsters anything in school these days? Back to Wales, duck, where he came from. He was always talking about it – it happens when you get old, you know. Sentimentality, I suppose."

"Whereabouts in Wales? Did he ever say?"

"Somewhere in the north, as I recall. He spoke the language, you know. He told me North Wales Welsh and South Wales Welsh are two quite different languages, did you know that?"

Celia shook her head. "I don't know anything about Wales. I've never been there."

"No, me neither. But Canon Jones spoke about it often. He always intended to retire back to his home town: where the mountains meet the sea, he used to say. There, that would be the north, wouldn't it? The mountains – Snowdonia?"

Celia dimly recalled past geography lessons: *the highest mountain in England is Scafell Pike, the highest mountain in Scotland is Ben Nevis, the highest mountain in Wales is Snowdon. . .*

"I guess. What about Canon Jones's daughter? Do you remember her?"

"Young Jenny?" A distant, faraway look of regret passed across his face. "Aye. I remember her, all right. And her mother, too. Such a shame, it was, what happened to that family."

It was the first time anybody had mentioned Genevieve's mother. Somehow, in Celia's feverish desire to trace Genevieve and Gethin, she had given little or no thought to the fact that Genevieve had a mother of her own. *My grandmother*, she realized, with a thrill of excitement.

"So what did happen to the family? To Canon Jones, and Genevieve and – what was her mother's name?"

"Let me think, now. Cecily, was it? No, Simone. That's right. Simone. French, she was."

Simone. . . Celia heart thudded in her chest, so loudly she thought the verger must surely hear. But he drained his mug, oblivious of course to Celia's thoughts.

"Elegant lady, always smart-looking. Nicely turned out, as my wife used to say. Gloves and that. You don't see it any more these days, more's the pity." He gave Celia a sideways glance; not suspicious, more curious. "What's your interest in them, then?"

Time to tell the truth. Tell the truth and shame the devil. The phrase popped into her head, from heaven only knew where.

Celia looked him straight in the eye.

"She was my grandmother. Genevieve is my mother, I'm trying to find her. I'm adopted," she added. "She had me adopted when I was a baby."

Jeffrey the verger nodded phlegmatically, quite unmoved, as if adopted children came to the cathedral in search of their natural parents every day of the week.

"Right. Gotcha."

That was all. No exclamations of surprise or disapproval, just simple acceptance.

"So what did happen to them?" she prompted him. "Why did you say it was a shame?"

'Well, Mrs Jones died, didn't she? Turned out she had some kind of cancer, poor thing, and was dead within six months. And poor bloke, too. He never got over it. It must have been shortly after she died that he retired, now I come to think of it. And that was on top of all kinds of trouble with the daughter – young Jenny. Genevieve." He looked at Celia again. "You do look a bit like her. I can see it now."

"What sort of trouble?"

"A family feud of some kind. Never did get to the bottom of it. Well, I wouldn't do, would I? None of my business. But it was plain there'd been some bust-up or another – she just disappeared one day and never came back, not even for her mother's funeral. That shocked a lot of folk here, you know. There's always gossip about people's lives, cathedral or no cathedral."

Celia felt bombarded by so much new and unexpected information.

"Such a respectable family, they were, too," he went on. "It wasn't at all the type of thing anybody would have expected. They always seemed so upright, Canon and Mrs Jones; decent, you know. A touch old-fashioned, if anything. Mrs J never worked – the word was, he wouldn't let her. Nicely brought-up, Jenny was – bright, went off after college to do her nurse's training and everything."

"She trained as a nurse?"

"As I recall, aye. I think it was a nurse. Might have been a teacher, though." He thought about it, then shook his head, firmly. "No, it was definitely a nurse. There was talk she might come back and look after her mother once she knew she was ill, but not a bit of it. Whatever it was they'd rowed about, it obviously went deep. Sad. After that lovely wedding, too."

"Wedding?" Celia stared at him, not understanding. "You mean they got married after they came here?"

The verger laughed merrily. "Not *their* wedding, Jenny's of course!"

"Genevieve's wedding? You mean she got *married*?"

"That's right."

'But – are you sure?" she cried wildly. "Are you sure you're not getting her muddled with somebody else?" It made no sense, none. How could Genevieve have been married?

"Sure I'm sure." He laughed again. "Right

here in the cathedral, it was. We were all calling it the Wedding of the Century. It was the same year Prince Charles and Lady Diana got wed. Same year, same month. When was that, now? Eighty-two, was it? Eighty-one? A beautiful do – the sun shone, the bishop married them, the choir sang, and her train stretched right down the aisle just like Princess Di's. Mind you," he added, sucking on his teeth, "look how that wedding turned out, all the unhappiness and rifts and family arguments. They all said that was a fairy tale, too, didn't they?"

He looked again at Celia. "Oops. Gone and put my foot in it, haven't I?"

Celia tried to look unconcerned, to smile nonchalantly, but the smile came out lopsided. The verger put out a fatherly hand and patted Celia's shoulder, gently.

"Just because your mum was married once upon a time, doesn't mean she still was when you came along, does it? Who knows what happened in the meantime, eh? Anything could have happened. No mother would give her child away unless she really had to. I can't claim to know a great deal about women, but I know that much. She must have been in dire straits to have thought adoption best for you. Don't you go imagining any nonsense about her not wanting you, duck – don't go torturing yourself."

His kindness brought the tears back to Celia's eyes. She found herself snuffling, embarrassingly, ridiculously, and without a tissue. He handed her a pristine white hanky, without another word, and then busied himself with his back to her while she composed herself.

"Thanks." She blew her nose, feeling a little better. "I don't suppose you happen to remember the name of the man she married, do you?"

The verger blew out his cheeks with a whistling noise through his teeth. "Phew. Now you're asking. No, hang about." He held up a finger, his face clearing. "Yes. I do remember."

Celia leaned forward hopefully. "So what was it? His name? Was his last name Cavendish?"

"Cavendish? No, his surname was Butcher. You remember that actress, Genevieve Bujold?" He looked at Celia's blank face. "No, of course you wouldn't, you're far too young. She was French, like Jenny's mum. A real beauty, and a tidy little actress, too. Anyway, I remember my wife was taken with the similarity of the names. Genevieve Bujold – Genevieve Butcher. See?"

"Kind of." Celia finished her tea, and stood up. "So her married name was Butcher? Thanks ever so much. You've been really helpful."

"Glad to have been of assistance." He smiled at her. "So what will you be doing now?"

232

"Off to Wales, I suppose. Looking for Canon Jones. He's my only lead."

He looked doubtful. "Are you sure? It's a big place, Wales. There must be thousands of Joneses."

"I'll be fine. Honestly. I have my sources." She thought of Phoebe and smiled, cheered slightly, and held out the handkerchief. "Thanks for this. I'm afraid it's a bit soggy."

But the verger shook his head.

"No, no. You keep it, love. Have it with my compliments." He stood up, too, and patted her shoulder again. "I've got granddaughters about your age. I've been very fortunate in my life. A wonderful wife and kids, and now I'm blessed with four lovely grandchildren. Family life's a precious thing. You go careful on your travels, duck. You mind how you go."

CHAPTER 14

Celia had always promised that she would never, under any circumstances, hitch-hike anywhere. Who in their right mind would willingly get into a car alone with a total stranger? It would be madness, foolhardy in the extreme. As it turned out, however, Celia had no choice. When she got back from the cathedral to her room at the pub she packed hastily, cramming her things into the rucksack in her keenness to get going again. She had so much more information now, thanks to Jeffrey; surely Phoebe would be able to come up with something from the Net? She looked at her watch; still not nine o'clock yet. It was Thursday: double study-period first thing, so with any luck she'd catch Phoebe before she left for school. Deciding to skip breakfast – the smell of stale fat frying creeping up the stairs was in any case turning her stomach – Celia pulled the drawstrings of the rucksack tight, shrugged on her fleece, and looked around the room for her wallet. There wasn't far to look. Bed, rickety wooden chair, chest of drawers: she looked underneath it, opened each drawer to its fullest extent, got down on her hands and knees and peered under the bed. She unmade it, first pulling back the duvet in case the wallet had somehow become tangled in its folds, and then, panicking, stripped it down to the stained mattress, but to no avail. She even searched the unravelling wicker waste-paper bin, tipping its contents on to the floor and scrabbling frantically amongst the empty sandwich cartons and Fanta can from last night, the used tissues and sweet papers and the wrapper from the tiny sliver of guest soap provided on the washbasin.

The wallet wasn't anywhere to be found. Celia realized, with a desperate plummeting of both heart and stomach, that in her hurry earlier on to get out she had – stupidly, carelessly, *irresponsibly* – left her wallet behind in the room. She had been robbed while she had been in the cathedral listening to the verger's revelations, and she now had precisely no money at all.

"Feebs?"

"Hiya!" Delightedly. "How's things? Have you found her yet?"

Celia closed her eyes, and leant against the side of the telephone booth. She could feel the cool smoothness of the glass beneath her cheek.

"No."

"So where are you now, then?"

"In Lichfield."

"Lichfield? Where's that?"

"Midlands. Just north of Birmingham."

"Oh, right. What are you doing there?"

Hiding in a phone box, waiting for the heavy hand of the law on my shoulder for running off from that pub without paying my bill.

She felt a small stab of exasperation.

"Talking to you on the phone."

"Ooh, sarky or what!" Amused; unoffended. A slight pause – just a beat. "Is everything OK?"

Yes, everything's fab. My mother is turning out to be not just impossible to find but schizophrenically multi-personalitied. I've had a God-awful row with my father which totally buggers any possibility of asking for help or, God forbid, going back home, and I've almost certainly ploughed my GCSEs so Lady Mags won't want to touch me with a bargepole. I was almost raped three days ago, I've just been robbed, I've broken the law, and to top it all I haven't a clue what to do next. Everything's just hunky-dory.

She opened her eyes. "Not really, no. I've got no money. My wallet's been stolen."

"Oh no – God, that's really pants! Haven't you got any money at all? Is that why you reversed the charges?"

"Yeah – I hope that's OK."

"Christ, yes! No problem, honestly! But why don't you just go to the bank and get some more out?"

"There is no more," Celia said, dully. "It's all gone. I've spent it all."

A longer pause while Phoebe digested all this. "Bloody hell. You are in a mess, aren't you? Boss assaults you, lost your mobile, lost your money –"

"OK, OK! Rub it in, why don't you?" Celia yelled, the irritation boiling over and turning to rage, frustration and impotence. "I rang you for some help, not to make me feel worse!"

Immediate contrition. "Sorry. Sorry! I will help, of course I will, if I can. What would you like me to do? Only I'm not sure I can help much with the money thing, I'm a bit strapped myself at the moment."

"It's OK." Celia took a deep breath, closing her eyes again momentarily. "It's all right. I wasn't ringing to ask for money."

Briefly, she outlined to Phoebe what she wanted her to do. Then she hung up, and waited for her friend to call her back.

It took Phoebe forty-five minutes to find what she was looking for. It was the longest three-quarters of an hour of Celia's life: she lurked inside the phone box for a while and then, driven out by a succession of people wanting to use it (*why this one?* she wanted to cry; *why this one, when there's probably an empty one just down the road?*), on the pavement outside, pulling the collar of her fleece up around her neck in a rather pathetic attempt at disguise, and sure with a sick and thudding certainty that everyone who passed was a plain-clothes police officer, armed with a warrant for her arrest on the charge of defrauding the pub where she had stayed overnight. It was only when the phone rang – finally, blessedly – that Celia realized the curious stares of the passers-by were almost certainly due to her being bundled up in her fleece in temperatures that must already, at nine-thirty in the morning, be well into the seventies.

She yanked open the door of the booth and snatched up the receiver.

"Hello? Phoebe?"

"Yup. Sorry it's taken so long."

"So what's the story? Did you find anything?" Impatiently.

"I think so, yeah. Hang on a tick – I down-loaded it and printed it all off." A moment's silence punctuated with faint rustlings as Phoebe obviously consulted her notes. "Yes, here we go. Snowdonia. I fed the names of all the places along the north coast within striking distance of the mountains into the search engine, to see what it came up with."

"And?"

"And it came up with – " Another rustle. "Brynmor. It's even got its own little website. Bless! And you'll never guess what the subtitle is on the homepage."

Celia sighed, silently. Phoebe was her best friend; she'd got Celia out of more than one hole during this project already. But how she did love to string things out, to eke out the drama.

Celia humoured her. "Go on then. What?"

"Where the Mountains Meet the Sea. I'm not kidding, it actually says that!"

It was more than Celia had hoped for, and well worth the wait. Mindful of how Jeffrey had described Gethin Jones's home town, where he had retired to, it was the exact brief she had given Phoebe: look for somewhere in North Wales where the mountains meet the sea. But past disappointments made her cynical.

"Are you sure? It actually says that – you're not just trying to make me feel better?"

Phoebe snorted. "As if! Come on, Seal, why would I lie? It actually says it: *Beautiful Brynmor: Where the Mountains Meet the Sea.*" Her attempt at a Welsh accent owed more to Pakistan than to Pwllheli. "And there's pics as well; mountains, sea, the works. It looks fab, dead picturesque."

"Thanks." Reassured, Celia felt suddenly better. What did lack of finances matter? She'd find a way to get there, somehow. "I mean it. Thanks a million – I owe you one."

"Actually," said Phoebe, nonchalantly, "you owe me about one hundred by now. I'm still fending off your parents, you know. Lying to them that we talk regularly, that you're perfectly fine and that you're only not calling them because it's a generation thing and you feel happier communicating to them via me."

"Yeah? They're still hassling you? Sorry."

"It's no hassle. Did I say it was a hassle? They're worried. I feel sorry for them, if you want to know the truth. I know how mine would feel if it were me who'd done a runner."

"I haven't done a runner!" Celia flared up, suddenly furious. "You know what I—"

"OK, OK. Don't get out of your pram. I know that, you know that. I'm only trying to tell you how they feel. Can you really not give them a call, tell them that you're still alive and kicking?"

"No."

Celia's voice was flat. It was out of the question, totally. She needed all her resources right now to concentrate on the task in hand. What she didn't need was her parents messing with her head; her father bawling her out again about the pregnancy/Josh thing, her mother making her feel guilty.

"I can't. Absolutely not. Don't ask me why, I just can't."

"I wasn't going to ask you why." Phoebe sounded suddenly weary. She sighed. "It's up to you. It's your life. I'm not going to tell you what to do."

Celia hitched lifts from a wallpaper salesman going to a conference in Wolverhampton, a young couple with a new baby on their way to visit relatives in Telford, an elderly man going to Shrewsbury who, despite his advancing years, drove his equally elderly Ford Fiesta as if he was in pole position for the Renault Formula One team, a glamorous thirty-ish career woman in an obviously company-owned BMW on her way to Chester who swore like a guardsman at everything else on the road, and finally, most daringly, a lugubriously silent Irish lorry driver en route to Holyhead to catch the ferry home. The whole journey took nearly eleven hours, including protracted and frustrating stops in-between lifts. To make matters worse, the heat and the dust seemed to have started off some kind of hayfever, which made her sneeze and cough continuously.

It got easier after the first lift, a journey of

only half an hour or so, during which time Celia sat folded in mute and terrified silence on the back seat amongst the wallpaper samples, hugging her rucksack for comfort and certain that the softly-spoken and inoffensive driver was at any moment going to turn off the dual carriageway, produce a scimitar and thoroughly molest her. The relief she felt when he dropped her off quite unmolested along the A5 was mingled with a faint but definite disappointment that this was all there was to it, what she had been avoiding all these years, terrorized by parents and teachers and over-emphatic media scare stories.

The weather changed near Oswestry. The blue cloudless sky became hazy, then silver, then darker and darker grey, until by Chester it had started to rain, great heavy drops the size of fifty pence pieces driving smearily against the windscreen. But a worse problem for Celia than the weather or even the hayfever was lack of food. All the drivers ate something at some point on their particular leg of the journey, unwrapping pies and packets of sandwiches, or stopping at service stations, but none of them suggested Celia might like anything. The most she was offered was a couple of Polo mints by the wallpaper salesman, which she declined nervously, on the somewhat unlikely basis that they might be spiked. On the one hand, she realized that somebody offering her a lift didn't also assume responsibility for her entire welfare; why should they spend any of their money on her, a complete stranger? But on the other hand, as extreme hunger made her increasingly bad-tempered and resentful, she wondered why nobody appeared to realize or care that, while they merrily stuffed their faces, she was sitting empty-handed (not to mention empty-bellied) beside them.

Eventually, the lorry driver came up trumps. He stopped at a Little Chef somewhere west of Chester, with a hissing of air brakes, and inclined his head towards the building.

"You coming in?"

Celia's stomach gave a plaintive little growl. "I can't. I'm broke."

The Irishman shrugged. "Sure, and haven't I just been paid? It'll be my treat."

The food, when it arrived, was possibly the best Celia had ever tasted. Following her host's lead she went for the All-Day Breakfast: their plates were piled high with rashers of bacon, eggs, sausages, tomatoes, hash browns and fried bread, followed by toast and marmalade, all washed down with copious cups of strong tea. The lorry driver finished first, wiping his plate clean with the last of the toast and then, leaning back in his chair, folded his hands beneath his stomach and sighed appreciatively. But Celia had to admit defeat. She laid the knife and fork down on the plate, regretfully.

"All done?" The Irishman raised an eyebrow.

Celia nodded, and pushed the plate away. "I'm stuffed. Thanks very much. It's really kind of you; I was starving."

"I'd never have guessed."

It was raining in earnest when they left. High up in the warm fug of the cab, Celia dozed as the lorry ploughed along the A55, eating up the final kilometre. The wipers swept hypnotically against the windscreen; the radio was on, tuned to some obscure station that played endless Country and Western.

> *Please don't take my man*
> *You picked a fine time to leave me*
> *Give him all the love you can*
> *Bring more love*
> *Brynmor love. . .*
> *BRYNMOR, LOVE!*

Forcing open her eyes, confused and disorientated, Celia sneezed, and struggled to sit up.

"Whaddya say? What?"

She was giddy with sleep, woozy and slightly nauseous.

"Brynmor. Another two miles, so the signs say."

He came off the dual carriageway and put her down on the edge of the village. It was nearly ten o'clock, and still pouring with rain. Celia watched the lorry driver reverse expertly into a turning and then drive off, back towards the main road. He waved as he passed her, a brief salute with his right hand. She watched him go, the huge wheels churning up spray from the road, until the red tail lights disappeared into the gloomy distance. Celia's heart sank, down and down; it was such a real physical sensation that she almost expected to see it spilling out on to the puddled pavement. All the while she had been hitching lifts, sitting passively in other people's vehicles, she had been able to convince herself that everything would be fine once she reached her destination; that things would fall into place, that she would be able to cope. But now she was here, she realized she had only been kidding herself. She felt utterly dejected, abandoned; watching the lorry drive off was one of the lowest spots of the venture so far, and she hadn't a single clue what to do next.

Well, I can't stand here all night, that's for sure. She hoisted the rucksack on to her back and trudged into the village.

Brynmor was small and within a pebble's-throw of the beach, with the impressive dark bulk of the mountains backed up behind. That was the good part. The bad part was that it was extremely run-down. The short high street was lined either side with shops, obviously quite grand in their time with curly wrought-iron balustrades and overhead arcading, the original glass replaced now with perspex; but at least half the shops were empty, the lower windows boarded up, the upper ones smashed or missing completely. The perspex arcading was yellowed and cracked, the balustrades rusted, the shopfronts grimy and shabby with peeling paint and drifts of litter gathered in doorways.

The street was deserted, with neither person nor car to be seen. Celia wondered what had happened to the place; surely it should be busy and bustling with holidaymakers at this time of year, so close as it was to the twin tourist honey-pots of beach and mountains? Where were the guest houses and cafés and restaurants, the ice-cream parlours, the gift shops, the amusement arcades? It was like a ghost town, something out of one of the naff cowboy films Dad loved to watch on TV. Celia half-expected to see a ball of tumbleweed drift along the street, followed by a black-Stetsoned outlaw on a snorting, pawing stallion.

Where the hell am I going to stay tonight? Even if there were any guest houses in sight, I've got no way of paying to stay in one.

She walked the length of the main street, regretting her choice of attire that morning, when it had been hot and sunny, of shorts and flip-flops. It was not a long journey. It took precisely five minutes. Despairing, she retraced her steps and then turned down a side road on the left to see where that led.

She found herself going down a steep hill, at the foot of which lay the railway station. Beyond the station the dual carriageway thundered past and then, further yet, she could see the pale exposed sands of Brynmor Bay. The tide was going out, its choppy grey surface dimpled with the incessant rain like beaten pewter. On the far horizon, where the gunmetal sea met the leaden sky, desultory lightning flickered. Celia had no doubt that, given a sunny summer's day, the scene that lay spread out before her would be attractive, inviting even. This time yesterday, she recollected, it had been a beautiful evening. She had watched the gold- and rose-tinted clouds in the darkening blue of the sky through the coach window, on her way to Lichfield. But this evening it was already deep twilight, the rain casting a forbidding and cheerless pall over everything.

She followed the road around to the right, past the railway station. The footbridge over the single track had been painted in bright shades of red and green in an attempt to cheer the place up; a somewhat fruitless attempt, Celia thought, as the station had the same desolate and abandoned air as the rest of the village. Is this really the place Genevieve's father spoke about in such glowing terms to Jeffrey the verger, she thought: the place he grew up in and loved so much that he retired here? *Perhaps there's been some mistake; perhaps there's another Brynmor, or maybe Phoebe didn't search for long enough and there's another North Wales village where the mountains meet the sea.*

But she knew, in her heart of hearts, that there had been no mistake, that this was the right place, God-forsaken and neglected though it was, and that she, heaven help her, was stuck there.

She plodded along the road, sunk in misery. She was getting wetter and wetter, the backpack heavier and heavier. Hayfever was making her nose run, and she felt shivery and faintly unwell. Rivulets of rain dripped down her neck, inside the collar of her fleece and T-shirt and along her spine. Her feet slid about on the flip-flops which squeaked with each step, the thong digging painfully between her toes. As shoes, they were worse than useless. She stopped abruptly, swore, and removed them.

Bloody things!

Holding them in her hand like a weapon, suddenly close to tears, she looked around wildly for a bin to throw them in. Directly in front of her, across the road, was a large empty house, a mansion almost, clearly once smart and imposing but now, like so many of its Brynmor companions, disused and boarded up. The front door, though, stood wide open to the elements. Cautiously, still clutching the flip-flops, Celia crossed the road. She stood on the pavement and peered up the pathway to the front door.

Shall I? Dare I? At least it'll be out of the rain.

She found herself inside, without even having consciously made the decision. The front hall was lofty and once grand; in the dim light filtering in from the street lamps outside, Celia could make out a patterned mosaic floor, a sweeping staircase. It smelt of damp and decay, and there were piles of pigeon droppings on the floor. Five doors led off the hall. She pushed open the nearest, her heart beginning to thud anxiously, the nervous puffs of her breath visible in the dank damp air. The door squeaked protestingly on its hinges before swinging open.

A person-sized hole had been made in the

boards across the once-gracious French windows, letting in enough light for Celia to see bare floorboards, some missing, and a huge fireplace of some pale stone. She went warily over to it, feeling her way, her damp bare feet sticking slightly on the wooden floor. It was darker in there than in the hallway, but it seemed dryer. She reached the fireplace and dropped her backpack thankfully on to the ground. With her back against the wall, she slid down the length of it until she was sitting on the floor. Then, pulling the rucksack towards her, she lay down half on it, half on the dirty floorboards, wrapped herself into a foetal position, and closed her eyes.

She must have slept because the light made her jump with fright. It was shining directly into her eyes, and she couldn't make out who was holding it, only that it was a rough male voice who was shouting at her, over and over:

"What you doing here, girl? What you doing here, then?"

CHAPTER 15

Terrified beyond any rational thought, and still at least three-quarters asleep, Celia rolled over, across the dust and grime on the floor, in an attempt to escape from the beam of light that held her captive. Groggily, she tried to sit up, and then to stand, but was forced back down on to the ground by first an arm and then the full weight of someone across her shoulders and upper body.

"Get off me! Get off!" she yelled, and was racked by a fit of coughing.

Memories of Magnus Armstrong came flooding back, memories of him standing behind her in the kitchen, pressing against her, fondling her; trapping her.

You're a dirty girl. . .

Terror and panic combined to give her a strength she didn't know she had. She thrashed around under the weight of her captor, the stench of long years of dust and decay from the floorboards mixing in her nostrils with the animal reek of stale sweat, though whether hers or his she didn't know.

"Get *off*!"

They rolled around on the floor, locked together as if in mortal combat. Celia gave another mighty heave; there was a loud crack, like firewood snapping, and this time she managed to dislodge him. Still wriggling and flailing like a salmon on a line, she crawled out from underneath him and scrambled to her feet, bruised and panting, her heart hammering beneath her ribs like a steam engine. In the struggle, he had dropped the flashlight. It lay against the hearth now, illuminating both him and the room, and Celia could see in its sideways beam that her assailant was little more than a boy, a sallow stringy beanpole of a youth a few years older than her. He sat up slowly, rubbing the back of his head and frowning.

"Ow," he said, a whining edge to his voice. "That hurt."

Gasping for breath, Celia bent and grabbed her backpack and stood holding it against her chest, like a shield.

"I'm warning you," she said, in what she intended to be a low and dangerous voice, but which came out as a squeak. "I've got a knife in my pack, and if you don't let me go I'll use it!"

The boy shrugged, and clambered to his feet, still aggrievedly rubbing his head.

"Suit yourself. *Duw*, I've got a lump the size of

an egg. That's marble, that fireplace. Bloody hard. I'm going to have the mother of all headaches in the morning."

Celia couldn't believe what she was hearing.

"What?" she yelled, incensed. "You wake me up in the middle of the night by shining a torch in my face like some kind of terrorist, you scare me to death by yelling at me, you physically attack me, and then you've got the front to moan about your head? What kind of nutter are you?"

He stared at her. "You're mad, you are. Scary."

"*I'm* mad? What about you, then? What are you playing at?"

He shrugged again. "Not playing at anything," he muttered. He bent, warily, to retrieve his flashlight. "Drugs, is it?"

"What?"

"You come in here to shoot up?"

"No, I bloody didn't!" Celia was appalled. "For your information, I came in here because –" She stopped, checked herself. Why should she have to explain herself to him? "Why did *you* come in here, then?" she challenged him, pugnaciously.

"To get out the rain." He shuffled his feet slightly, like a little boy, caught out. "And there's some nice cast-iron fireplaces, upstairs. I wanted to check them out."

"Steal them, you mean," Celia accused him.

"Yeah, so? What's it to you?"

Sensing she had him at a disadvantage, she pressed on. "So why jump on me, then? What was that all about?"

"You frightened me, didn't you? I wasn't expecting to see anyone in here."

"*I* frightened *you*!"

"Yeah." He lifted his chin, defensively. "I thought you was a junkie, didn't I? You could've killed me!"

"Oh, right. So you thought you'd get the first blow in and scare me to death." Scornfully, dismissively, reasonably certain she was in no more danger from him, Celia began to walk towards the hall with as much confidence as she could muster.

"Where you going now, then?" he challenged her.

"What's it to you?" she shot back, in his exact tone.

"Yeah, OK. One all," he conceded.

She paused, in the doorway. "Is it still raining?"

"Yup. Tipping down."

"Bugger." She sneezed, and coughed again.

"Bit damp, aren't you?" he observed, cheerfully. Drops of water were gathering along the hem of her shorts and dripping down on to the floorboards with small dull thuds.

"So?"

He lifted a shoulder. "So nothing. None of my business, is it? I'm off upstairs to check out those fireplaces. Stay here if you want."

"Oh, how kind of you," Celia said, caustically. "What a perfect host you are."

He gestured towards her backpack. "You really got a knife in there?"

"What do you think?"

"I think you're a scary lady. What's your name?" he asked, suddenly.

"Why?"

"Just wondered. I'm Gareth."

Celia laughed suddenly, struck by the absurdity of the situation, him introducing himself to her as though they were at a party.

"Well, hello, Gareth," she drawled.

"Were you going to stay here all night?"

"That was the plan, yeah. Until you came dropping in, like the bloody SAS."

"So you've got nowhere else to go?"

"God, what is this? University sodding Challenge?"

"I could help you, that's all."

"How are you going to do that, then? Invite me back to your penthouse apartment?"

A hurt expression crossed his face, clearly discernible even in the torchlight.

"No. I live up the Bryn, on Hafod Mawr. The

big field, bottom of the mountain," he added, seeing her lack of understanding. "We're travellers. Come and kip out with us for the night, if you want. One more's going to make no difference, is it?"

She only went with him because, as he had observed, she had nowhere else to go. That, and the sheepish way he'd shuffled his feet when she'd challenged him about the fireplaces. He was just a big kid. She had nothing more to fear from him, she was certain of that. It had to be better than staying in the big house. It was creepy, sinister; the kind of place you could imagine a body being discovered, walled up behind the fireplace, desiccated beyond identification after years of entombment. She thought of the little attic room at the Eagle and Child, of all the state-of-the-art toys she'd had to play with in Jessica's room at Elizabeth Lodge; of her own bedroom, at home. How had it come to this, that she be reduced to seriously considering staying the night in such a place as that? It was unimaginable. Anything had to be better than that.

The rain had eased to a thin mean drizzle. He led her along a narrow lane that climbed up towards the mountain. She could hear sheep bleating close by, and in the distance a dog barking, or perhaps it was a fox. She felt shivery, curiously dreamlike, in a trance-like state caused by interrupted sleep and a let-down of the adrenalin rush she'd experienced when fighting, as she'd believed at the time, for her life.

The boy led her up a narrow farm track. Celia stumbled along it after him, stones and clods of earth digging through the thin soles of her flip-flops. The moon came out suddenly from behind the clouds which were driven along the sky by the wind, like eighteenth-century galleons in full sail.

"Nearly there now."

She saw an untidy collection of vans and tents in the field nearby, illuminated by the moon-light. A dying fire sent up a thin drift of smoke into the air, and she could hear two voices arguing shrilly inside one of the vans.

They walked together across the damp grass, and Celia stumbled again and nearly fell. The boy put out a steadying hand, and then took her pack from her back, suddenly gallant.

"Here – let me."

He rapped his knuckles against the door of a scruffy cream-coloured caravan.

"Who is it?" A gruff voice from within.

"S'me – Gaz."

The door opened, and a blaze of light spilled out. Celia found herself looking up at the most beautiful man she had ever seen. He had the face of a dissipated angel, with black shoulder-length dreadlocks and flashing dark eyes. Only a stubbled chin and multiple piercings – along the top curve of both ears, in his right nostril and left eyebrow – stopped him being too pretty to be male.

"Who's this, then?"

His voice was soft, with a Celtic lilt. He looked her up and down, dismissively, and Celia felt herself blushing.

"I found her up at Plas Coch," the boy told him. "Asleep, she was. I said she could come and crash out here for the night."

"Did you, now." The man rubbed a hand over his chin, thoughtfully.

"Uh huh." The boy grinned suddenly. "She's a scary lady. Don't mess with her."

An older woman appeared in the doorway behind the man. She was slender, with a mane of corn-coloured hair strung with multi-coloured braids.

"Don't tease, Gareth," she chided him, gently. "Were you really sleeping at Plas Coch?"

Celia nodded. "Yeah."

The woman shuddered. "You're braver than me. That place has bad vibes. I'm Lowri," she added, and smiled at Celia. "We don't have much, but you're welcome to share it."

"Thanks." Celia was taken aback. "You're very kind."

The man held the door open wide, and Celia stepped inside.

"So who are you, scary lady?" he asked. "What brings you here?"

Celia looked at him, at his dreads and rings and studs. His gypsy-like beauty was breathtaking. She wondered what other body piercings he might have. He was exactly the type of person her father would have forty fits about Celia "mixing with", as he would no doubt put it. As if Celia was a cake ingredient, or a bottle of tonic water. God, he was such a snob.

Who am I? Genevieve's daughter – Gethin's granddaughter; Simone, Jessica?

She lifted her chin.

"Celia," she said. "My name's Celia, and I'm looking for my mother."

She spent the night in the cream caravan, on a rear bunk piled high with blankets. It looked as if its normal use was as a dog's bed, as the blankets had a liberal sprinkling of animal hairs; but she slept deeply and soundly, despite the dog hair and the rain which had started again, ricocheting off the tin roof with a noise like a hail of bullets. Gareth and Lowri slept somewhere else in the van, but shortly after Celia arrived the

259

man kissed the woman soundly and opened the door, disappearing off into the night.

When Celia woke, the van was deserted. She knelt up on the bunk, and peered out of the tiny window above her head. Lowri was standing about twenty metres away, holding a blue plastic basket piled high with laundry on her hip and talking animatedly to a younger woman whose right arm was in plaster. Close by, two toddlers with dirty faces and wearing only drooping disposable nappies made mud pies. An emaciated tan-coloured dog sniffed around them, and then cringed as the younger woman shouted at it, lifting her un-plastered arm in an angry gesture of banishment.

Celia hurriedly pulled on some clothes and left the caravan. Lowri looked up at her as she passed, and smiled briefly. Otherwise nobody spoke to her as she passed through the field. At the top end, three men were crowded around an ancient rusting car with its bonnet up, doing something elaborate and noisy to its insides. As she drew closer, Celia recognized the dreadlocks of the man from last night, and an inexplicable thrill of excitement shivered briefly along her spine. He didn't look up. None of them even acknowledged her presence.

Celia found her way down to the beach. The rain had stopped. It was clear and sunny again, but with a fresher feel to the stiff breeze that blew in off the sea. Her hayfever seemed a little better. Maybe it was being by the sea, she'd read somewhere that helped. The tide was right out, the sea reflecting the exact clear limpid blue of the sky, and the smooth yellow sands of the bay stretched away into the distance, invitingly clean and unblemished. Swarms of seabirds clustered together on the sand, stalking around and squabbling, their cries breaking the perfect peace of the morning. Celia took off her DMs and, knotting the laces together, slung them around her neck. Then she trudged along the sand, her head bent, deep in thought.

She was unaware of the time, didn't know how long she'd walked. A sudden cry from behind, and then another, made her stop and turn. Behind her, as far as she could see, a single line of footprints stretched along the beach, back the way she had come. Hers. Only hers. It seemed somehow symbolic. There was a figure a few hundred metres away, right down by the water's edge, clad in an acid yellow garment. As Celia watched, it lifted an arm and waved, then began to jog towards her. She was suddenly, sharply, reminded of her first morning at Silverdale: the sea, the beach, the birds, and her alone with her thoughts.

Perhaps it's Richard Daley, with his dog; come to find me, to see how I've progressed with my search. . .

It was Gareth. He grinned as he approached. "Hiya!"

He too was barefoot, wearing a fluorescent yellow fleece. He seemed irrationally pleased to see her.

Celia grunted. " 'Lo."

"What you doing here, then?"

"Playing tennis, what does it look like?"

"Tennis?" He looked around, presumably for the racquet and net, and Celia felt a stab of irritation. On the other hand, perhaps he really was stupid. The way he'd jumped her last night, maybe she shouldn't take any chances.

"I'm having a walk," she said. "By myself," she added, tersely.

"Oh, right." He didn't take the hint. "What you doing later, then?"

"Why? You asking me for a date?"

Again, he took her at face value. "Date? You must be joking. Anyway, you fancy Byron, don't you?"

"Byron?" she frowned. "What are you on about?"

"I could see it in your face," Gareth was saying, gloomily. "Everyone fancies him; well, all the women, at any rate."

She realized, with a flash of insight, that he was talking about the dreadlocked hunk of last night.

"So he's called Byron, is he?"

"So he says." Gareth scowled. "Reckon his real name's Brian, myself. He's not even Welsh – comes from Cheadle Hulme, or some such. Dead posh."

"He sounds pretty Welsh to me," Celia mused. They began walking along the beach together, following Celia's footsteps. "How old is he? Has he got a girlfriend?"

"What is this, University sodding Challenge?" Gareth mocked. "I haven't a clue how old he is. And he's got hundreds of girlfriends, I daresay. My mum included."

"Your mum?" Celia stared at him.

"Yeah. Lowri. She's my mum."

"Don't you mind?"

"Nah. She's a pretty good mum, as mums go."

"No, I mean about. . ."

"I know what you mean. Why should I mind?" He humped a shoulder. "He can do what he likes. They both can. It's what living here's all about." He glanced at her, sideways. "Were you serious, what you said last night? About looking for your mother?"

Despite herself, Celia found herself telling him her story. He was curiously easy to talk to;

he didn't interrupt, in fact he said nothing the entire time she spoke. It was almost like reading from a book. The words flowed from her as if written down inside her head, and when she reached the end – her, here, now – she stopped, breathless and yet oddly calm and cleansed.

They had reached the end of the beach, the slipway she had walked down earlier. She perched on the end to put on her boots, looking at Gareth's feet as she did so. They were pale, thin and bony, like prehistoric sea creatures.

"Aren't you going to put yours on?"

"Didn't bring any. Can't be doing with shoes, they only get holes."

She had the distinct feeling he was trying to impress her. A black and white bird flew low overhead, crying plaintively.

"Oystercatcher," remarked Gareth. "There it goes, look – wow, wish I could fly!" He suddenly sounded very young; Edward's age. Celia knotted her laces tightly.

"I need to ask around about Canon Jones," she said. "Any ideas?"

Gareth followed her cautiously up the slipway. "I'll ask Byron when we're back at the camp. He knows everybody round here. Or perhaps you'll want to ask him yourself – give you a chance to talk to him?"

He was teasing her. Celia gathered her dignity around her, like a cloak, and ignored him.

"It might take some time," Byron mused, later. "But I'll ask around for you, yeah? See what I can do."

His eyes were darkest navy-blue, his voice warm and caressing. Celia shivered with lust.

"Thanks," she managed. "It's really kind of you. I do appreciate it."

Somewhere in the background, Gareth snickered like a horse.

"You cold?" Byron asked, noticing the shiver. "The wind's changed direction," he observed. "North-westerly. The heatwave's over."

He was right, on both counts. The heatwave was over – it rained again that night, and the ensuing days were overcast and chilly – and it was three days before he had any news for Celia. She hung listlessly around the camp during that time, fighting down her frustration and telling herself to be patient, that it would be worth the wait. Nobody questioned her while she was there, asked her what her business was or where she came from; she was simply accepted, left to make her own way, and after an initial period of feeling in the way, surplus to requirements, she realized this was merely the travellers' way and was grateful to them for their lack of interference.

On the evening of the third day, Byron sought Celia out. She was in the van, rinsing out some clothes in the sink and dressed only in a T-shirt and knickers. He came in without knocking.

"Hello," he said, gravely. He didn't seem to notice she was in her underwear.

She blushed. "Oh, hi." Coughing, she sat down abruptly on the scuffed velvet banquette which, at night, converted into Lowri's bed. And Byron's, too, for all Celia knew. She pulled the T-shirt down as far as it would go, to cover her thighs. "How are you? Would you like some tea?" She looked around wildly, wondering where Lowri had hidden the kettle.

"No, thanks." He obviously wasn't there for social chit-chat. "I've found someone who knew your Canon Jones. Olwen Hughes. She was his cleaning lady for years. Works at the chemist's now."

"God." Celia put a hand to her mouth. Her heart had leapt to her throat; it throbbed there, huge and pulsating and expanded with anticipation. She was very close to her goal now; she could sense it. She was so filled with excitement, she could hardly form her words. "Where is he now, does she know? Did she tell you? Shall I go and talk to her?"

"Hold your horses." Byron touched her arm, lightly. It made her skin tingle. It was only later she realized it was a gesture of kindness rather than flirtation. "There's no point. Gethin Jones is dead. He died two years ago."

CHAPTER 16

It wasn't the first time the travellers had settled at Brynmor, and they had been at Hafod Mawr now for almost three years. They liked the place. It was easy to see how the time had slipped by, each season blending seamlessly into the next, and why they kept returning. Brynmor was a ravishingly beautiful place to live, if you could overlook the run-down qualities of the village.

"It was the road," Byron explained to Celia. "In Victorian times, when the railway came, it became a great holiday spot. But the dual carriageway changed all that. It was built to make things easier, to improve the road to Anglesey for the holidaymakers. But it put a stop to passing trade, and one by one things began to close down. Town planners – they've been the death of this village, make no mistake."

"And you'd know," Gareth put in, under his breath, "coming from Cheadle Hulme."

"You don't need to be local to recognize the cause of the problem. It's not just here, boy – it's happening everywhere."

Byron's provenance was uncertain. Nobody knew for sure where he came from, although Gareth stuck rigidly to his Cheadle Hulme conviction.

"You listen to his voice," he insisted. "Manchester. Greater Manchester."

"It sounds Welsh to me," Celia said.

"Nah. *I'm* Welsh. He just pretends to be. He's Manchester. Can't you hear the difference? He's just a posturing ponce."

Gareth had lived with the travellers all his life. He had been born, or so he said, in a tent in the shadow of Cader Idris, and had moved all over the country ever since.

"But what happened about school?" Celia wanted to know.

"School?" He spat, in disgust. "School's useless, never learnt anything at school. Living's what you learn most from. You stay here with us, girl. We'll see you all right."

"Actually," Lowri had told her, later, "he's got eight GCSEs. But don't let on I told you. He likes his little pretences, does Gareth. He likes to make out he's cynical, a man of the world, but the truth is he's anything but."

Celia had already realized this, back on the beach that first morning, when Gareth had talked about Brynmor, shining-eyed with fervour: "I love it here. It's home. Anyone with an ounce of imagination can see past all the closed-down shops and stuff."

She could understand how he felt. She was beginning to feel it herself. When she followed him that first evening to the camp at Hafod Mawr she had intended to stop for one night; but she ended up staying for almost six months.

When Byron told Celia that Gethin Jones was dead, she collapsed. She subsided on to the floor, sliding off the seat with thumping heart and tunnel vision and a terrifying feeling that someone was sitting on her chest, preventing her from breathing. She truly thought she was dying herself. However, this response to Byron's news, so melodramatic as to be almost Victorian in its nature, was due to illness rather than hysteria. It turned out that what she had thought was hayfever was in fact the onset of a particularly nasty flu-like virus.

"Combined with a deep-seated chest infection," said the doctor who came to examine her, bending over her where she lay on the dog blanket, "and exacerbated by not eating properly, and unsatisfactory living conditions. She'll have to have something more suitable to sleep on than this. How long have you had that cough, young lady?" as she was wracked by yet another spasm.

She couldn't answer, was unable to order her mind or her thoughts, which kept wandering away in the most peculiar and random manner. She simply lay there, helplessly, as Byron attempted to answer the doctor's questions on her behalf.

"Name?"

"Celia."

"Celia what?"

"Just Celia."

"Address?"

"Hafod Mawr. She lives here, with us."

"Doctor's name and address?"

"She doesn't have one." The doctor looked up from his prescription pad, sharply, and Byron glowered. "She doesn't have to have one, does she? There's no law against it. She doesn't want to be a drain on NHS resources."

"Ever suffered from asthma?"

"How the hell do I know? I'm not her keeper, am I?"

"So you presumably won't know her date of birth?"

"Not exactly. But I know she's nineteen. And she's a student."

Nineteen. Responsible for herself. And a student, so not liable to pay for any medication. How quick-witted Byron was. That much filtered in, past the grey fog that surrounded her.

Or maybe someone just told her about it afterwards.

The doctor left a prescription for antibiotics and painkillers, which Gareth was dispatched to fetch, and Lowri appointed herself chief nurse. She removed all the hairy blankets from the bunk, shaking her head as she did so – "That Gareth. He will keep letting the dog sleep on the bed; why didn't you tell me it was in this state?" – and made it up properly, with clean sheets. She cooked Celia regular nutritious meals, and ensured she took both her medication and plenty of fluids, according to the doctor's instructions.

The illness knocked Celia for six.

"It's not surprising," Lowri declared, much later. "All the emotional upheaval you've been going through – your chi must be knocked completely off balance. I'll ask Cynthia to give you some crystal therapy; that will sort you out."

Celia knew nothing about her chi, nor crystal therapy. She only knew that, for what seemed like an eternity, she could barely raise her head from the pillow, and for another couple of aeons after that she felt weak and wobbly, unable to gauge how much energy she would need to do anything, and frustrated by her lack of stamina and inability to do the simplest task. Lowri made her stay in bed, and insisted on bringing her meals to her.

"I like it," she said simply, when Celia protested feebly for the umpteenth time about what a nuisance she was being. "You're not a nuisance at all. I like having someone to look after. You ask Gareth if you don't believe me – he's always scolding me for fussing around him."

Celia found herself rather surprised by all this, by Lowri's chicken casseroles and steak pies, and her insistence on Celia finishing her course of antibiotics and, if necessary, visiting the doctor for more. If she had thought of travellers at all in the past, she supposed she had imagined them essentially as flouting convention; shunning doctors' intervention when ill, preferring instead to treat themselves with herbs or some such, and certainly all vegan or, at the very least, vegetarian. And how did Lowri manage to cook such conventional, *normal* food, when her cooking facilities were so primitive?

"Don't be a prat," Gareth scoffed, when Celia said as much. "What's wrong with meat? I've no time for all this veggie bollocks. I've been known to rip legs off cows in fields, me, when I'm hungry."

Typically, Lowri was less confrontational. "We do use alternative therapies. But if you're really ill, as ill as you obviously were, then it's foolish to turn your back on orthodox medicine."

"But I thought you were vegetarian?"

"I am. But Gareth isn't. We're all different here, just like anywhere else in society. This way of life is about choice, and having the freedom to practise that choice. And," she went on, gently, "what's primitive to you is normal to me. I may not have a Neff double oven and fan-assisted microwave, but I'm perfectly used to coping with what I do have. It's not a problem."

Celia realized to her shame that she had been guilty of pre-judging. For all her lip-service to freedom of choice, her ranting in the past at her father for his narrow-mindedness in condemning anyone whose lifestyle was different from his own, she was just as bad. She had always considered herself so open-minded, but in reality she was just as much a fascist as Dad was. It was a sobering thought, and one she was not all happy at discovering about herself.

"How long have I been here?" she asked Lowri one morning. The leaves on the trees through the window of the van looked dusty and dry, as if readying themselves to fall; the heather on the Bryn had turned a glorious purple.

Lowri smiled her sweet unhurried smile. "Does it matter?"

274

"I suppose not." She subsided back, amongst the fusty pillows. "I'm so fed up with lying here. I want to get up, get on with things."

"All in good time." Lowri bent and put a mug of camomile tea on the floor beside her.

"So what's the date today?" Celia tried a different tack.

"I'm not sure." Lowri straightened up. "The fifth, sixth? Somewhere around there."

Celia reared up in alarm. "Of *August*?"

"Celia, *cariad*." Lowri plumped the pillows and settled her back down again. "You've been ill. Seriously ill, mind – the doctor was all for carting you off to hospital."

"You never told me that," Celia muttered, mutinously.

"You were here when he said it. Only you were too out of it to take much notice."

"So why didn't I go, then?" She knew she sounded ungrateful, ungracious, but couldn't seem to stop herself.

"Would you have preferred that?" Lowri's green gaze was suddenly gimlet-sharp.

Celia sighed. "No. Sorry. You've been so kind – you're *being* so kind. . ." She trailed off, at a loss, at odds with the world and everyone in it.

"Byron tells me your Canon Jones is dead." Lowri changed the subject with breathtaking directness.

"Yeah." Celia bent her head and let her hair swing forward to cover her face, her cheeks flaming suddenly (*stupidly*!) at the mention of Byron's name.

"So what will you do next?"

"God knows. I haven't thought that far ahead. I can't believe this is it, the end, full stop – it's too depressing."

"You can stay here, you know. For as long as you like. As long as it takes."

"Can I?" Marginally cheered, she said: "You really are kind. But won't Byron mind?"

"Byron? What's it got to do with him?" Lowri frowned, not understanding.

"Well, there's not much room in the van now I'm here, is there? I couldn't help noticing he's had to, er, make other arrangements."

"Make other. . .?" Lowri's face cleared as light dawned. "Oh, *Iesu mawr*! You mean you thought he and I. . ." She gestured, and then threw back her head and laughed, a glorious gurgle of laughter deep in her throat. "Oh God, girl! You're not serious!"

"But Gareth said. . ."

"Oh, Gareth! That lad's so jealous of Byron he'd have you believe he's servicing the entire village. No, my love; there's nothing between Byron and me. We've known each other since we were kids – we're related, you know, way back. Twenty-eighth cousins, or some such non-sense."

Celia couldn't resist pressing her for more information. "So he hasn't got dozens of girl-friends then?"

Lowri shrugged placidly. "Haven't a clue. His business, isn't it? But I doubt it. Too much of a free spirit, is Byron. A commitment-phobe, some would say."

Celia contemplated privately that sex and commitment weren't actually the same thing, but decided some things were best left unsaid.

Gareth took to regaling her with stories as to how near death's door they had all considered her.

"Byron says you went blue round the lips," he said, all but smacking his own with relish at the drama of it all. "He said when you fell off that seat, he thought he'd killed you."

Celia remembered feeling much the same. She recalled how she'd been dressed that morning, in her tatty Simpsons T-shirt and old grey knick-ers, and blushed anew at the memory.

"You really fancy him, don't you?" Gareth, noticing her red face, sounded gloomy rather than crowing.

"Oh, piss off," Celia muttered, pushing her hair back behind her ears.

"You do. I know you do. I suppose that means

you'll be staying here then, hoping you might cop off with him."

"Gareth," she said, loftily, "why don't you act your age? Of course I won't."

"Oh." His face fell. "Aren't you staying, then? Lowri said she thought you were."

"I meant, I'm not hoping I'll get off with Byron." *Liar!* she told herself, with a little shudder of excitement just at the opportunity of mentioning his name. There was always hope. Besides, she didn't think it was just her imagination, but Byron definitely seemed to be becoming more attentive to her of late.

"So you are staying, then?"

"May as well," she sighed. "There's nowhere else for me to go."

The extent of her despondency at Byron's news, that Gethin Jones was dead, was largely masked to begin with by her being ill. But when she started to shake off the physical symptoms of the illness she was aware of a more familiar feeling alongside the gloom deep within her. All her old impatience was back, all the avid eagerness to get on with her search, along with a good deal of frustration that being ill had wasted so much time. She couldn't believe that she had come to the end of the road, that the trail had brought her this far only to culminate in a cul-de-sac, so to speak. Gethin Jones might be dead, Genevieve apparently disappeared off the face of the earth, but Celia's hopes simply refused to pass away. There had to be some way of continuing the search for her mother, of getting a new lead; there just had to be.

She was aware that this optimism might be totally unfounded, that she could merely be setting herself up for yet more dashed expectation and thwarted hopes and dreams, but she had to try. She couldn't just droop feebly around the camp for the rest of her days or, worse, drag herself back home, beaten, her metaphorical tail between her legs. That would be just too pathetic for words. So as soon as she was physically able, and without telling anyone where she was going, she walked to the chemist's shop in the village. A bell pinged melodiously as she opened the door.

"Can I help you?"

Celia peered at the rectangular badge the assistant wore pinned to her white lab coat. *Nest Williams*, it proclaimed. *Pharmacist*.

"I hope so, yes. Could you tell me if Olwen Hughes works here?"

She was immoderately pleased with herself for remembering the name. She had carried it with her, deep in the recesses of her mind, throughout the long dark days of her illness.

She was his cleaning lady for years. Works at the chemist now...

"She does, yes."

"Oh, good." Celia swallowed, nervousness and excitement combined. *Close again, so close...* "I wonder if I could have a word with her, please? If it's convenient?"

The pharmacist regarded Celia with curiosity. "Sorry, love. She's not here."

A tiny, barely perceptible prickle of disappointment. "Oh, right. Could you possibly tell me when she'll be back? I'll hang around till then."

The pharmacist smiled in a kindly way. "You'll have a long wait."

"Is it her day off?" *Typical – of all the days for me to choose...*

"Not exactly. She's away in New Zealand, visiting her daughter. She hasn't seen her for over ten years, and she's never seen her grandchildren."

Hope seeped slowly from Celia, like water round an ill-fitting bathplug. *New Zealand. Bloody great.*

"So when will she be back?"

The pharmacist shook her head regretfully. "She's gone for four months, love. The holiday of a lifetime for her, it is. We're not expecting to see her much before the beginning of December."

*

280

A fair came to Brynmor over the August bank-holiday weekend.

"It's cool," Gareth told Celia, fervently. "They come every year, there's dodgems and waltzers and the gallopers an' all."

"The gallopers?"

"Yeah, you know. The horses – the carousel."

He was such a kid.

"You're such a kid," Byron told him, with amused scorn.

"I'm not!" He was immediately on the defensive.

"Yes, you are – a great big kid. How're you ever going to get yourself a woman if you get all excited about *funfairs*? Big turn-off, son. Trust me."

"I'm not your son. Don't bloody patronize me, you bastard!"

It wasn't just harmless baiting on Byron's part. There was such antagonism between them, Celia could feel it. And Gareth would always come off worse. Compared to Byron, he *was* a kid. He looked like one, and he acted like one. He just didn't have what Byron had, his looks, his self-confident swagger, his sex appeal, and he would probably never have it, however old he grew.

Celia felt sorry for him.

"I like funfairs," she objected. "Does that make me a kid, too?"

Byron glanced at her, appraisingly. "Oh no, *cariad*," he said, softly. "You're not a kid."

There was a sudden electric spark between them. The tone of his voice, the look he gave her, made the hairs on the back of her neck stand on end. Gareth began to stomp off in a huff, and Celia put a restraining hand on his arm.

"I'll come to the fair with you," she declared. "If you want me to."

The fair was a swirl of noise and colour, of excited children's voices and tinny piped music and "Roll up, roll up!", of flashing lights and brightly painted rides and the all-pervading fairground smell of hot machinery and candyfloss and frying onions. Celia, caught up in the atmosphere, was reminded of when she was a child, when a trip to the fair was thrilling and memorable. She was in party mood, and dragged a distinctly less enthusiastic Gareth from ride to ride until he refused to go on any more.

"Why not?"

They were by the waltzers. Gareth shrugged. "Don't feel like it, that's all."

"Oh, go on, Gaz." She linked arms with him, persuasively. "Be a pal. They're my favourite."

He pulled his arm away, sulkily. "No."

"Oh, stuff you then." She was suddenly annoyed with him. What was his problem this evening — hadn't she sided with him against Byron, offered to go to the fair with him? Why couldn't he just forget about the stupid slight, and enjoy himself? "I'll go by myself."

She stepped up to the still-spinning stalls, pressed on all sides by other eager would-be riders. The attendant lifted the bars and released the occupants, ushering Celia inside one, and all of a sudden Gareth was there beside her.

"I thought you said. . .?"

"Changed my mind, didn't I?"

They smiled and laughed as the waltzers began gently undulating, then screamed and clutched at each other as they gathered speed and spun crazily around, careering seemingly out of control, and threatening to spin right off. When the ride ended, they half-fell off and staggered drunkenly across the grass, laughing hysterically and still holding on to each other for support.

"Oops!" said Celia, tripping over a rubbish bin. "Who left that there?"

Suddenly, Gareth had his arms around her and was trying to kiss her. His face was close to hers, his eyes closed, his lips pulled back over his teeth, and he was grasping her so tightly she could scarcely breathe.

You're a dirty girl. . .

She absolutely did not fancy him. She wriggled from his grip, hastily.

"Gareth! What are you trying to do, strangle me?"

Tried to make a joke of it, but failed. He opened his eyes, and the look of pathetic disappointment on his face almost made her laugh. It was if they were in a drama class, and he'd been told to do hangdog.

"I thought you liked me."

"I do like you. You're a top guy." Trying to make him feel better, less rejected, but failing at that, too.

"But not in that way."

"It's not you, Gaz. Honestly. It's me."

He laughed, bitterly. "Yeah. Sure. I'm not your type, right?"

"Gareth." She swallowed. She wanted to say the right thing. "I haven't got a type at the moment. I don't want a relationship right now, I'm too messed up."

"Except with Byron." He threw her a look that was a challenge. "You'd shag him, right enough. If he offered. Wouldn't you?"

"Oh, for Pete's sake."

It was pointless. She began to walk off, angrily. He ran to catch her up.

"You would, wouldn't you? Wouldn't you?"

She stopped, and turned to face him, breathing heavily.

"Yes," she said, through gritted teeth. "Yes. I would. Since you ask. Satisfied now?"

They stood and glared at each other, furiously. Celia wanted to say more, to make him understand. To tell him what a hard time she'd been having over the past weeks, was still having, with the frustration of having to hang around waiting; how she just didn't need this from him. The trouble was, if she began to say all this, to let everything spill out, she didn't think she would be able to stop.

Two girls strolled past, arm in arm.

"Cheryl got three As and six Bs," one of them said, "but Sal only got five Cs and two Ds."

"I know," said the other, "but she didn't do any work, did she?"

They stared at Celia and Gareth as they passed, curiously.

"Ooh er," Celia heard one of them say, "looks like a lovers' tiff!" and they both giggled inanely.

A whole chain reaction of thoughts began to set itself off inside Celia's head. All the anger left her, instantly. She couldn't even remember what she had been feeling so annoyed about. She started to walk off again, purposefully.

"Hey!" Gareth caught hold of her arm. "Where are you going? You can't just go off like that!"

"Why not?"

"Well. . ." He gestured with his free arm, towards the fair, the unspeakable dangers that obviously lurked within. "You go off by yourself, anything might happen to you!"

"Nothing's going to happen to me. I can look after myself." Then she saw his face. He looked as if he had been whipped. He already had a king-sized hang-up about Byron, and she'd made it worse. She'd hurt his feelings, and she felt guilty. "Look, I'm sorry. I do like you, you know I do, but not like that. I'm sorry if I misled you."

Gareth gave a small grimace, trying to brush it off, to save face. "It's no big deal. I thought it was worth a try, that was all. Any chance for a snog."

She let that one go. "Yeah, well. Whatever. I'd rather we were just friends, OK?" She looked around. "Any idea where the nearest phone box is?"

Dad answered. He sounded surprisingly calm; amazingly so. And pleased to hear from her too, instead of the usual instant hassle.

"Celia. Sweetheart." It sounded as if he had a cold. "Where – I mean, how are you?"

A good sign. Mum had obviously been getting at him, telling him not to quiz her the next time she rang. She felt a surge of emotion. It felt astonishingly like fondness.

"I'm cool. I really am, Dad. There's no need to worry about me."

"That's good. It's so nice to hear your voice, love."

Then Mum was on the line. "Hello, Celia. How lovely of you to call." Her voice was thick and hoarse with cold, too. Probably something Eddie had brought home from school.

"I just wondered –" Celia cleared her throat, nervously. "I just wondered whether my results had arrived?"

"Oh heavens, Celia, yes! Your GCSEs! I'm sorry, love; we were so overwhelmed at hearing from you it went right out of our minds. Just a moment."

Noises off, Mum's hand over the receiver as she rummaged around and spoke to Dad. Then she was back. She read out the results. Apart from History, which Celia had bombed spectacularly, she had passed them all. She had even managed three As. She stood there in the phone box, beaming, too chuffed with herself to speak for a moment.

"Wow!" she managed, at last. "How about that! I never thought I'd get an A for English Lit."

"Well, you did. Well done; we're proud of you!"

Don't say that – oh, please don't say that. . .

She had a huge lump in her throat, and tears pricked at the back of her eyelids. She bit her tongue and stared hard at the graffiti scrawled on the phone box until the feeling wore off. For a moment, a treacherous little moment, she had wished she was back there with them, celebrating her unexpectedly good results. For a moment, she had felt homesick.

"So how are you, then?" Mum asked, deliberately neutral. "How are things going?"

"Oh, really good." Celia injected masses of enthusiasm into her voice. "I wasn't too well a while back, but I'm much better now. I'm living with a really cool bunch of people, and everything's fine. I'm at a funfair right now – listen." She opened the door of the booth and held the receiver out, into the night air and the distant sounds. "Can you hear?"

"So have you found her?"

"Genevieve? No, not yet." Pointless to tell the truth, that she was unlikely to get any nearer to finding her this side of Christmas. They would be bound to insist she came back home.

"Oh, Celia." Mum was all at once in uncharacteristic tears, and Celia realized, with a sudden stab of alarm and regret and guilt, that neither of her parents had colds at all.

"Come on, Mum," she muttered. She didn't

know what to say, had no experience of comforting her mother. Mum was the comforter, the coper, not her. "I'm OK. You can hear I am. Can't you?"

"It's not that." Her voice was unclear, indistinct. Celia could barely hear her.

"What? What is it, then?"

"Oh, Celia," she said again. "Oh, darling. I'm just so scared. . . I'm so terrified that when you find her you'll like her better than me."

CHAPTER 17

Celia's reaction to what Nest Williams, the pharmacist, had told her about Olwen Hughes's whereabouts had been one of mixed dismay and frustration, with a not inconsiderable dose of anger thrown in for good measure. Tears of disappointment sprang to her eyes, and she found herself clenching her fists at her sides, white-knuckled, and white-hot inside with the all too familiar feeling of being impeded and thwarted by circumstances beyond her control.

Her choice was stark: give up and go home, or stay in Brynmor until Olwen's return from New Zealand. Going back home to wait was no choice at all – it was impossible, unthinkable. Somehow, Mum – or, more likely, Dad – would be bound to find some way of keeping her there for good, some reason why she shouldn't return in December. In her more reasonable moments, Celia knew that in truth her parents could do little to keep her at home, short of chaining her up night and day, but the way she had come to feel about her search for Genevieve had little to do with reason. She was so close now, she couldn't give up. She had waited nearly seventeen years to find out the truth about her mother. Surely she could hang on another few weeks?

And so the time went by. The hot days of the summer changed almost imperceptibly into a mild and golden autumn. Celia's birthday came and went, and more than a week had passed before she realized it. In general, life at Hafod Mawr had a comfortably established pattern, with little need for calendars or clocks, and Celia did her best to settle into it. She got up when she woke, ate when she was hungry, or when Lowri or one of the others prepared a meal and invited her to share it, and went to bed when she was tired. She began helping out some of the other travellers at car boot sales and craft fairs, and managed to make just about enough from her trips to pay for her basic needs.

But inside her, the impatience for Olwen's return gnawed away like a small vexatious rodent. She tried asking in the village about Gethin Jones, but she was largely met with blank stares and shakings of heads.

"A quiet man, he was," the man at the newsagents told her. "Kept himself to himself."

"I knew who he was, of course," said the landlord of Brynmor's only pub, a run-down looking establishment with a peeling sign over its front door: *Y Llew Goch*. The Red Lion,

Gareth told her. "Never came in here, though. *Duw*, no – not a drinking man, your Canon Jones." He ran a filthy cloth over the surprisingly shiny brass beer taps, and gave her a gap-toothed grin.

"I didn't know him personally," the woman at the post office told her, "but I'll tell you who did." A small flame of hope kindled inside Celia. "Olwen Hughes, at the chemist's. She used to clean for him, years ago it was now, but she'd remember him, right enough."

The flame flickered, and went out.

At last, December arrived. The first of the month was imbued with so much significance, it reminded Celia of waiting for Christmas, or her birthday, when she was small.

She was outside the chemist's first thing, waiting for it to open.

"Oh, hello." The pharmacist recognized her as she unlocked the door and rolled up the shutters.

"I just wondered if Olwen Hughes is back yet?"

"She's not, no." The pharmacist's thunderous face told Celia that the news wasn't good. Her words confirmed it. "She rang the other day to say she's decided to stay with her daughter for Christmas."

"Oh no!" Celia said, appalled, her own face falling.

"You may well say that." The pharmacist folded her arms and pressed her lips together. "She's left me in the lurch without so much as a by your leave. And at the busiest time of the year – all those coughs and colds around, not to mention this latest flu epidemic. I told her straight, if she's not coming back until the new year she may well find she's no job to come back to." She peered at Celia. "I don't suppose you've got any experience of working in a chemist's, have you?"

"Me?" Celia said, flustered and taken aback. "No, I haven't."

"Oh well." The pharmacist began to tidy the shelves. "It was worth a try. What was it you wanted to see her about, anyway? Something important, was it?"

How could she begin to explain? *The only remaining link with my mother – the possible key to my identity. The last resort. My final hope.*

Celia gestured, helplessly. "It was rather. I suppose I'll just have to wait a bit longer."

"Nothing I can help you with, then?" The pharmacist opened the till and began to tip bank bags of pound coins and fifty pences into it.

"Not really. Unless –" Celia frowned. "You didn't happen to know Gethin Jones, did you? I think Olwen Hughes used to be his cleaner."

"That's right, she was. I remember. A very quiet man, he was. Private. I never really knew him at all. He's dead now, though," the pharmacist pointed out.

"I know. You don't know where he lived, by any chance, do you?"

"I do, yes." She nodded. "Up Cwm Lane, it was."

"Do you remember which number?"

The pharmacist sucked her teeth, doubtfully. "Now that I can't say. Next door to Oak Cottage, it will have been, though."

"Oak Cottage?"

"That's right. Oak Cottage is Olwen's house. Canon Jones was her next-door neighbour."

The following day, winter arrived. When Celia woke the next morning, pushing back the curtain above her bunk, she could see that the towering mass of the Bryn, so recently blazing purple and gold with heather and gorse, was now completely white. It had been snowing.

She pulled on her DMs and ran outside, absurdly excited. Byron was bent over his old van, fiddling as usual with its innards and swearing at it in Welsh. He threw down a spanner in disgust, spat after it, and straightened his back as Celia approached.

"Morning, sweetheart. *Iesu Grist*, it's cold!"

He looked at her, clad only in her combats and T-shirt, and she shivered.

"Yeah. I think I need to buy something warmer."

"Try the Oxfam shop in Bangor," he suggested. "Great student hang-out. Loads of bargains. I got this there." He held out the hem of his sweater, a huge garment knitted in rainbow stripes that hung almost to his knees. "Grungy but warm."

"It's fab," she said, enthusiastically. "Really funky."

He studied her shrewdly, an amused smile hovering on his lips. He had quite clearly twigged that she would enthuse about plus-fours and a cravat, if he was inside them. He knew, and she knew he knew, and the knowledge made her blush.

Turning back to the caravan, she muttered something about breakfast.

"Fancy a walk first?" Byron said, casually. "Up the Bryn? There's a druid's circle up there, it looks amazing in the snow. The climb'll warm you up."

It took almost an hour to reach the top. Byron managed it easily, his lean rangy figure ahead of her making short work of the ascent, drawing further and further ahead and finally disappearing, but it was a struggle for Celia. She scrambled up the last bit, red-faced and gasping. Byron was there, standing tranquil and utterly non-panting by the druid's circle, a mini-Stonehenge, leaning against one of the standing stones out of the wind and lighting a roll-up. The sweet stench of cannabis drifted across the air.

"God," Celia complained, "you might have waited for me."

Byron laughed. "You don't have to call me God. I let my mates call me Byron."

He put out a lazy arm, and drew Celia backwards towards him. Her heart began to thump even harder, but he was only showing her the view, the mountains, stretching out in magnificent snow-clad splendour all around, as far as she could see.

"Look. That's Drum over there, and there – right in the distance, see – that's Tryfan. Beautiful."

"It's stunning," she whispered. *Just like you. . .*

"Worth the climb?"

"Oh, yes."

He tightened his grip on her, his arm around her shoulders. The wind whipped a stray piece of her hair across her face and into her eyes. He tucked it back under her beanie hat, tenderly, and drew a gentle thumb across her cheekbone. Celia scarcely dared breathe. *Omigod he's going to*

*kiss me! Does my breath smell? Why didn't I brush
my teeth?*

"Pretty lady," he murmured, and then something else in Welsh, something soft and caressing.
Celia thought she would die of pleasure, of the
romance of it.

"What does that mean?"

"I was just trying to remember what I've got
to buy in town today."

So much for romance. He let go of her
abruptly, dropped the dog-end of his spliff and
ground it out with his heel. "Lots to do this
morning – I've got to try and get that old heap of
a van started, if we're going south."

"Going south?" Celia stared at him, uncomprehending. "What do you mean?"

"The forecast is bad for the next few days.
Snow this early in December is a bad sign, it
looks as if we're in for a hard winter. We've
decided to cut our losses and go down to
Dorset, until the spring at least. We're on the
move. Didn't Gareth tell you?"

"But you'll come with us," Lowri said. "This is
your home, this van."

"But I can't. I've got to talk to Olwen." Celia
sat with her hands wrapped around a mug of
tea, staring blankly ahead of her. She had
stumbled down the mountain in Byron's wake,

seeing nothing, aware only of what he had said. The travellers were leaving Brynmor. They were moving on. Where did that leave Celia?

"Who's Olwen?" Lowri's face was blank. Had she really forgotten?

"The woman from the chemist's. She was my grandfather's cleaner, before he died." She looked up at Lowri, desperation on her face. "I've got to talk to her. She's my only lead."

"She's the one who's gone to Australia, right?"

"New Zealand."

"Didn't you say she was coming back early December?"

"Well, she's staying until after Christmas now." She rubbed a weary hand across her eyes, suddenly close to tears. "I just don't know what to do."

"Only you can decide." Lowri smiled, gently. "It's only Dorset. Not another planet. You can always come back here in the new year to talk to her. Or take the chemist's phone number, and ring up to find out when she's back."

She made it sound so simple, and Celia suddenly realized that it could be. It didn't have to be difficult, a life-or-death decision. It was up to her to decide how to cope with it.

"Can I really come with you?"

"Of course. Everyone's expecting you to. It's not a problem."

"It seems a bit of a cheek." She sipped at her tea, not convinced.

"Why?"

"Well, I come bowling in here and before you know where you are, you're stuck with me."

"Don't be daft." Lowri smiled again. "You're welcome to come, or not. Just as you choose."

"I don't want to be a nuisance, burdening you with all my problems."

Lowri took Celia's mug from her. "You haven't been a nuisance so far; why should you start being one now?" She opened the door of her tiny fridge and took out some eggs. "Want some breakfast?"

"Please."

"I'll tell you what," Lowri said, glancing around conspiratorially, not wanting to be overheard. "Gareth wants you to come. He'll be gutted if you don't, is what he said."

"Yeah?" It was nice to be wanted, if only by Gareth.

"Mm hm. He's become very fond of you."

Celia gave a little laugh, which didn't quite ring true. "A bit too fond, to be honest."

"I did wonder." Celia couldn't see Lowri's face; she had her back to her, was busying herself poaching the eggs.

"I do like him. But as a friend. I haven't led him on," Celia said, truthfully.

"I'm sure you haven't. It's Gareth, he's always been prone to these crushes. He sometimes seems ever so much younger than sixteen."

"Sixteen?" Celia was puzzled. "But I thought you said he'd got eight GCSEs? How can he, if he's only sixteen?"

"He did them a year early. He's bright, like I told you. God knows who he gets *that* from, not me, that's for sure." Lowri put a plate of eggs in front of Celia. "So will you come with us, then?"

"I do want to." Celia was suddenly embarrassed. "I don't want to hurt Gareth. I'll have to try to put him straight, but I don't want to upset him."

"I know you don't. You're a good girl." Lowri touched Celia's hair, briefly. "Your mum must be missing you."

Celia didn't want to be reminded of home, of how much Mum might or might not be missing her. Lowri was kind-hearted and doubtless meant well, but Celia wished she hadn't mentioned Mum. She suddenly had no appetite.

A few days before leaving for Dorset, Celia went up to Cwm Lane. Oak Cottage was about halfway along, and next door to it was a small empty house, with a sagging slate roof and a narrow front garden overgrown with nettles and bramble cables. The wooden front gate swung open in the cold wind, its once-cheerful sky-blue paint scabbed and peeling, and screwed to it was a tarnished brass plate bearing the cottage's name. *LICHFIELD*. Proof, if any were needed.

Curious, Celia walked along the narrow path that led to the front door. There had been a sharp frost overnight, and the snow on the cracked paving stones scrunched slightly underfoot. Celia stepped on to the garden and peered in through a window, shading the glass with her right hand. It was a small living room; she could dimly see a grate on the far wall, a cast-iron fireplace of the type Gareth had been coveting all those weeks – no, months – ago; Celia was surprised he hadn't—

"Can I help you?"

A polite voice, enquiring rather than accusing, but it made Celia jump nonetheless. A small, plump, fifty-ish woman stood on the path before her, in pink sheepskin slippers and a cardigan, her arms wrapped around herself against the cold.

"Who is it you're looking for?" she asked.

Caught out, Celia began to blush. "Er – well – nobody, actually. I mean, I just wanted to look at—"

"Well, there's nobody here, as you can see," the woman interrupted, firmly. "So I think you'd better go, don't you?"

Clear off, before I call the police! She didn't actually say the words, but Celia could sense them hanging unsaid in the air between them. She was looking suspiciously at Celia. She glanced down at herself, at her muddy DMs and stained, torn combats, and the old army-surplus greatcoat she had picked up, following Byron's tip, for two quid at the Oxfam shop in Bangor, and realized how grubby and disreputable she must look.

Then she noticed that the door to Oak Cottage stood open, the light from the hallway spilling out on to the path and piercing the murky afternoon gloom.

"Are you Olwen Hughes?" Yet how could she be, when the pharmacist had said she was spending Christmas in New Zealand with her daughter?

The woman took a startled step backwards. "I am. And who might you be?"

"I'm Celia," she said, aware of grinning delightedly, inanely, and in all probability looking like the village idiot. She couldn't help it. "I've been waiting to talk to you. I'm Canon Gethin Jones's granddaughter."

It was as if Celia had worked some kind of sorcery by mentioning Gethin Jones's name. Olwen Hughes's whole demeanour changed. She invited Celia in to her own house, as if she were an old friend, offered her the most comfortable chair and settled down for what she clearly hoped was going to be a long chat.

"But I thought you weren't coming home until after Christmas," Celia said, puzzled.

"My daughter persuaded me to stay. But then Nest was so annoyed when I rang to tell her, and I thought of all the Christmas cards that wouldn't arrive in time, and well – to be honest, I need my job. I can't afford to lose it on a whim. So I got my original flight, and Jackie and the family are all coming over here in the summer, and it's all worked out for the best after all." She looked at Celia, her expression kindly. "And now here you are, peering through Canon Jones's windows, and wanting to ask me about him. What was it you wanted to know?"

"Everything." Celia sighed, hardly daring to believe, after having to be patient for so long, that she really was sitting talking to Olwen Hughes at last. "Anything you can tell me. I'd be really grateful."

"He was such a lovely man," Olwen sighed. "A gentleman. There's not many like him around these days, and that's a fact."

"So you knew him well?"

"Oh, yes. He came from here originally, you know. A Brynmor boy, born and bred. And then he retired back here after he left the cathedral. I never knew he had a granddaughter, though." She stared into Celia's face as if hoping to find some traces of the old man there, some resemblance.

She began to tell Celia about Gethin. A picture began to emerge, of a reserved and solitary man, courteous and polite in an old-fashioned type of way. It was clear she had been fond of him.

"Did he tell you much about himself?"

"Oh, *Duw*, no!" She looked horrified at the thought. "He wasn't the type to talk about himself, not to me at any rate. I knew his wife had died, but that was about the extent of it. He kept himself to himself." *A quiet man – private.* It fitted with what others in the village had said about him. "We have a saying in Welsh, *doeth pob tawgar.*" She smiled. "It means *wise is the silent.*"

"And was he wise?"

"He was. Oh, yes."

Celia could feel the question bubbling up inside her. "Did you ever meet his daughter?" she asked, eagerly.

Olwen Hughes shook her head, and Celia cursed herself for having allowed the hope to build up again. Hadn't the verger at the cathedral told her there'd been a family rift, that

Genevieve had disappeared one day and never come back? *Sentimental reunions don't happen in real life, only in books*, she told herself angrily.

"I didn't even know he had a daughter," Olwen went on. "Not until after the funeral. She wrote to me, thanking me for arranging it all. I was shocked. I never knew he had a daughter, you see," she repeated. "He never mentioned her. Not once."

"She wrote to you?" A buzz of excitement, the familiar shiver of anticipation. "You didn't keep the letter, by any chance?"

The older woman stood up, and opened a drawer of the heavy oak sideboard.

"I think so; I don't like to throw that kind of thing away, official correspondence, so to speak." She rummaged around, tutting. "Now, where is it? I know I answered it. I felt I had to apologize for not letting her know her father had died, even though I didn't know she existed until then. Ah, here it is." Triumphantly, she held up a white envelope with a typed address label on the front. "The solicitor contacted her, you see. About the will. It must have been the first she heard of her father's death. I daresay it was as much of a shock to her as hearing from her was to me."

"May I see?" Celia could hardly breathe. She felt as if time was standing still, there in that cramped little cottage room with the fire burning merrily in the grate.

Olwen Hughes handed it over. "Of course you can. She's your mother, isn't she? I was forgetting."

The envelope bore a London postmark. It was dated March two years ago. Carefully, Celia drew out the contents – a single sheet of ordinary white paper, folded twice. It felt like handling the Holy Grail. The actual body of the letter was as Olwen had said, simply thanking her, in formal, unemotional language, for making the arrangements for her father's funeral. It was signed with an illegible squiggle, and underneath, in bold capitals, VIV CAVENDISH.

But at the top of the page was a printed official letter heading. CAVALCADE , it proclaimed proudly, in red, and then, in slightly smaller letters underneath, EXECUTIVE EMPLOYMENT AGENCY, and an address and telephone number in central London. Centred at the very bottom of the letter, beneath the signature, were the words *Director: Genevieve Cavendish*.

It was her. Celia had found her mother.

CHAPTER 18

"May I ask who's calling?"

"Tell her – tell her it's Simone."

"Just a moment."

After quite a bit more than a moment, the same cool efficient voice was back on the line.

"I'm afraid she's in a meeting just now. Can she call you back?"

Celia hopped from foot to foot in agitation. "It's difficult. I'm in a call box. It's really urgent – couldn't she just –?"

"Hold the line. I'll try again for you."

The silence that ensued was so long, Celia almost hung up and went away. It would be the easiest thing, she reasoned. Just to walk away. No explanations. No need for justification, on anyone's part. No—

"Can I help you?"

A different voice. Contained, composed. Could there be just a hint of curiosity?

"Is that –" Celia took a deep breath. "Is that Genevieve?"

"Who is this?" Sharp, now. Annoyed at being disturbed.

"It's —" Another pause. Just who was she? "You called me Simone. On my birth certificate. But I'm Celia now. Celia Duckenfield."

"Is this some kind of joke?"

"No. It's no joke."

"How old are you?"

Didn't she remember? "Seventeen."

"You're not old enough. It's not time yet. I'm not ready. You're not supposed —" She corrected herself. "You're not *allowed* to come looking for me until you're eighteen. That's what they told me."

"So why did you write that letter, then? For me to have when I was sixteen?" Celia tried to keep the anger from her voice, but failed. She couldn't help it. Hadn't she realized what wheels that letter would set in motion; didn't she have an inkling of what Celia would have been going through?

"That letter. . ." she said, slowly. And then, in wonderment, "My God. It is you. It really is."

Celia was to go to London, to the Cavalcade offices, the following afternoon.

"We can chat in my office, and then we'll go out somewhere nice for dinner," Genevieve had enthused. "My treat. My God," she said again. "This is amazing. I can't believe it's really you. I just can't believe it."

She had laughed, and she had cried. She had

308

exclaimed, over and over, how amazing it was, and that she couldn't believe it, and all the time Celia stood in the phone box in Brynmor, clutching the telephone and feeling curiously detached. The whole thing felt unreal. Shock, she supposed. She hoped Genevieve wasn't really in a meeting; what would the other people be thinking? She suspected that it had just been the usual ploy to avoid having to take an unwanted call.

When she told the others that she had found Genevieve, tearing breathlessly across the field and into the van, she was disappointed by their reaction, which was understated to say the least.

"Have you?" said Lowri, distractedly. Byron was sitting on a chair in front of her, a towel spread across his shoulders. She had cut off his dreadlocks and was dying the remaining hair a vivid scarlet. "That's good. Hold still, By, it'll drip in your eyes."

"So you'll be off, then, will you?" He glanced at himself in the mirror Lowri held. "*Duw*, I look shocking. Still, it hides the grey."

"Off? No. Only to meet her." She felt uncomfortable, in the way. As if she was interrupting them with her paltry bit of news. And she thought Byron looked awful. What on earth made Lowri choose that red for his hair? Shocking was about right. "I'll be back later, the next morning."

Genevieve had said nothing about staying over, but there was no way Celia would be able to get back to Brynmor that night. If necessary, she would have to find a hotel. She had just about enough money for her train fare, but not enough for accommodation as well. Perhaps she could borrow some from Lowri.

Gareth wanted to go to London with her, but she wouldn't let him.

"Don't be a prat. What will you do?"

"Walk," he said, in his most lugubrious voice. "Think."

"Oh, do me a favour. Do your walking and thinking here – I couldn't stand the responsibility."

There was a party that evening, in Dan and Cynthia's van; not because of Celia's news, but because Dan had suddenly come into some cash from an unspecified source and he wanted to share his good fortune with everyone else.

"So you're off to London," said Byron softly, in her ear. She had managed to manoeuvre herself next to him.

"That's right." She took a swallow from the bottle of lager he handed her.

"You've found your mother."

"Mm hm." Bizarrely, she didn't want to talk about it. She had a superstitious feeling that talking about it would somehow jinx the whole meeting.

"Cool. So that's you sorted, then."

"Hardly." *How could he think that? Doesn't he have any idea what being adopted is all about, that you don't just find your mother and fall into each others' arms and live happily ever after?*

"Hardly." He mocked her voice, gently, her posh southern Lady Margaret's accent, and she reddened. "Course it is. You've got the perfect excuse now, haven't you?"

"Excuse for what?" She didn't understand.

"For going home. Back to Mummy and Daddy."

She pulled a face. "I'm not going back there. No way."

He laughed, throwing back his head so she could see his fillings.

"Sure you are. You don't need to carry on living like this. You've just been playing at it. You can go back any time you want. Little rich bitch, roughing it with those funny hippy folk. We won't see you back here again. Trust me — I'm a gypsy, I know these things."

There was no malice in his voice, just a smug certainty that he was right. She looked at him sideways. His hair glowed like a Belisha beacon in the dim gas lights of the van. He looked ridiculous; she much preferred him with dreads.

"Gareth says you come from Cheadle Hulme," she said, provocatively.

311

"Gareth knows jack shit." He upended his lager bottle into his mouth and stood up, suddenly. "I'm going for some fresh air. Coming?"

She had scarcely got outside the front door before he had his arms around her and was kissing her, probing insistently at her lips with his tongue. At first she kissed him back, instinctively, but after a short while she realized she was only going through the motions. Her heart wasn't in it. Only yesterday she would have given her eye teeth to have Byron kiss her, but today she just wasn't interested. She didn't bother to question why. It wasn't important.

She pushed him away, firmly. "I really don't want to do this."

"Sorry. My mistake." This clearly wasn't to be a Magnus Armstrong encounter. He let her go immediately, grinning inanely, and she realized he was so stoned he could barely stand. "No offence, pretty lady. Whoever captures your heart will be a lucky man."

He dipped his head cheesily, in mock salute, and stumbled back into the van, leaving Celia feeling as if she had had an significant experience even though, in reality, very little had actually happened.

The next morning, Gareth insisted on walking to the station with her.

"I'm never going to see you again," Gareth intoned, mournfully.

"What are you on about? I'll be back in the morning."

"No, you won't. Byron said so. He knows about these things."

"Yeah, right. Sure he does."

"He does. You don't know. He's always right."

"Like hell he is. He called me a little rich bitch."

Gareth scowled. "He's a tosser. But there's other things he knows about, things you can't explain. Look, you're taking all your stuff." He indicated the rucksack on Celia's back.

"I've only got things for overnight. The rest is in the van. Of course I'll be back, I'm coming down south with you at the weekend."

"Don't go." He stepped forward, lifted a hand as if to touch her and then, changing his mind, let it drop at his side. "I don't want you to go. I love you," he muttered.

Celia bit her tongue, hard, to stop herself smiling. Poor Gareth. He was quite sweet really, in a damp, clingy kind of way.

"Gareth," she said, firmly. "You have to stop this. I really like you, you know that. But I don't love you. And you don't love me either, not really. It's only properly love when the other person feels the same. You'll find that out some time. I hope you find it out soon; you deserve it."

She leant forward and kissed his cheek, gently, and then patted the spot she had kissed as if to seal it into his skin.

"Bye."

Oh hell, she thought instantly, *perhaps I shouldn't have done that*. But the look on his face as she turned to go into the station told her otherwise. He looked as proud as if she had given him the Crown Jewels.

"The first thing you've got to do," said Genevieve firmly, ushering Celia into her office and gesturing for her to sit down on a squashy blond leather sofa, "is stop calling me Genevieve. I loathe the name."

Celia couldn't take her eyes off her. She looked young, much younger than her actual years. Her shining bell of hair was the colour of runny honey, with tiger stripes of caramel and cream, her make-up immaculate with the kind of perfect understatement that takes years of practise and at least half an hour to apply. She was dressed in trousers and a long tunic top in a soft, fluid jersey the exact caramel colour of the stripes in her hair. Round her neck was a single heavy piece of amber on a twisted copper wire, and on her feet she wore narrow shoes of burnished chestnut leather. The whole effect was designer-label, elegant, and incredibly well-groomed. Apart from the grey-green eyes, Celia could see no resemblance to herself whatsoever. She didn't know if she was disappointed or relieved.

"Were you called Genevieve because it's French?" Celia managed to say, eventually. Lamely.

"French?" Genevieve frowned. "How d'you mean?"

"Genevieve's a French name, isn't it? I always thought it was because of your mother being French."

Genevieve raised her eyebrows.

"You know my mother was French? My God, you have been doing your homework, haven't you?" Then she laughed. "Actually, it was because my father was a fan of the film. You know? Genevieve? With Dinah Sheridan?" She saw Celia's blank expression, and laughed again. Celia remembered Jeffrey the verger, in the cathedral. *Of course not, you're far too young. . .* "No, I don't suppose you do. It was about a car."

"A car?" Celia couldn't believe they were having this conversation. It was too surreal for words.

"Sure. Apparently he fell in love with the film – or perhaps it was Dinah Sheridan, who knows – and Bob's your uncle. Or should I say,

Genevieve's your daughter. And it's a Celtic name, not French: it comes from the Welsh for white wave. My father was Welsh. Did you know that, too?"

Celia nodded, slowly. They looked at each other, for a long moment. Genevieve looked away first, and sprang to her feet with a bright smile.

"Well, anyway. You must call me Viv, everybody does. Would you like some coffee? Tea?"

"No thanks."

"A cold drink, then? Juice? Coke?" Celia shook her head to both. Genevieve looked at her watch, which looked like a Rolex. "I suppose it's too early for gin. Are you sure there's nothing you'd like?"

I'd like answers to all my questions. I'd like you to stop wittering on about your bloody name, and sit down and talk to me!

"Jesus," Genevieve was exclaiming, earnestly. "I just can't believe it's actually you sitting here. In my office. Little – little Celia. All grown up. Oh bugger it, I'm going to have a gin anyway, even if it is only half-past four."

She opened the front of what looked like a filing cabinet, but what turned out to be a fridge. After a moment she turned back with a brimming glass in her hand.

"Are you sure you won't have one? Well,

cheers, anyway. Here's to you. Oh, sweetie." She sat down again, next to Celia. "What fun we're going to have! We're going to be such friends, I can tell!"

Celia smiled, politely. Now she was actually here, she felt shell-shocked. She had been unsure what sort of reception she was going to get, had prepared herself for suspicion or reticence, even for open hostility, but had not expected all this thrilled enthusiasm. She could hardly just come out and bluntly ask why Genevieve had had her adopted. It would be unnecessarily brutal.

"This is a really wicked office," she said, instead.

Genevieve beamed. "Isn't it groovy? I adore it." She took another large swallow of her gin. "I've worked bloody hard to get here, I can tell you. All my own efforts. From nothing to twenty branches, all over London and the home counties, in well under twenty years – I reckon that's pretty impressive, myself. It impresses the hell out of me, at any rate." She drained her glass. "Now, shall I have another little drinkie? Oh, why not – it's a celebration, isn't it! But only if you join me. I never drink by myself, it's one of my cardinal rules."

Celia accepted a Coke, thinking that it would give her something to do with her hands.

"I thought you were a nurse," she said, when Genevieve sat down again.

"Bloody hell." She regarded Celia gravely over the top of her glass. "Did you hire a private detective, or something?"

"No." She couldn't help feeling a small spurt of pride. "I found you by myself."

"All your own efforts too, eh? Chip off the old block, aren't you?"

She put an approving, beautifully manicured hand on Celia's knee. Celia felt faintly uncomfortable. This moment, actually meeting Genevieve, was something she had yearned for and planned for what felt like her entire life. But the gesture felt inappropriate: it was too much, too soon.

"I did train to be a nurse," Genevieve told her. "But it wasn't my idea; it was my father's."

Like doing History instead of Drama. . . Celia felt a connection with her, for the first time.

"Yeah. I know the feeling," she said. "Dads who know best."

"Or think they do," said Genevieve, grimly. "I realized fairly soon after qualifying that I was a pretty lousy nurse. My heart just wasn't in it. I resented the long hours, and the money was rubbish. But there was something about it I enjoyed. I liked talking to the patients, being a shoulder for them if you like. I was good at it, too." Celia thought suddenly of Stanley

318

Cavendish, back in Silverdale. *She had the knack of getting people to open up. The magic touch.* "I did think briefly about going into psychiatric nursing, but I couldn't bear the thought of all those nutters." She giggled. "Dreadfully non-PC, aren't I? But there you go. At least I'm honest. After a while, I decided what I really wanted to do was help place people in the perfect job – it's so satisfying when you're doing something you enjoy, and I had the skills to help other people do just that. So here I am." She gestured with her glass-free hand.

"Why did you have me adopted?"

The question came out utterly by itself; the words just spilled from Celia's lips with no conscious decision on her part. She felt as helpless and abashed as if she had just vomited on to the pale cream velvet-pile carpet.

An expression of discomfiture flitted briefly across Genevieve's face.

"Let's not talk about that just now. There'll be plenty of time for all the recriminatory stuff later. Let's just spend some time getting to know each other first, hmm?"

She leant forward, persuasively, and Celia noticed how very much like her own Genevieve's eyes were. It was an odd sensation, like staring at herself in a mirror.

"Sorry," she said. "Bad timing. But I just really

need —" She looked down at the carpet, tongue-tied, at the spot where her words would now be lying. She wished she could sweep them up and swallow them again. But she couldn't. They had escaped, and there was no turning back.

"I really need to know," she said, simply, looking up again.

Genevieve sighed. "OK," she said. The excitement and enthusiasm were gone from her voice. It sounded flat and strained. "All right. I guess you deserve an explanation."

And so Celia finally came to hear Genevieve's story, and thus her own.

"I suppose," she began, slowly, "the simple truth of the matter is that I wasn't ready for a baby at that time in my life."

"But you were married!" Celia burst out. "And you didn't even put my father's name on my birth certificate!"

Genevieve didn't express surprise that Celia knew.

"Married in name only. The marriage was a mistake; we'd separated on and off practically from the word go. I didn't want him to have any connection with you – he left me for good when I told him I was pregnant."

That thought had never occurred to Celia. "What a bastard!"

"I thought so too, at the time. He wasn't really, though. He was just immature – not ready for the responsibility. You know that feeling you get when you meet a really gorgeous man for the first time, that you can't wait to jump into bed with him?" Celia thought of Byron, and blushed. Genevieve, seeing the blush, misinterpreted it. "Perhaps not. I keep forgetting how young you are. I should have stuck to going to bed with him, but my parents talked me into marrying him. They thought he was such a catch, and they also couldn't bear the stigma of having a daughter living 'over the brush', as my father so quaintly put it." She grimaced.

"But everyone lives together these days," Celia pointed out. "It's no big deal."

"These days, yes. Not so twenty years ago. And my father was a clergyman, a cathedral canon. Such a scandal, my dear. He couldn't bear the thought of all the tittle-tattle. And as for my mother – " She left the sentence unfinished, eloquently.

"What was your husband's name?"

"David Butcher. He was a commodities broker, in the City. Rolling in it. My mother thought he was wonderful, the snob."

"And was he my father?" Celia whispered.

"Oh, yes. Well, in as much as he was there at the conception," she said, crisply, taking another slug of her drink. "If that's your idea of being a father."

"So why do you call yourself Cavendish?"

"It was the name of some people I worked for up north somewhere when Dave and I split up the last but one time. They wanted a live-in carer for the wife – they'd had some personal tragedy, and she'd gone round the twist. Weirdest six months of my life, I can tell you. Anyway, it seemed like a good opportunity for me to see once and for all if I was cut out for mental nursing and to get away from things for a bit, to get my own head straight. I didn't tell Dave where I'd gone, but he found out somehow and started piling the pressure on for me to go back – I really love you, Ginny, I promise I'll change, all the usual crap. Like a fool I fell for it and went back to London to see him a couple of times, to talk things through." She stared into her glass, rattled the ice-cubes distractedly. "It was a difficult situation. I'd tried hard to shed him from my life, and then there he was, back in it again. I hadn't even told the Cavendishes I was married, I'd told them my name was Jones, my maiden name. When I started going back to see him I told them I was visiting my parents."

"Why? Wouldn't they have understood if you'd told them the truth?" The subterfuge seemed unnecessary.

Genevieve shook her head. "Lord knows. I didn't want to take the risk, have them thinking I'd tried to fool them and telling me to get out, or whatever. The really daft thing is, I told them my parents were living in Devon. God only knows why I said that, either. We'd moved away years before, when I was a little kid. I'd been happy there, I suppose. All my friends were there. You know how important your friends are when you're little. I don't recall making many after that. Anyway," she went on, "one night when I was visiting David we'd both had too much to drink and the inevitable happened." She glanced at Celia. "And you were the result. I went back to the flat a few weeks later to tell him the glad tidings, after I'd found out for sure, and discovered him in bed with his secretary. In *my* bed!" she added, indignantly, still infuriated after all the intervening years. "The silly sod didn't even have the imagination to see what a cliché it was – I mean to say, his *secretary*." She shook her head, exasperated at the sheer folly of men. "Yeah, you're right. He was a bastard. Anyway, I decided to stay with the old girl and her husband for as long as I decently could, and when I left to have the baby I called myself Cavendish and used their address, so Dave couldn't find me. Besides, I rather liked the name. I still do. Genevieve Cavendish – it has a ring to it, don't you think? Better than Butcher, or Jones, at any rate. After the baby was born – you, I mean, God, I still can't get over it! – I kept the name, borrowed some money from a friend to set up this business, and the rest, as they say, is history. I'm officially Cavendish now, I changed it by deed poll when I opened the tenth Cavalcade branch."

She swallowed down the rest of her drink in one gulp, and almost absent-mindedly got up to fix herself another.

"So why didn't you have an abortion?" Celia asked, baldly.

Genevieve stopped in her tracks, her hand still on the open fridge door.

"Hell's teeth," she said. She looked shocked. "You're very direct, aren't you?" She carried on pouring her drink, and didn't answer until she was sitting down again.

"To be frank, I did consider it. There was a time when I thought it would be the easiest option. But when it came to it, I couldn't quite bring myself to do it. I thought I was cool about abortion – liberal-minded, you know – but when it was applied to me, it just felt like murdering a baby. I guess it was all that church upbringing: it went deep, deeper than I'd imagined."

"So you decided to give me away instead."

Celia hadn't intended it to sound accusing, but she did, nonetheless.

"Ah, Simone, don't say that!" she pleaded. She didn't seem to notice she had used the wrong name. "I couldn't keep you. When I left Dave I had nothing. I couldn't bring up a baby properly, I could barely look after myself."

"I thought you said he left you when you told him you were pregnant?"

"Did I?" She looked confused. "Well, whatever. The fact is, we weren't together any more, and I was penniless. Literally. I wanted the best for you – I wanted you to have two parents who'd adore you, and give you all the things you deserved. I even specified I wanted you to go to a churchgoing family, although Lord knows why, given the hassle the church has caused me over the years. I think I must have gone a bit doolally, all the hormones I expect."

"But why did you write that letter for me to have when I was sixteen? I thought you were sixteen when I was born, I thought it for years."

"Did you? How funny." She drew her forefinger around the rim of her glass, musingly. "It never occurred to me that you might think that. Like I said, I went a bit bonkers; two days after you were born I got terribly emotional, and felt I had to try and explain why I'd done it. The nurses said it was the baby blues. I thought you might be old enough to understand by the time you were sixteen, that's all. There was nothing symbolic about it. I'd forgotten all about that letter until you mentioned it yesterday, on the phone."

"Couldn't your parents have helped you out?"

Genevieve's face darkened. "I'd sooner have died than ask my parents for help."

"Did you have a row or something?"

"A row? My entire childhood and adolescence was a row."

"I know what you mean."

Genevieve's face contorted. "No, you don't. You can't possibly. My father was a bully who enjoyed tormenting me, and my mother was too adoring and too weak to stand up for me."

"What?" Celia was shocked. This wasn't the picture painted by the people she had spoken to. They had talked about the wise and popular Gethin Jones whose sermons packed them into the pews. Surely Genevieve must be over-dramatizing?

"You don't know the half of it," Genevieve said, bitterly. "Nor did anybody else. Every-body thought he was wonderful, the perfect father. The perfect Church family, in fact. They didn't know what went on behind closed doors. He wanted to control every single little detail of my life, and she just stood back and let him. He was a cruel, vindictive man, and he made my life hell. I was twenty-five before I had the courage to stand up to him, and by then it was too late. He'd forced me to train as a nurse and then had me married off to somebody he considered suitable. Even the wedding was his choice. Dave and I would have settled for a register office and a quick pint afterwards, but that wasn't good enough for him. He wanted his little girl to have the full fairy tale works, just so the cathedral could see what a wonderfully close family we were." Her voice was full of resentment.

"Perhaps he just loved you?" Celia suggested, timidly.

Genevieve shook her head, vehemently. "Is it love to lock your ten-year-old daughter in her room every night to make sure she does her homework? Is it love to choose all her O- and A-level subjects for her, to decide what she is going to wear every single day? When she comes home with a hamster, desperate for a pet, is it love to force her to hand it over personally to the vet, to have it put to sleep? Is it love to forbid her having boyfriends until she's twenty-two, or to tell her constantly how fat, ugly, lazy and stupid she is? That's not love, Simone. That's bullying. And my mother was too weak to stand up for me," she said again, her voice harsh and strident. "'He's tired, darling,'" she mocked, in a bitter parody of her mother's French accent. "'He doesn't mean it. Be a good girl, now, and do what he say.' God, if I had a pound for every time she said that."

She was silent for a moment, reflecting. "Even once I was married it took me a while to realize I was free of him. David insisted we kept on visiting them – even he didn't understand what my relationship with my parents was really like. He always thought I was exaggerating. But one day we were round there, and Dad was telling me how awful I looked, and Mum was making excuses for him. As usual. I'd put on weight, he said, and the colour of my top made me look ill. That was it. A petty thing, I know, but it was the last straw. I stormed out, and never saw either of them again. My mother died a few years later, and he didn't even bother letting me know she was ill, let alone that she'd died, so I couldn't go to her funeral. I didn't go to my father's either. He moved back to Wales, back to his home town, after my mother died, and he didn't tell me about that, either. That's how much he loved me, Simone."

"You keep calling me Simone," Celia pointed out. "If you hated your mother so much why did you call me after her, on my birth certificate?"

"I didn't hate her." Genevieve smiled, wearily. "It wasn't as strong as hate. Perhaps she was scared of him too. God knows. Anyway, by then I felt nothing for her. I had to put some name on the certificate; the nurses asked me what my mother's name was, and that was that. And I look around at all this –" she gesticulated, "and I'm so bloody glad I've been able to prove the bastard wrong, that I'm none of the things he said I was. Are your parents nice?" she asked Celia, suddenly.

She was caught on the hop, stunned at what Genevieve had told her.

"I guess so, yes. They're OK."

"I've thought about you every day," Genevieve told her, standing up. "And every day I've been reassured that I did the right thing. I'd have been a crap mother. With the example of parenting I grew up with, I couldn't have been anything else. Now come along; we've had enough soul-searching for one day. Drink up that Coke, and let's go and *party*!"

Genevieve showed her to a small bedroom off the office that reeked of chic minimalism, with an en suite bathroom.

"You'll want to freshen up, I expect. I stay

329

here overnight sometimes. It's easier than flogging all the way back home to Windsor."

"Windsor?" Celia stared at her. It was only a handful of kilometres from where she lived. It had taken her all these months to find Genevieve, she had come all this way, and all the time she lived less than fifteen kilometres away. "I live in Ascot."

"Do you?" The irony was lost on Genevieve. Of course; she was unaware of the extent of Celia's search. "That is so fab! We're practically neighbours – we'll be able to go out often, really be mates."

She left Celia to it, saying she had some e-mails to send. There was a telephone in the bedroom. Celia looked at it. Surely Genevieve wouldn't mind?

Phoebe answered on the second ring. "Hello?"

"Feebs, hi! It's me, and you'll never guess what – I've found her! I've actually found her! I'm with her at the moment, at her office – she's a really high-powered businesswoman, but so cool with it, she looks really young, dead funky, and she acts young too, and you'll never guess where she lives? Windsor! We're just about to go out for dinner but I wanted to—"

"Celia." Phoebe cut across her, urgently. "Shut up. Just shut up and listen." And she told Celia that she had to go home, now, because her brother Edward had been in a road accident and was lying in hospital with suspected brain damage.

CHAPTER 19

The streets of London were full of Christmas decorations. Every shop window bore over-the-top displays of tinsel and baubles and gaudily trimmed Christmas trees, every street was hung about with cut-outs of Santas and snowmen and prancing reindeer, and festooned with lights of every colour. Their bright cheerfulness was horribly incongruous, the celebratory note they struck almost indecent in its unseemliness. Celia wanted to tear them down, smash the lightbulbs, scream at the carrier-bag-clutching shoppers hurrying through the drizzling dusk: "Don't you know my brother is dying? Don't you care?"

She hadn't known what worry meant until that day. Genevieve had insisted on driving her, not just to Waterloo but all the way to the hospital where Eddie had been taken. Celia sat beside her in her company BMW on the very edge of the soft beige leather seat with her stomach churning, clutching together hands that were cold as death.

She hadn't known what praying was, either.

Please God let him live please don't let him die. . .
I'll do anything I promise anything I'll become a
better person only please God please please don't
let him die. . .

They stopped at traffic lights. The colour of
the stop light was reflected smearily on the wet
tarmac, red as blood.

"I'm sure he'll be all right," Genevieve said.
For the thousandth time.

You don't know that. How can you know that?

"Yeah," Celia said, dully.

"When did it happen, did your friend say?"

"Tuesday."

"Tuesday? But that's two days ago!"

"I've been away."

"Do you need to ring anyone?" Genevieve
indicated the car phone, attached to the dash-
board.

Celia stared at her with unseeing eyes.
"What?"

"Whoever you've been staying with? Let them
know what's happened, tell them you won't be
back tonight?'

"I wasn't staying with anyone tonight," Celia
said.

Genevieve digested all this. "I'm not sure I
understand."

"I left home in June."

"Sorry, you've completely lost me now."

"I've been looking for you. I thought you realized."

The car gave a sudden lurch. "I see," said Genevieve. "Let me just get this straight. You've been away from home looking for me since June?"

Celia couldn't summon the will to reply. It seemed unimportant now, in the light of what she was going back to.

"When you told me you'd been looking for me I didn't appreciate. . . I assumed the adoption agency. . ." Genevieve tailed off. "So where were you ringing from yesterday?"

"Brynmor. North Wales."

"I know where Brynmor is. You mean you came all this way without knowing where you were going to sleep tonight?"

"It doesn't matter. I'd have found somewhere." Celia gnawed at her top lip. "Can we go any faster?"

"Of course. Sorry." The car accelerated. "If I'd known, you could have stayed with me. It wouldn't have been a problem. You should have told me."

When they arrived at the hospital, Genevieve wouldn't go in. She dropped Celia outside the front entrance. It was plastered with notices: STRICTLY NO PARKING! KEEP CLEAR FOR AMBULANCES AT ALL TIMES!

"You don't want me there," she said, "getting in the way. You need to be with your family at a time like this." Then, realizing what she'd said, she pulled a wry face. "You know what I mean." She handed Celia a small rectangle of laminated card, gold printed with black. "My business card," she said. "It's got all my numbers, e-mail and everything. My home number's on the back. Don't be a stranger – call me, let me know how he is."

Celia put it in the pocket of her Oxfam jeans without glancing at it. "Thanks. I've got to go."

She fumbled with her seat belt, with the door handle, her fingers feeling as dextrous as a pound of sausages. Genevieve leant across her.

"Here, let me." The door sprang open. "Try not to worry. I'm sure he'll be fine, honestly."

The lift was on a go-slow, stopping at every floor; the corridors were endless and identical. They too were hung with gaudy Christmas decorations, and the wards beyond as well; if it seemed tacky and out of place in the streets it was doubly so here, amongst the sick and dying. Celia tore pell-mell along the passageways, her heart pounding in her ears, fearful at what she was going to find and repeating her mantra over and over: *please don't let him die please don't let him die.*

The ward was quiet, calm and tranquil. A

nurse showed her to a cubicle, cream flowery curtains drawn around the bed. But nothing could have prepared her for the shock of seeing Edward. He lay quite still in the hospital bed, his arms arranged neatly outside the blue waffle blanket. A drip with a bag of clear fluid suspended above was attached to his left arm, the business end tucked discreetly under a bandage. But it was his head that was so shocking. It was hugely swollen, grotesquely misshapen, with tufts of hair sticking up here and there like a lavatory brush and a long line of black stitches like railway track above his right eyebrow. His face beneath was the colour and texture of a squashed tomato, both eyes merely puffy slits in the middle of livid dark-purple bruising. His nose resembled an enormous piece of pulpy red plasticine, the nostrils caked with dried blood, and there was more stitching under his chin.

Mum was sitting on a chair, holding his right hand between both of hers, and Dad stood with his back to Celia at the foot of the bed, reading something aloud from a newspaper.

Celia gave a choking cry and stumbled forward.

"*Eddie!*"

Mum and Dad turned instantly.

"Hello, Celia, darling." Dad put his arms

336

around her and kissed her, and Mum got up from the chair, smiling gently.

"It's so lovely to see you. How clever of Phoebe to find you. Look, Edward; look who it is!"

At fourteen Edward was as tall as Dad, but he looked somehow shrunken lying in the hospital bed, small and vulnerable, a little boy again. His wrists, lying motionless on the blanket, were pitifully thin and bony. A huge knot of distress worked its way loose inside Celia's chest and lodged in her throat, choking her. She hugged her parents, unable to speak, half-blinded with tears.

"Dad was just reading Eddie the report on yesterday's match," Mum told her. "United won again, did you know?"

The nurse who had accompanied Celia stepped forward.

"Time for temperature checks," she said, "and your medication. Are you going to be good this afternoon, young man, or are we going to have to fetch the doctor again?"

Celia looked wildly around. *What's the matter with everyone?* she thought, hysterically. *My little brother is lying in a hospital bed with seven bells knocked out of him, and they're all acting as though everything's quite normal! Are they mad, or is it me?*

Edward began to make strange grunting

noises in the back of his throat. Mum and Dad turned instantly back to him.

"Come on now, son," said Dad, bracingly. "You know you've got to be brave."

The nurse was more severe. "That's enough of that. You don't want to worry your sister, do you? She's come to see you, and all you can do is lie there making that silly noise!" She turned to Celia. "You can talk to him, you know. He's quite conscious – he can hear everything you're saying. Go and say hello, he's been looking forward to seeing you."

Celia looked anxiously at Mum and Dad for support, and they nodded encouragingly. She sat down on the chair by the bed, where Mum had been sitting, and took her brother's hand.

"Hiya," she said. The lump in her throat moved slightly. "What have you been up to then, you dozy pillock?"

It seemed cruel, but Dad smiled his approval. "He had a bit of an argument."

"Yeah? How does the other guy look?" A feeble joke, but the best she could manage.

"He was on his bike," Mum explained, smiling down at Edward tenderly, "without his helmet. He was turning into Church Avenue and a car came round the corner, out of nowhere, Mrs Amberley said. Driving far too fast. She saw the whole thing."

"He bounced off the bonnet," Dad went on, "and went, as the saying goes, arse over tit into the road."

Another noise from Eddie. It could have been a laugh – it was impossible to say. The nurse busied herself around him with various tasks, and Dad drew Celia outside the curtains. He gripped both her shoulders for a moment, tightly, wordlessly.

"Thank you," he said. "Thanks for coming back."

He looked tired, his face grey and with lines Celia hadn't noticed before. She gestured helplessly.

"Of course I came back," she said, her face working. "I was worried sick. Is he going to be OK?"

"So the medics say. There's no permanent brain damage, thank God. That's what they were anxious about initially."

"Are they sure?"

"They've done two brain scans. They're as sure as they can be. They say it's mainly bruising and a few fractured bits and pieces, and there's no reason why he shouldn't make a complete recovery in time. He was lucky; they had another kid in a couple of weeks ago who'd come off his bike, same sort of accident. He didn't make it. And he'd been wearing a helmet.

Eleven years old, and now he's dead. Imagine what his family must be going through." He passed a hand over his eyes, wearily. "Anyway, the main thing is Eddie's going to be OK."

"Yes, but –" But he looked so dreadful, so horrendously mangled and battered. How could somebody who looked like that make a complete recovery?

Dad patted Celia's arm. "I know. I know what you're thinking. But he is going to be all right, love. We've got to hang on to that. They say the most important thing at the moment is for us to act as ordinarily as possible with him. What you said was perfect. You couldn't have said anything better, truly."

Back in the cubicle, the nurse was ministering to Edward. She pushed two small white capsules between his grazed and swollen lips. The grunting noises increased, and he began to kick his feet beneath the bedclothes and beat his arms about, in a kind of frenzy.

"That's enough of that," the nurse commanded, bossily. She put a restraining hand on his forehead and held a beaker with a spout, the sort toddlers use, to his lips. "Try and swallow some of this, now. It'll help them on their way."

Her mission accomplished, she bustled out starchily. Anguished, Celia sat down on the chair beside Edward again and took his hand. As she looked at him, two tears slid out of the slits that were his eyes and began tracking down the wreck of his face.

"Oh Eddie," she whispered. "You poor little sod."

He squeezed her hand weakly, twice. It was a code they had invented when they were little, sitting side by side in the back of the car on long journeys: once for are you OK? twice for I'm OK.

It finished Celia. She bent her head over her brother's hand and wept and wept as if her heart would break, all the tears she hadn't shed over the six long months since slamming the front door behind her at the start of her search for her mother.

"You'll never guess who I saw in the holidays?"

"Surprise me."

"Josh."

"No! Really? God."

"And guess who he was with?"

"Rudolf the Red-nosed Reindeer?"

"Ha ha. No, somebody less good-looking than that. Emma Price."

"Emma *Price*? Shit!"

"Yup. They were on the up-escalator in the mall, doing a spot of face-sucking. They nearly fell off the end."

"You are *joking*! Emma Price." Celia considered the implications. "I always thought he had better taste than that. She's only Year Eleven. How did he meet her, anyway?"

"Dunno. Didn't bother asking. Frankly, I was just stunned that a first-year university student would lower himself to snog a scrotty little Lady Mags Year Eleven."

"Watch it. We were scrotty little Lady Mags Year Elevens not so long ago," Celia reminded her. "Anyway, what's all this about university? I thought he was going to RADA."

"Didn't get in, apparently," said Phoebe. "Talking of which, how's college?"

"It's cool. Hang on a sec." Celia pushed her bedroom door closed with her foot, and picked up the receiver again. "Actually, it's bloody hard work, but in a cool sort of way."

"Let's face it, it's got to be better than LM. How did you manage to get your parents to agree to college? I thought they'd ground you until the next millennium when you came back."

"Yeah, me too."

Her whole homecoming had been unreal. Edward's accident had taken over, it was as if it had soaked up all the excess emotion until there was nothing left to spare for Celia's return. She had gone back home with her parents that evening as if on autopilot; they were in the car and halfway home before she realized nobody had actually suggested she should go with them.

"We have to talk," Dad said back at home, opening the front door and switching on the hall light. Just that. Not a hint of repression or anger. *We have to talk.*

The lights on the Christmas tree shone brightly, incongruously, into the hallway.

"Not now," Mum said, gently. "In the morning. Would you like a bath, love?" she asked Celia. "There's plenty of hot water. I can't face cooking – shall we send Dad out for a take-away?"

And so order was re-established, not with the bang of angry words and raised voices and recriminations but the relative whimper of normal everyday, familiar things. The bliss of a long hot soak in the bath. Celia couldn't remember the last time she'd had a bath. Going into her room and choosing a CD to put on while she dried her hair. Proper pyjamas instead of a T-shirt. Central heating, and carpet underfoot. Yet everything felt unreal, as it had when talking to Genevieve from that telephone box in Brynmor. When she went downstairs again Dad was back, and they ate egg foo yung and chicken chow mein and discussed Edward anxiously, and all the time Celia had the same sense of unreality. It was as if she was observing herself from a long way away.

"The consultant said he should be home for Christmas, all being well," Mum said. She glanced at Celia and smiled, and Celia knew exactly what she was thinking. The family, together again. At last. She couldn't bring herself to say, I might not be staying. She was no longer sure what might or might not be doing. Her priorities seemed to have changed, subtly, without her even being aware of it.

Edward was indeed home for Christmas, and in the new year Celia started at the local college. To her enormous surprise, Mum and Dad listened to what she had to say about Lady Margaret's and agreed that she could just as easily do her A-levels at college.

"So long as you do proper courses," Dad began. "You'll never get into university with some of those playing-at-it subjects."

"But I might not want to go to university," Celia pointed out, calmly. She didn't quite know where the calmness came from. She'd never managed it before when Dad got into do-as-I-say mode.

"Granted," Dad replied.(Equally calmly. Astonishing.) "You're right. It should be your decision. It's your future."

"So how's Ed?" Phoebe was saying, in the here and now.

"He's OK. Recovering. Should be back at school after half-term, the doctor reckons."

"And what about your mother? Are you going to see her again? You never did finish telling me about her."

Celia thought about all the other things she hadn't told Phoebe, like Byron and the travellers. Byron had been right about her not coming back, after all. She still had a pang about the things she had left behind, in Lowri and Gareth's van. They'd be in Dorset now; untraceable. She didn't tell her about discovering Genevieve's business card, either, in the pocket of her jeans when she was putting them in the wash. She had stared at it for several seconds, and almost threw it away before deciding to keep it. It was a week or so afterwards that Genevieve rang her. Another thing Celia hadn't told Phoebe about.

"May I speak to Celia?" an unfamiliar voice had said.

"This is Celia."

"Oh, hi, sweetie. I didn't realize. It's Viv. Genevieve."

"How did you get my number?" All she could think of. Stunned at the irony, that *Genevieve* should be ringing *her*.

"I looked in the phone book. Surname

Duckenfield, lives in Ascot – not too many of those." Genevieve laughed. "It's how I thought you'd found me. I never imagined—"

"I didn't look in the book because I didn't know you lived in Windsor," interrupted Celia, curtly. She didn't know why she was being curt. It was hardly Genevieve's fault.

"I wanted to know how your brother was – Ernie, is it?"

"Eddie. He's OK. He's coming home next week."

"Brilliant. You must be so relieved."

"We are."

A pause. A distinctly uncomfortable pause. Then:

"Look," said Genevieve, awkwardly. "There's something I need to say to you."

And she told Celia how she'd been thinking since they met, that perhaps they'd taken things too quickly, that she needed time to think things through, that *Celia* should have time to think about whether she really wanted Genevieve in her life.

"It's entirely my fault," Genevieve said. "I was just so bowled over by this lovely young woman standing in front of me when I'd had this image in my mind all the time of a tiny baby – daft, isn't it? Of course you weren't a baby any more. I think I got a bit carried away."

"Are you saying you don't want to see me any more?" Celia asked, flatly.

"No! God, no! Not at all! I just think –" She was clearly groping for words, for the right way of putting it. "I think we need to put a bit of space between us. That's all. Just a bit of thinking time."

I've had seventeen years' thinking time, Celia felt like saying, but didn't.

She looked at Genevieve's business card now. It was rather battered from having been lost in her pocket for a month, the gold tarnished, the lettering smudged.

"She was OK," she told Phoebe. "I expect I'll see her again. I put so much effort into tracking her down."

"Blimey, you've changed your tune!" Phoebe exclaimed. "When you rang that evening you made her sound like a cross between Madonna and the Businesswoman of the Year."

"She's OK," Celia repeated. "She's no superwoman. She's mixed-up. Like the rest of us. The problem is," she said, "I wanted to find my mother, and she wanted us to be friends. Mates. It didn't seem kind to tell her I've got plenty of mates of my own age."

She thought of their brief meeting, of all Genevieve's revelations. It was only much later that she had realized Genevieve had asked her nothing about herself.

"So you're not seeing her again," Phoebe declared.

"I didn't say that. I'm sure I will see her again."

She picked up the business card from where it lay, on top of her chest of drawers, and looked at it. Genevieve was right. They both needed time to think things through properly, to decide how to proceed with this new and unconventional relationship, to see if it could work for both of them. Now Celia knew where to find her there was no need to rush into anything. She had all the time in the world. In the meantime, there were more pressing things to think about. Such as. . .

"Feebs," she said, wheedlingly. "I've got a pig of a Sociology essay to hand in by next Monday – any chance of your coming round tonight to lend us a hand?"